The Uprising
Mackenzie Duncan Series
By Adrianne James

Copyright 2014 by Adrianne James
Published by Star Bound Books

Cover Design by Gonet Design
http://www.facebook.com/gonetdesign
Editing by Rogena Mitchell-Jones Manuscript Service
http://www.RogenaMitchell.com

THE
UPRISING
THE MACKENZIE DUNCAN SERIES

Star Bound Books

Other titles by Adrianne James

Young Adult Titles:
Life on Loan
Overexposed

New Adult:
The Mackenzie Duncan Series
The Tempering: Book 1
The Enlightening: Book 2
The Uprising: Book 3

Coming Home Line
(NA Contemporary Romance)
The Billionaire and The Barfly:

COMING SOON

Mages of Vale Series

Forever Forbidden Series

Acknowledgements

I had a hard time with this book. I fell more in love with Mackenzie with each book I wrote and so when it came time to say goodbye, I just couldn't do it. I wanted THE UPRISING to be perfect, to answer all the questions that were opened up in the first two books and to leave the fans of The Mackenzie Duncan Series with a smile, I don't think I would have been able to push through if it weren't for my husband constantly asking how many words I got in when he came home from work, my amazing friend Julianne for compiling a list of every wolf I ever mentioned and ALL the details available, not to mention reading bits and pieces whenever I started to doubt myself, Rogena Mitchell-Jones, editor guru and life saver when I need you to edit and edit FAST, and every reader out there who sent me messages or left reviews wanting to get their hands on the final Mackenzie Duncan book. Thank you. All of you.

ONE

Leaves and branches whipped past Mackenzie Duncan's face, some in a blur because of the sheer speed she was running while others dug into her skin, slicing her face as easily as a knife would. Not that it lasted long. Her werewolf blood made sure to heal her before the blood dripped down her cheek.

She slowed, looking back, hoping to see Liam. He had just been with her. Her stomach lurched when she didn't see him. If something happened to him, she didn't know what she would do. Except, she did. She would finish what they had started out to do. She would find the Royal lines, and she would stop Margret from regaining the power she craved. Then she would make her pay for everything she had ever done to Mackenzie and Liam.

When all she could see were still trees, Mackenzie stopped. Two steps back in the direction she came, holding her breath as she went, a tear fell down her cheek. She wiped it away almost as quickly as it had fallen. She would not cry over something that might not be true. Liam could be fine. He would be fine.

The silence she found herself in was short lived. A loud thunder and cracking branches that started off soft and slow grew into such a cacophony that Mackenzie felt surrounded. Turning around in circles, she tried to get her bearings, to prepare for whatever was about to break through the trees at her, but it was everywhere.

"RUN!" Liam had screamed before she saw his blond hair peeking between the greenery. Mackenzie didn't wait; she ran. She had always been fast, but after the night that changed everything, she was nearly impossible to catch. As a wolf, she was even faster.

Knowing that Liam was behind her filled her with relief, but it was short lived. Mackenzie skidded to a halt when a five-foot-tall black and white wolf stood before her. Its yellow-green eyes locked on her own, and its teeth bared.

Mackenzie's body vibrated with anxiety and fear. This couldn't be it. They traveled across an ocean and into France looking for other packs to help her find the Royal line to stop Margret's reach, and after only a week, without finding a single pack willing to help, it was going to be over.

The animalistic growl she had become so familiar with rumbled from deep in her chest, and she smiled at the wolf in front of her before giving into the beast. Mackenzie fell to the ground as bone after bone broke and reshaped and healed in its proper place. What used to be an agonizing transition, now just a normal part of her life, Mackenzie stood back up, tall on all fours. She bared her own teeth and growled right back at the wolf.

She didn't move forward. She didn't mean it or its pack that was quickly coming to stand behind it any harm. She wanted to talk to them. She needed to know if she and Liam were on the right track. Who knew how far Margret had gotten in only a week.

A warm hand glided against Mackenzie's back and without even looking, she knew it was Liam. She could almost sense when he was around. If it was because of their sire bond or simply because of their emotional connection, she wasn't sure.

She dare not take her eyes off the multitude of wolves before her to look at him, though. When the black and white wolf shook and howled, she knew he was changing. She had only seen it happen a few times before when Geoff was showing her. Her heart clenched in her chest at the same time as her blood boiled thinking of him.

She wished that she didn't miss him so damn much. It would be easier if she could forget everything they ever had and just hate him just as she did Margret.

Once the wolf cracked and popped and transformed back into human form, a man stood tall in front of them.

"Qui êtes-vous? Que faites-vous sur notre terre?" He spoke in seemingly fluent French. Mackenzie didn't understand a word he was saying and honestly, didn't think it was the time for Liam to pull out the English to French dictionary.

"I wish I knew how to tell you I don't speak a lick of French. I shouldn't have taken Spanish in high school." Liam was mumbling, and Mackenzie could feel him fidgeting beside her.

"I said who are you? And what are you doing on our land?" the man asked. Mackenzie huffed in relief.

Thank goodness that he spoke English. They might not get themselves killed after all. "Our land is clearly marked. You are trespassing."

"We know. We came in search of others. We mean no one any harm. We need to speak to your pack leader." Liam stood his ground and shockingly, his voice never wavered.

"Why?"

"We would rather talk to them, honestly. We bring news from the United States." Liam didn't continue. They had already spoken about how much to say before trusting anyone else. Mackenzie had already trusted too many and paid the price for it dearly.

"Are you lone wolves?" The man looked back and forth between Mackenzie and Liam, distrust blatant in his eyes.

"We stick together but have no pack we call home."

"She has to change back. No shifting. And you will respect our leader. We will kill you if we think for a second you intend to hurt him."

"Understood. But she needs privacy to change back and dress." Mackenzie finally took the time to look at Liam. She would never have requested that. The man stood before them as naked as the day he was born. It was just how things were. She had seen more than her fair share of naked men and women since she began turning with the light of the moon. They had seen her, too.

"Where you are from nudity is sacred?" The man was clearly confused. He sighed and looked at the group behind him. "The men will turn, but the women will not."

As if on cue, five of the eight wolves turned their backs and the man before them did the same. Mackenzie willed her humanity back into her body, picturing everything she had to live for, everything that made her happy and light and full of love.

Mackenzie took a breath in as a wolf and then breathed out as a human.

She looked to Liam with a question, but his face gave nothing away. He watched the group before them with untrusting eyes. Mackenzie dressed quickly and assessed the situation. They were only two and here was a group of eight taking them deeper into the forest to meet the rest of the pack. They were in over their heads, but there was no turning back.

The pack surrounded them as they walked deeper and deeper into the dense trees. Mackenzie could hear the animals running away as if they knew the true nature of the humans invading their domain. They probably did. Mackenzie could smell the difference between animals, between those that hunted and those that were hunted. The animals themselves could probably do that, too.

"What are your names?" the man asked.

"Mackenzie," she said, "and this is Liam. What's yours?" Mackenzie was trying to be cordial. She needed this pack to trust her and Liam, which would be hard considering the rocky start they were already on. Perhaps when she told them that her father, Darren, had sent them, they would have a little more faith. But then again, being part of the Royal line might no longer be something to be respected. Margret was a Royal. A Royal set on bringing back the old ways and ruling over all Werewolves.

"I am Nicholi. We are almost there. When we enter the compound, you will speak directly to our leader. You will address him with respect and do as he asks. If you attempt to harm him in any way, we will kill you."

"We understand," said Liam calmly. They didn't have to worry about that. They were not there to fight. At least, they hoped that wouldn't be the case. Liam slipped his hand into Mackenzie's and gave it a reassuring squeeze. The warmth from his hand spread through her, calming her and reminding her that he was there. That after everything, he would always be there.

Mackenzie was uneasy. It felt like there were more eyes on her than just the eight wolves that surrounded them walking into this unknown pack, in this unknown forest, in a place where even if they managed to get out of a bad situation, there was a greater chance of encountering a worse one.

Every snapped branch and every birds call made her jump. Liam tugged on her hand, causing her to look up at him. The question in his eyes was clear, 'what's wrong.' The problem was not knowing the answer. She didn't know what was wrong. All she knew was that trusting random packs in the past had screwed them all over, and she was wary of doing it again.

Instead of answering him, she just shook her head a little. When they were actually alone, she would confide her worries in him. She trusted Liam completely. Even if he did try to kill her once. But at the same time, she understood and would have done the same. Hell, when she saw the wolf that bit her, she did do the same. She may be his sire, but they were so much more than that. He was hers, and she was his. It took her longer to realize that than it did him, but nevertheless, she knew that of all the people in the world, she could trust Liam.

The trees grew sparse, and Mackenzie began to hear the voices of others off in the distance. Nicholi whispered to the man in front of the group who then ran ahead. Weres had better hearing than most, but they all knew that and adjusted accordingly. When he whispered, he must have spoken barely above a breath since Mackenzie had no clue what had been said. More secrets. Just what she needed.

Nicholi stopped in front of them and held a hand up in the air causing the rest of the wolves with them to stop. Mackenzie's head whipped around, trying to take in every detail, every scent, in preparation for a quick getaway. Whatever was going on, it didn't feel right. Watching Nicholi, she could see his skin beginning to prickle and the slight shake in his stance. He felt it, too. He was worried.

Liam leaned into her ear and whispered just a hair above a breath, "Something's wrong." All she could do was nod her agreement. When the wolves around them started to become uneasy, her body began to tremble, aching to change forms. Instinct raged through her, vibrating every bone, pulling at every muscle, fighting to take control from her.

Nicholi turned to them, worry clearly etched on his face. "If you had anything to do with this attack, I will kill you myself."

Before either Mackenzie or Liam could respond, a blood-curdling scream pierced through the trees. The ground thundered as wolves charged past them. They were running in formation, five wolves surrounding a sixth. As they pushed through the group, Nicholi cried out a mix of anguish and anger, collapsing to the ground as he changed forms.

When he stood tall on his four legs, his eyes narrowed and his teeth bared at Mackenzie and Liam. He pawed forward, a growl resonating from his chest. With Liam's hand still firmly in hers, she could feel the temperature rising in his palm, the vibration of his body needing to be set free, and the twisting of muscles under the skin that told her Liam had lost control and was in the process of changing to Wolf himself.

"This wasn't us. I swear." Mackenzie could feel her voice wavering. She just hoped that Nicholi understood that the waver was from the fight to stay human and prove that she wasn't a threat to him and not from fear of being caught in a lie. "You need to help your pack. We can help. Let us help."

In the few seconds it took Mackenzie to talk to Nicholi, Liam had changed. His large paws moved uneasy on the ground, and when Nicholi bared his teeth again, Liam moved in front of Mackenzie and returned the snarl.

"Liam! Stop!" she cried out. It was not the time. She knew he was trying to protect her, but if they didn't get on the same side and quick, she and Liam would be toast. They were outnumbered and way outmatched.

But Liam didn't back away. He didn't move. He kept himself planted in front of her, ready to jump if needed.

"Nicholi. We can help. I am going to change. Then we are going to go in there and stop whoever is hurting your pack together. Okay?"

She could see the wolf in front of her wavering between wanting to keep them away and wanting to believe her. She hadn't planned to tell him what they were doing, but if she wanted to gain his trust, she had to—and even then, it might not matter.

"You can trust me. Us. Darren, great-great-grandson of Meredith and my father sent us to France to find as many packs as possible and warn them of a threat. Do you understand what I am saying? The fighting back there could be one of your own issues, or it could be something bigger. Something we have been dealing with for a while now. *Let Us Help.*"

The aggression in him lessened and slowly, he backed up. It was enough of a gesture that Liam's growl stopped, and Mackenzie felt safe to change. An agonized howl echoed off the trees as Mackenzie let the hurt and need help to fuel her change.

When she stood tall, full of muscles and covered in brindle fur, she took off like a shot. The wolves that followed her soon took the lead as she slowed, letting them enter first. The cries and sounds of war grew louder and louder with every stride that they took. Fear began to seep into Mackenzie. What would they see? Would they really help or just make things worse?

Once the final trees cleared, there was no more time for her doubts or fears. The scene before them was bloody and violent. Wolves were tearing into each other, dead lying on the ground without their heads, but what caught Mackenzie's attention the fastest were the two small children huddled under a picnic style table, crying and calling out for their mother.

Mackenzie could see two wolves, one brown and one grey, covered in blood and matted fur wrestling just in front of the children. She didn't think. She just ran. She plowed into the fighting duo sending them both crashing to the ground with a thud. Mackenzie didn't know which wolf was the attacker at first, bracing herself for either to lunge at her.

The children cried out again, and when the brown wolf's head snapped in their direction, she knew. She leapt at the grey wolf, jaws already open. Mackenzie landed on top of the grey wolf and its putrid breath washed over her when it snarled in response. She didn't wait another second afraid to lose the control she had, and bit down. Fur and flesh coated her mouth, and when she pulled away, she saw the gaping hole in its shoulder where her mouth had just been. Spitting the offending material from her jaws, the two kicked and bit and wrestled to the ground.

With the beast twice her size pinning her to the ground, she knew that it wasn't over even if the cocky wolf on top of her did. She had been in that position before. She had nearly died, too. But she didn't. She wouldn't. She refused to be taken out so soon.

One of the children screamed, distracting the grey wolf for just a second. A second was all she needed. Mackenzie used her hind legs and kicked as hard as she could, throwing the wolf off her. It flew into a nearby tree, and with a crack, it fell to the ground. Its body lay twitching, and she pushed herself up to stand. She moved slowly at first, the injuries to her body still in the process of healing, then quicker as she felt the final bone in her back leg grow stronger again.

She looked over her shoulder at the children crying and their mother, yet again, in the battle just feet from them. She wanted to go and help her, but she knew if she didn't finish off the grey wolf, the minute its spine healed, it would try to kill her again. She wouldn't be weak. She wouldn't be trusting that someone would save her. She would save herself before she even needed it.

Mackenzie towered over the convulsing wolf, pure hatred in its stare. She place a paw on its head, with claws digging into its already blood soaked fur, and bit down on its neck. Two solid snaps were all it took to drain the life of the bastard who attempted to do the same to her.

She didn't stop to reflect on what she had done. She didn't stop at all. Once she knew that the grey wolf wasn't going to come after her again, she turned to run back to the children's mother. Only she was too late. Their mother's body lay just feet from them. The wolf that had been fighting with her was now stalking the table, circling it, taunting the children beneath it. Her head was dangling from its mouth.

Anger boiled inside of her. The tears on the children's face her fire. She placed herself between the children and their mother's murderer. It spit the head from its mouth, and as it rolled away, a wolf howled in the distance. The cocky wolf growled once more at her before darting off. When Mackenzie looked up to see what had happened, she saw of the few remaining wolves still standing; half ran off together, leaving Nicholi's pack to pick up the pieces of their now destroyed home.

Mackenzie scanned the area, looking for a sign of Liam. Her heart raced when he was nowhere in sight. A whimper fell from her lips when she spotted the broken white wolf on the ground, half hidden by a bush. Approaching slowly, afraid to see if she had lost him forever just a few short weeks after truly having him, her heart beat wildly in her chest.

When his body began to twitch, a breath she hadn't realized she was holding escaped from her lungs, and she ran to him, nuzzling him with her snout. When his yellow-green eyes opened and locked on hers, her heart flooded with relief.

Mackenzie closed her eyes and relished the warmth that loving Liam filled her with and turned back. She ran a hand through Liam's fur. "Stay put, finish healing. I'll be right back."

Mackenzie stood and ran back to the children who were still under the table, the older boy pressing the younger girl's face into his chest, not letting her see their mother, but his eyes never leaving her.

She crouched down to look under the table, and the children cried out, scooting back away from her. "It's okay. I'm not going to hurt you, promise. Let's get you into a house or something, okay?"

The boy looked at her skeptically, but the girl, she bit her lip before nodding and pulling away from her brother. She placed her hand in Mackenzie's and led her to a building. The door had been broken into, and the place was destroyed, but it was obviously a home. The little girl released her hand and ran off into the house, and the boy just watched Mackenzie.

When the girl ran back in, she was carrying a robe. She held it up for Mackenzie to take. With a smile and a quick thank you, Mackenzie covered herself and tied the robe closed. The little boys' eyes narrowed.

"That was mommy's robe."

"I'm sorry. I can take it off. I can find something else to wear." She wasn't sure how to handle the situation. She hadn't thought about her state of undress when she went to the children to begin with, but at that moment, it would feel really strange disrobing and walking around in the nude.

"No. She tried to help mommy. She can wear it." The little girl said through tears. The few tears that fell were soon joined with more and more until the poor girl was sobbing. Her brother went to her to try to console her, but nothing worked.

"Mommy fought strong. She protected our pack leader and us. She died a hero."

Mackenzie listened to the boy who didn't look more than seven or eight with awe. She didn't know if she would have handled what he had seen with such strength, and she was a full grown woman.

Nicholi burst into the house from behind her, covered in dirt and blood. "JAMISON! MADDIE!"

Tears filled his eyes as the children filled his arms. He placed kisses on their heads and pulled back to look at them, and then pulled them tight for another hug.

"Mommy..." Maddie croaked.

"I know, sweetheart."

"I tried to protect Maddie, Dad. I did. I didn't let her watch. I promise."

Mackenzie stood back, silently watching as the family reunited and dealt with the loss.

After a few moments, Mackenzie excused herself and went back outside to see if she could do anything to help with the rest of the pack. Liam stood waiting for her and took her in his arms, kissing the top of her head.

"You are amazing," he said. "Come on. I think they need help moving all the bodies."

Mackenzie nodded and followed behind Liam. As they worked together with the new pack to give their fallen a proper goodbye, questions loomed in her mind.

Was this Margret? Or did France have its own super power?

TWO

As the last of the fallen wolves had been moved to their version of a church, Nicholi came out of the house with his children in tow. A woman rushed over to him, gave him a hug, and took the kids with her when she left the area.

Mackenzie watched as he gave instructions to the others in the area. She watched as he stood tall and spoke clearly and certainly. Then his eyes landed on her. Liam stood nearby, but a quick yet subtle hand gesture told him to stay put. Nicholi was not going to hurt her. They had earned his trust. She didn't know how she knew, but she did. The feelings of unease and worry were subsiding the longer the enemy pack had been gone.

"You saved my children," Nicholi stated. It wasn't a question. And from his stance, arms crossed, standing tall, and eyes perfectly fixed on hers, he wasn't expecting a response. "You tried to save my mate."

There was no waver in his voice. No tears on his cheeks. Nothing to indicate any sense of emotion whatsoever at that moment. But Mackenzie knew he was churning inside. She saw him just before with his children in their completely destroyed house. She saw the fear in his eyes when he entered and the sheer joy when he spotted his kids.

Mackenzie just nodded. She didn't know what to say, honestly. She could agree with him and seem eager to be praised, or she could deny it and jeopardize any good will he had started to feel for her and Liam.

"Thank you."

Nicholi turned from her and addressed the group. "You were all very brave. But we are no longer safe here. Go collect your things. We are going to the winter grounds."

When he turned back to her and Liam, he said, "You are welcome to come with us to speak with our leader. Please, wait outside for me. I must say goodbye to my mate."

Liam nodded and squeezed Mackenzie tightly to his side. His lips pressed into her hair for a brief moment, then lead her out, leaving Nicholi to grieve for his wife and all of the other fallen members of his pack.

Outside, Mackenzie was expecting a crazy madhouse of people preparing to leave their home and lost loved ones behind. Instead, it was somber, many walking house to house, holding hands and collecting small bags.

A soft hum began from a few. The few turned into many, and then the many turned into all except

Mackenzie and Liam. The agonizing tune made her want to weep alongside those who had lost their families. The unity of the pack in their grief made her hopeful. They stood together in both battle and in the aftermath.

This is what they were fighting so hard to protect.

"Come. It is time to go." Nicholi had come out; eyes were rimmed red, but not a tear was shown. He was strong and if what she assumed was correct, he was strong for his pack. He must have been a second in command.

They trekked through the woods the same way they had entered. Maddie and Jamison stuck with the woman who had led them away, but their eyes rarely left their father. Once, the little girl looked over at Mackenzie, who was still in her mother's robe, and gave a little wave. Mackenzie responded in kind with a little smile.

Little was said in their four-hour journey. There was little that needed to be said. As the moonlight spread over the trees and the owl's called out before hunting their prey, the pack arrived at their winter grounds. It was further south, and much warmer than where they had been before.

The winter grounds had a clearing that held a few handmade greenhouses, as well as plenty of wooden cabins. The large fire pit in the center was already surrounded by five men and one woman. They all stood when the pack entered the area, relief evident on their faces. Mackenzie watched as some scanned the group only to turn and walk away stiffly. Her heart hurt for them. Whatever was going on, this pack was taking a huge emotional hit.

"Gather around the fire, everyone," an older man with salt and pepper hair and a full beard said with a thick French accent, "Even our visitors."

Mackenzie had been surprised by his use of English, but if he intended to speak to them as well, it made sense. She and Liam moved forward with the crowd. The fire crackled and cast an orange glow across everyone's face.

"We have suffered a great loss today at the hands of another. We had also made friends when we needed it the most," he said then looked to both Liam and Mackenzie. "As a pack, we will go on. We will grow stronger as our young ones grow older. We will not let Alice destroy us. Justice will be had, but not now. We must keep our heads. They have strength, but we have intelligence. We will use it. Now, eat and get a good night's rest."

Mackenzie's heart beat wildly. Who was Alice? Why had she attacked? Liam's hand tightened on her own, causing her to look up at him. His yellow-green eyes were wide and laced with confusion. She gave him a little shrug of her own, trying to tell him silently she was just as in the dark as he was.

When the pack began to disperse, all heading to their winter quarters for a much-needed night's rest, Liam gave her hand a tug and led her forward to the leader.

Three men who sat around him stood abruptly, muscles flexed and vibrating. Mackenzie stopped in her tracks and just looked at them. Liam's irritation showed through clearly, but she hoped she appeared cool as a cucumber. She was not after their pack leader. She thought she had proven that already. Their hands were full. They might not even want to help with the Margret situation, and she couldn't say she would blame them if that were the case.

"Let them be. Sit, sit," the leader said, motioning to the logs next to his. His henchmen sat down, surrounding him again, and Liam and Mackenzie sat as well. No one said anything for a while. They all just stared into the fire. The longer she sat there, the more memories of the attack flashed in her mind. She couldn't get the image of the decapitated head dangling from that wolf's mouth from her mind. A tear streaked down her face, and her heart was heavy. In her time as a Werewolf, Mackenzie had seen many things, done many things, but nothing was as bad as that. Nothing compared to two children watching their mother murdered only to have it rubbed in their face by a gloating wolf. She hoped that one day they were able to forget the horrible scene of how their mother died, and remember that she did it to protect them, because she loved them. Their mother saved them.

"America is a very long way from France." The leader's voice was even. His eyes never left the flames, and his posture stayed as it was. Mackenzie waited a minute to see if he was going to continue, but he didn't.

"It is," she said carefully. How much should they tell them? She had planned to tell them everything, but if they are being attacked, maybe they were just getting a piece of what they gave on another day. What if this Alice wasn't bad? What if she was doing exactly what Mackenzie and Liam were trying to do? What if this pack was a superpower like Margret was?

"You are here for the same reason we are. Another pack believes it has rights to your pack. But you are looking for help. We handle our problems alone."

"Another pack believes it has rights to all packs. The daughter of the Royal Werewolf is seeking to reinstate herself as the leader of all of us. Every pack, on every continent, no matter who is leader. She has already taken a good amount of the packs in North America. If her control gets too much larger, she will be unstoppable. No single pack will be able to handle this problem alone." Liam's tone was sharp. Perhaps he took offense at the comment. Maybe he didn't want to be looked at as weak. Mackenzie felt the sting from the leader's words as well but hadn't intended to say anything.

"Then our enemy is your enemy. Alice is working under Margret's orders."

Mackenzie felt like she had been hit with a wrecking ball. Margret's reach was farther than she had ever realized. Had this pack plans to handle things alone?

"If Alice is under Margret, then how do you plan to handle it alone?"

"We move from place to place. We have multiple pack homes to keep us safe."

"Running? Your plan is to run away? And what happens when they find all of your hiding places?"

"Then we make another. Packs have survived war after war by staying out of the way. By not interfering."

"Is that why—" Liam started, but Mackenzie placed a hand on his arm and shook her head when he looked to her. She knew what he wanted to know, but pissing them off wasn't the best idea. The leader running away and leaving the pack behind to deal with the attack was a coward's move. A leader should be there to lead, to fight, to protect.

"If you could just point us in the direction of any pack from the Royal line that might not be all too happy about Margret trying to take over the world, so to speak, we will leave first thing in the morning."

"You wish to seek out the Royal family? Why would they wish to speak to you?"

"Because my father is Darren, great-great-great-grandson of Gwendolynn."

"I know of one pack, but they are hard to find. I can only give you a direction to go. From there, you are on your own. You may sleep in the far cabin."

Mackenzie stood and thanked him, pulling Liam along with her. She could see the irritation pouring out of his eyes, but there was nothing to say to convince them actually to do something besides run. They were afraid of fighting, of war. Most people are. At least they would have a better plan on where to go in the morning.

The cabin was small, but it had a bed. They hadn't slept in a bed in weeks. It didn't matter that the mattress looked to be forty years old or that there was no bathroom. What mattered was that they were about to sleep in close quarters on a bed without having to take shifts sleeping or being the look out.

Even still, when the door closed, Mackenzie pulled down a latch that was at the top of the door to lock it. Then Liam moved a table that had been beside the bed in front of it as well. It wouldn't stop anyone who really wanted to get in, but it would definitely slow someone down.

Once that was done, Mackenzie finally looked at Liam. His strong but lean body stood tall by the bed as he pulled his shirt from his head, exposing his chiseled chest and abs. When he caught her ogling him, he smiled and held a hand out for her to take.

Mackenzie took the five steps that covered the distance from the front door to the bed on the far wall and linked her fingers with his. The warmth that radiated from him soothed her aching heart and muscles and caused her to melt into him. With a little tug, he had her in his arms and held her close. Mackenzie felt a feather light kiss on top of her head and a smile crept onto her face. She tipped her face up to look into his and pressed her lips to his.

That moment, the feeling, was one that she had only ever felt with Liam. She felt completely her own, but at the same time, completely his.

"You and me. Always," he said when he pulled back. Mackenzie nodded in agreement. She stepped back just enough to pull the covers on the bed down and climb in, making sure to scoot over to give Liam room.

With his arms wrapped around her, their sides pressed so closely together they might as well be one person, Liam sighed.

"What are we going to do?" he asked. He didn't have to elaborate. She knew what he was talking about. He often would start conversations in the middle of his thoughts, and most of the time, she knew exactly what he was talking about.

"We keep with Darren's plan. We find the royals that want things to stay as they are with packs ruling themselves. We can't be the only ones willing to fight to keep Werewolves from going back to nothing more than peasants to 'royalty.' We can't be the only ones who think that growing ranks by biting humans and killing pack leaders or anyone who disagrees with her is wrong."

"But what if the royals we find are in on it? You heard them. Margret has already gotten here. Whoever this Alice is, they are fighting for Margret. We have to be careful."

Mackenzie was quiet after. The ceiling held little details, but her eyes never left it laying there on her back in the bed. So much had changed in such a short amount of time, and it didn't seem to be slowing down at all. Knowing who to trust and who not to trust used to be so easy for her. Now, all she did was question the motives and truth behind every word anyone besides Liam or her father said. Geoff had even fooled her. She had thought at one point that she and Geoff would have been a great couple. She trusted him. She had a love for him. She fought for him. And he was on Margret's side and that he was Margret's son. He turned her into a liar and made her the reason that so many had died. Did he know that Margret was on the verge of being untouchable? Did Geoff know it was only a matter of time before the world of Werewolves fell to their family?

"What are you thinking about?" Liam asked quietly. Mackenzie drew her eyes from the ceiling and locked them with Liam's eyes. She knew he wouldn't like that she was thinking of Geoff. They had fought long and hard over her, and for a time, Liam was sure that he was a consolation prize after Mackenzie had caught Geoff giving away their location to Margret.

"Honestly?" she asked. That was her clue to him that it was about Geoff. She didn't want to hurt his feelings, but she never wanted to lie to him. There were enough lies going on in their world to last a lifetime, and she didn't want to add to it.

"Always."

"I was wondering how much of this Geoff already knew."

Mackenzie felt Liam stiffen beside her and take a deep breath. She couldn't let him get angry over it. Or doubt her feelings for him. But he would also have to understand that Geoff wouldn't disappear from her memories simply because he wasn't in front of them.

She rolled to her side and started tracing circles on his chest with her fingertips. "Hey," she said softly. When his only response was a grunt and a far off stare at the wall, she said, "Look at me."

Liam's head turned slowly, turmoil clear on his face as he looked at her. "Just because I think about him sometimes, doesn't mean anything besides that he was part of my life, our lives, and part of this horrible fucking situation. I chose you. I chose you long before he left. I just didn't know how to handle it all. I love you. Not him. You. But if we are going to be able to stop Margret, we have to be able to talk about Geoff. He is part of the whole damn thing. And yes, I know you were right about him."

"I love you, too. And you are right. I just hate that he can still hurt you, hurt us, without even being in the same damn country."

"I know." Mackenzie leaned in and kissed him. When his hands gripped her waist and pulled her tight to him yet again before slipping under the fabric of her shirt, goose bumps covered her skin in anticipation.

A growl erupted from his chest as his fingers found her breasts and began playing with her hardening nipples. Mackenzie's heart raced, and her skin flushed. She nipped at his lip while kissing him, and when she pulled back for a breath, he ripped her shirt clean off her.

With a hunger in her eyes and lust in her voice, she said, "Make love to me."

Liam didn't respond with words. Instead, he worshiped every inch of her skin and loved her into euphoric bliss.

The next morning, the sounds of the forest permeated the small cabin. Mackenzie woke, tangled in sheets and Liam, and smiled. Sun was filtering through the cabin, and the warm air was pleasant, not overly hot or humid just yet.

She couldn't wait until this was how they woke up every day. Quiet mornings with the love of her life. Mackenzie sat up and stretched her arms above her head and glanced at her watch.

It was much later than she had thought. Surely, they would be able to hear the pack up and about. There were children and families, and after the day they all had, there were things to be done. The winter home should be ripe with activity. Only it wasn't.

"Liam, wake up," she whispered and shook his arm, "Wake up!" she said a little more urgently. Something was wrong. She could feel it.

"What is it? What's wrong?" Liam sat up quickly, but his voice still sounded asleep. As he was wiping the sleep from his eyes, Mackenzie jumped out of the bed and pulled clothing from her bag.

"Listen!"

"I don't hear anything, Mac."

"Exactly. It's nine in the morning. Don't you think we should hear something?"

As if the realization that something was really wrong hit Liam, he dressed quickly. All remnants of sleep gone, he was alert and ready to go before Mackenzie finished putting her shoes on.

Liam slowly moved the table from in front of the door, careful not to make it scratch on the floor or bang when setting it back down. When he lifted the latch, Mackenzie threw the door open, hoping to catch whatever was on the other side off guard.

Only there was nothing and no one to catch. The entire area was deserted. Mackenzie huffed to herself. She did it again. She trusted someone when she shouldn't have. They never planned to tell them where to find Evelyn. That would have been too easy.

"DAMN IT!" she yelled out into the trees. Liam placed his hands on her shoulders and began to rub, trying to push calm into her body with every pass of his pressing thumb.

"We found them without help. We will find another pack, too. We won't stop until we have found someone part of the Royal line and get them to help us put a stop to this insanity."

"That won't be necessary." The voice startled them, and they whipped around to see Nicholi coming through the trees. How had they not heard him? "I don't have long, but I couldn't just walk away after what you did."

"What happened? Where did they all go?" Mackenzie asked through gritted teeth. She was glad that Nicholi came back, but at the same time, his pack was nothing more than liars and cowards.

"They were worried about one of you giving away the location of the pack. I can understand that. You have no connection to us, and if you are questioned hard enough, you may tell them to save yourselves."

"Never." Mackenzie stood tall and proud. She knew she would rather die than see anyone else hurt because of her actions. It had happened too many times already.

"I came back to tell you where to go to find Evelynn like promised. You deserve that much. If our pack cannot stand up against Alice, I am in awe of your bravery to go against Margret. Evelynn's pack is found in the North, in the west of Paris by a good day's journey. If you follow that path," he pointed to a small but well-worn clearing in the growth between the trees to their right, "after a half day's travel, you should hit a road. Follow the road for three days and then head into the forest and make yourself known. The forest will be cut in half by a dirt road. There are several hunters and farmers living along the road, all spread out. There will be one building that stands out among the rest. When you spot it, you will know. That's where you will find Evelynn."

"Thank you. Will we see you again?" Mackenzie asked.

"If you need me, send word through Evelynn's pack. They will get me the message. I believe in your plans and I want them to succeed. No one wants to be under Margret's rule, and if I can help, I will."

"You just did. We better get going," Liam said. He reached out and shook Nicholi's hand and stepped back letting Mackenzie and Nicholi talk for a moment.

"I know I already thanked you, but it doesn't feel like enough."

"You didn't even need to do that. I did what anyone would have done if they had seen what was happening. Children shouldn't get wrapped up in war, and they should never have to watch their mother—" only, Mackenzie didn't finish her sentence. Not only were the words caught in her throat at the memory, but Nicholi went rigid, his eyes glossing over.

"Goodbye, my friends. And good luck."

Liam and Mackenzie headed toward the small path—finally with a little idea of where they were going.

THREE

There was a cool breeze flowing through the trees giving both Mackenzie and Liam a reprieve from the muggy warmth that permeated the forest. The sun was shining brilliantly, and the scenery surrounding them was absolutely beautiful. For a second, she was even able to pretend that they were taking a romantic stroll through the woods on a date instead of going in search of a member of the Royal Werewolf line to help them stop the biggest bitch of them all—literally.

"This is nice," Liam said as he linked their fingers together and began swinging their arms back and forth.

"Yeah, it is. Maybe we can come back one day and actually enjoy ourselves."

"I am enjoying myself. Right now, right here, with you. Margret isn't here. Her henchmen aren't here. No one is here, but you and me."

Liam gave her hand a tug like he so often likes to do and pulled her into his arms. He looked down on her with such light in his eyes that it warmed her from the inside out, filling her with joy. She couldn't help but think *this is it.*

"You know I love you, right?" she asked.

"Of course, I do, and you know I love you."

"You and me. Once everything is over, it's you and me." Mackenzie leaned in and kissed him softly, their lips pressing and melding against one another. Just as Liam's hand snaked up her back and into the hair at the nape of her neck to deepen their kiss, a rustle sounded from the low lying bushes near them.

Mackenzie jumped back, her eyes immediately searching the area where the sound had come from. When she saw a foot scramble to get out of sight, she knew that they were no longer alone.

"Hey, you can come out, you know."

When no one answered her, she stepped forward, ignoring Liam's protest. An assassin of Margret's would not have been heard or would have made the mistake of being seen before they were ready to strike. This person was hiding.

"Hey, you okay in there?" she asked a little softer this time. She could hear how fast their heart was beating and by the smell of body odor and lack of anything feminine, it couldn't be a girl. When there was no response, she motioned Liam to come forward. Perhaps talking to a man would be better.

Mackenzie leaned up and whispered in his ear, "Try something."

He looked at her with questioning eyes and a little shake to his head. "Just try. What if he's hurt?" Liam sighed dramatically then turned to the bush.

"Hey, come on out. Let us help you."

Again, they were ignored. "Let's just leave him be. Maybe he doesn't want our help."

"Maybe he just doesn't understand us. Give me the backpack," Mackenzie said as she reached for the large bag that Liam had been carrying. Unzipping it quickly, she pulled out a French to English dictionary.

Mackenzie began to flip through the pages.

"Bonjour," she said slowly and then flipped the page again "Avez-vous." She flipped again and again. "Besoin d'aide?"

"What the hell did you just say?" Liam asked quietly and quickly.

"Shh, I just asked if he needed help."

Mackenzie waited a moment to see if the boy would respond. When all she heard was his rapid heartbeat, deep breaths, and a little more rustling of the bush leaves, she tried again.

Mackenzie looked through the book again, holding the page of a word she needed with one finger while looking for more. "Êtes-vous blessé?" Then she looked to Liam. "I asked if he was hurt."

The boy crawled out from behind a bush and looked up at them. He couldn't have been more than fifteen. His hair was a tangled mess, and he was covered in dirt, but he didn't have a scratch on him. When Mackenzie locked eyes with him, she knew why.

His eyes matched her own. The yellow-green iris was the telltale sign of a bitten Were.

33

After figuring out that neither could understand each other, Mackenzie and the boy, who they learned was named Christophe, began trading the translating dictionary back and forth. The conversation was long, drawn out, and quite stunted but Mackenzie had to try to help this kid. He wasn't even old enough to be out of high school yet, and his life had been ripped from him.

"I... bit... wolf... by... Magic. Leg... healed. MAGIC!"

"Nous savons nous aussi." Mackenzie had hoped that she translated that correctly. She wanted him to know he wasn't alone. That she and Liam had both gone through what he was going through and that he would be okay. "Ça va... Ca va... Crap. Where is it? Bien se passer."

Mackenzie was getting tired of having to use the book, but she knew that not everyone was going to have learned English. She had already gotten (and healed) three paper cuts in their conversation alone.

"D'autres, comme nous." She tried telling him that they weren't alone. There were lots of other Werewolves out there, but this boy had yet to even turn. She had to be the one to tell him, and she didn't like it. The more she looked for the word Werewolves in the dictionary, the more frustrated she became. Apparently, Werewolf was Werewolf no matter what language you were speaking. "Les Werewolves."

"No! No! NO!" Christophe began chanting louder and louder with a frantic tone to his words.

Mackenzie and Liam stood quietly, waiting for him to calm down and accept it if he would. Mackenzie remembered when she first figured out what was going on. She was sitting in the library at Harvard after having been bitten while walking home one night. Everything was changing; she was getting stronger, more irritable, and her eyes had changed color. For her, it was the only explanation that fit, so she prepared for it. Liam, on the other hand, refused to believe even after being shown that Werewolves were real. He ran and tried to pretend life was the same as before she had bit him. Then, he tried to kill her. Their journey together was most definitely a long and complicated one.

"No. No." Christophe kept repeating the word over and over again, his face contorting into anger, his muscles all tightened and his voice began to get louder and more frantic. Liam grabbed the translation dictionary from Mackenzie and began rifling through the pages.

"Venir... avec... nous... si... vous... voulez." He turned to look at Mackenzie and quickly added, "I just told him he can come with us if he wants to." Liam offered the boy company before even talking to Mackenzie. Her head whipped around to look at him, completely in shock. They didn't have the time to babysit. They had a mission to do, and with the full moon just days away, they were going to be turning themselves. Keeping a new Werewolf in line while in wolf form is hard enough when you know them and their habits, but to do it in a forest they barely know, while possibly being hunted down, and while trying to keep their own hunger at bay if a human just happens to be around will be a nightmare.

"No!" Christophe yelled at them. He then began using his hands in a shooing motion before he stood and stormed off into the woods even further.

"I hope he makes it all right," Liam said in a sigh while putting the book back into Mackenzie's bag.

"I hope next time you check with me before offering to take on a pup while we have things to focus on." Mackenzie's tone was clipped, and she knew it, but damn it, she was irritated.

"I'm sorry for trying to help someone. I thought that was the damn point of this, to help people, but I guess it only counts if it's convenient?"

"Whoa, what the hell does that mean? All I was saying is that we have a lot we need to do here. We can barely communicate with him, and who knows if he is as scared and helpless as he seems. I would be more than happy to help him *find* someone to learn from, but right now, it can't be us. Help one or help thousands."

"Just come on. I think we need to go this way," Liam said and stormed off before even giving her a chance to respond. Mackenzie just watched him walk away, completely in shock at his anger for a few minutes before following him. She figured he needed some space and time to think. She could give him that, but she still thought she was right. There was no way to know if Christophe was being genuine or if he was an incredible actor. She had met far too many of those in the past few months.

After a good few hours of watching Liam's back, he stopped dead in his tracks, "Road."

"Road?" Mackenzie asked as she closed the distance between them. When she stood beside the man that both irritated the hell out of her at times and made her feel like she was flying at other times she saw the long gravel road that broke the trees into two halves.

There were no buildings or cars for as far as she could see, but it was a sign of civilization, and that was a good thing. They still had at least two more days ahead of them, but the road was one of the markers they were told to look for.

Liam reached over and linked his fingers with hers, giving them a good squeeze before leading the way out of the trees and onto the loose rocks that crunched under foot. The fact that he hadn't let go of her hand told her that he was done with his alone time. He had cooled off, and they were okay. Nothing else needed to be said.

"Which way? I don't think we came out on the road where Nicholi meant."

"He said north. So we go north."

"Which way is north?" Mackenzie asked a little embarrassed that she still had no clue how to orient herself. She had traveled on foot many, many times, but she usually had a map and a compass with her. This time, the map had gotten lost, and the compass was in the bottom of her bag buried under the few remaining clothing items she had.

"That way. Come on." Liam took charge, and Mackenzie was more than okay with that. She knew that when the time came for her to take back over, he would gladly step back. Somehow, without even ever having to talk about it, they knew when to let the other lead.

The sun had set, and yet there were still no buildings or people to be seen. Not a single car had driven past them in the hours and hours that they had been walking on the road. The trees changed a bit going from thick and dense to sparse to bare, and where the endless fields of wild grass flowing in the wind spread out.

It was absolutely beautiful watching the blades dance in the air. The more time Mackenzie spent outside of an actual house, the more she learned to love and appreciate nature. Perhaps it was just because she was close to turning for the month, and whenever the wolf was forced out, she felt drawn to nature in drastic ways.

Mackenzie stopped walking and pulled her hand from Liam's hand. She had to feel the grass. It was so high it would tickle the skin on her waist at least. With a grin, she pulled her shoes off and then began to undress. If she was doing it, she was going for it.

"What are you doing?" Liam asked looking back and forth down the road before turning his attention back to her.

"Look at it. It's too beautiful not to enjoy it. I need to feel it. Don't you get a pull, too? Look at the moon. In just a few days, it will be full. There isn't a cloud in the sky, and the moonlight is making the grass glow, and the wind is making it dance, and I just want to be part of it for a few minutes."

Mackenzie was standing before Liam completely in the nude, watching his eyes roam her body. When he didn't object, she smiled at him, and then she turned around and ran straight into the field.

The grass caressed her body, the dirt beneath her feet welcoming, and the moonlight that bathed her skin felt like home. As she spun, she tipped her head up to the sky and closed her eyes.

She heard him approach but didn't look. She could feel as he got closer and closer. Her body began to hum in a way that felt like she was on fire, but in the most delicious way. When she could feel his breath warm the skin on the back of her neck, she reached up. She wrapped her arm around his head and drew it to her.

Liam kissed her neck softly before letting his teeth graze her in the most tantalizing way. His large hands wrapped around her waist and pulled her back against his front, the heat from his skin searing into her, letting her know he, too, had shed his clothing.

The world around them did not stop. The wind still blew, the animals still moved about, and time did not stand still. Instead, the rush of nature fueled them, made their hearts race faster, and drove them to near insanity with need for one another.

Mackenzie pressed her ass back into Liam's hardened length, causing him to let out a groan of approval. Liam moved one hand up to cup

Mackenzie's breast and the other down to trace her slit before dipping into her wet folds and flicked her clit.

Her body shook with every tease of her nipple and every stroke of her clit until her knees buckled under her. Liam's strong grip held her to him as he lowered them both to the ground. The grass surrounded them completely; the blades tickling her skin with every movement. She dug her fingers into the dirt, spread her legs as much as she could, and arched into him.

Liam licked and nipped the skin along her neck and her back until Mackenzie was crying out for him to fill her. He gave her lips another pass or two before opening her up just long enough to thrust his body forward and to connect them together.

Liam moved so his hands held her hips as he pounded his body into hers. His fingers dug into her, claiming her. A growl came from deep within her chest that she didn't even attempt to hide. Liam responded in kind, and when Mackenzie looked over her shoulder to see him, their eyes locked. His focused stare as he filled her over and over with pleasure sent a feeling of ownership through her. He owned her, and she owned him. Something about that moment, the connection, was fate. She knew, without a doubt that they were mated.

She didn't know how Werewolves traditionally declared their mates, but she knew it had happened. They had claimed each other.

Liam's thrusts moved faster, harder, and he leaned over her, moving one hand to the ground for support and the other back to her clit to stroke. Mackenzie could feel every one of her muscles begin to convulse, a pulsating pressure in her stomach and pussy grew more frantic, and when Liam bit down on her neck, she exploded around him, crying out to the world around them without a single care if anyone could hear her.

After a few minutes, Liam moved off her and lay on the ground beside her. When she snuggled into his chest, he wrapped his arms around her and kissed her head.

"Did you feel it?" he asked softly. She nodded her agreement into his chest and placed her own soft kiss right above his heart.

"We're forever," she whispered back with a smile on her face.

The two lay there for a few more minutes before standing and redressing. Mackenzie looked back at the field and smiled. The call of nature was never to be ignored.

Mackenzie was beginning to worry that they had found the wrong road. They had been walking for close to four hours and had yet to see another forest to cut through like Nicholi had said.

"Looks like we might be seeing some civilization after all." Liam gestured down the road to what looked like the silhouette of a small building. Mackenzie could make out the outline of people moving about. She was just glad that they still had time before the full moon. She and Liam had come a long way, but it wasn't that long ago that Liam tried to bite a human as a wolf. The smell of human blood is more tantalizing than any other animal. She had to fight to keep him from destroying the girl and himself once he knew what he had done.

As they grew closer, a sign came into view. In large letters that looked to be hand painted on a wooden plank, were the words 'L'auberge de la Loire.' Mackenzie had no clue what it meant, but the stream of people going in and out with backpacks and maps in all states of cleanliness made it pretty clear it was a hostel.

She had heard her old friend—and only friend, back at Harvard talk about her trip to some country to backpack through and see as much as possible for as little as possible so she could have more money for clothes. Hostels were very low cost, and some were even free! They provided a cot to sleep on, a bathroom to use, and a roof to stay under.

"Feel like taking the rest of the night to sleep?" she asked. Liam looked at his watch then back to her.

"You mean all 5 hours until the sun comes up?"

"Sure, why not? It will do us good to get some sleep. Can't be all groggy if Margret or Alice comes by. We need to be fully alert. That means sleep. And this is right here."

"Whatever you want." Mackenzie led the way into the building. Most of the lights were off, but people were still moving around, talking and laughing and carrying on like it was the middle of the day. There was a counter with a thick piece of plastic separating them from the counter guy who sat on a stool reading a book. He looked up as they approached, but didn't say anything.

"Do you happen to speak English?" Mackenzie asked, hoping not to have to get out the translator again. The guy looked up and just nodded. She didn't know if he was just agreeing or if he really did understand her. "Are there any beds left for tonight?" He nodded again and pointed to the back. "How much?"

"Nothing. Just don't steal nothing and leave it like you found it."

Then he turned his attention back to his book.

"Okay, then, guess we go this way." Liam led the way to the very back where two empty cots were next to each other.

Once they put their bags under the cots and lay down, it was as if sleep was waiting to take them. In no time, the world went black around Mackenzie, and she fell asleep.

Mackenzie awoke suddenly when her cot was jarred. With eyes wide open, she was faced with some strange guy trying to get under her bed to her backpack. Anger boiled in her veins and through gritted teeth, she said, "Back the fuck up before I rip your hands from your body. Didn't your mother ever teach you stealing was wrong?"

When he didn't move, Mackenzie placed a single hand on his shoulder and shoved him away, which sent him flying into Liam's cot. Liam jumped out of bed ready to fight, even though from the look of his eyes he wasn't sure whom he was going to be fighting.

"You need to leave. Now." Mackenzie had sat up and swung her legs to the floor. With two hands gripping the side of her bed, she counted to ten in her head then back down to one. It was one of the few methods she had figured out to calm herself down since her change. When her anger got the better of her, things tended to break.

"You heard her. Go." Liam stood tall above the man who just smiled at them and stood up from the floor.

"No problem, Were," the man whispered with a knowing smirk before turning on his heel and leaving them. Mackenzie's eyes went wide, and her hands gripped tighter on the bed frame. The entire hostel was watching the altercation making Mackenzie very nervous. What had they seen? Or heard?

When the wood beneath her hand cracked, and small splinters fell to the floor, she snapped out of her worry and looked to Liam, who seemed torn between staying and going after him.

"Don't. It won't do any good. We just have to keep moving forward and look over our shoulders a little better. We have to keep going."

"What if they have someone follow us?" he asked. She knew he was thinking about the last time they traveled hoping to warn people about Margret. They only ended up getting them killed because they had a traitor in their midst. But neither she nor Liam was like Geoff. They weren't interested in ruling. They just wanted the killing to stop. If they could find the Royal Weres, maybe they could end the war before it became any bloodier.

"We just make sure they aren't. We pay more attention to our surroundings."

"Okay. Go back to sleep. I will keep watch and wake you in an hour." Liam pulled a book from his bag and began reading. Mackenzie wasn't sure she wanted to go back to sleep, or if she even could. The adrenaline was pumping through her body, and everyone around them kept looking their way. At one point, someone whispered about her breaking the bed. She was worried briefly until they attributed it to the poor quality and age of the bed.

Slowly, her heart slowed down, and when she could no longer feel the eyes of the room on her, she allowed herself to lie back and close her eyes, trusting that Liam would wake her when it was time.

FOUR

A gentle shake on her arm brought her from the depths of sleep. The hostel was buzzing with activity as people prepared to leave to continue on their journey. Mackenzie rubbed her eyes and sat up quickly.

"Why didn't you wake me sooner? You need to sleep."

"I'm not tired. I don't think I could have slept even if I tried, so I let you sleep. One of us has to be fully aware of our surroundings, right? I'll sleep wherever we end up camping tonight."

"Okay," she said. She didn't like it, but there was nothing she could do about it at that point. She would just make sure that Liam slept first when they made camp and would give him extra time. Hopefully, they would find the woods and not end up setting up camp on the side of the road out in the open.

"No one has been snooping around here since he left last night," Liam said quietly. If she didn't have the super hearing that comes with being a Werewolf, she never would have heard him.

"Good, but we should still get a move on and make sure to check over our shoulders, ya know?"

Liam just nodded his agreement and shoved the last of his things into his bag. Mackenzie grabbed hers from under the broken bed, and together, they moved down the narrow walkway that was lined with beds to the front door.

The person on the front desk said something, but Mackenzie was too determined to get out of there to really listen to the mumbled words being spoken.

"Let's keep moving. Who knows how far we have to go on this stupid road."

"Hey, we are going to find everyone we need to. You hear me?" Liam's kind words of encouragement were just what Mackenzie needed to hear. She looked up at him and smiled. Even with everything going on, the fighting, the deaths, the horrible possibility of being forced under Margret's rule, she could feel the love flowing between them.

"I hear you," she said, and then she leaned up to kiss his lips softly and linked her fingers with his as they started walking for the day.

"If we could just get to some tree cover, we could run and probably cut the trip in half."

"Yeah, just need those damn trees."

After what felt like an eternity, the road finally became surrounded by trees again, just as Nicholi had said they would.

"He said to make ourselves known. What does that mean?" Liam asked

"Not sure, but probably to make noise and not try to hide. Bad guys sneak around, ya know? Good guys have no reason to hide. So we don't hide. Don't give any pack that may be in there any reason to doubt our intentions."

"Unless bad guys are chasing them. Good guys hide when bad guys want to kill them. What if the pack in there has been taken over already?"

"We have to trust that Nicholi wouldn't send us into somewhere unsafe. He was really grateful for what we did for his kids. He stayed back to tell us where to go when the rest of his pack left."

"Right, he went against his pack. Tell me again why we trust him?"

"Can you tell me anything we have learned since being here that will help us find any of the Royal bloodline?" When Liam sighed and didn't answer, Mackenzie continued. "Exactly. We have nothing else to go on. Either we trust what he said by following his directions or we hightail it out of here. If he wanted us dead, he could have done so when he first found us."

"True," Liam said while scanning the tree line. "I guess we go in."

"Remember, make ourselves known." Mackenzie charged in, stomping and cracking fallen twigs and branches left and right, laughing all the while. Soon,

Liam joined in, and the two stomped through the trees as loud as they possibly could.

They called out things like 'Just passing through!' and 'Don't mind us! We're not the bad guys! See NOT HIDING!' Mackenzie hadn't felt so silly in a very long time. It was a nice change from all the serious and life changing events as of late.

There were a few times that a small crack or rustle of leaves caught her attention from the trees surrounding them, but decided to ignore it and keep moving. Perhaps whoever was out there was trying to let themselves be heard as well without going so far as to call out their innocence. Maybe they didn't even know what they were saying. They were yelling in English after all, and there was a good chance that whatever wolves were following them had never learned it.

The trees began to thin, and a dirt road came into view, splitting the forest in half. Mackenzie breathed a sigh of relief. They were getting closer.

"Just a little longer," Liam said with a grin.

"For this one. We have a whole damn family tree to track down."

"Baby steps, Mac. We have to start with one. We have to build that trust before we are pointed in any kind of real direction. So, you ready to go meet your great-great-something or another?"

Mackenzie shook her head with a smile on her face. Liam was good for her. He kept her grounded without losing the joy in the little things.

"Come on. Let's get this show on the road."

The road was long and looked to be completely isolated. As the trees turned to open fields, they saw farm houses and outbuildings spread out by miles. After probably ten miles, there was a large field that looked completely unkempt.

"It will stand out. You'll know it when you see it. Isn't that what Nicholi said?" she asked Liam.

"Yeah, he did. Look back there." Liam pointed to the back of the property. At the back of the overgrown field was a stone building. It was obviously abandoned many, many years before. With the type of stone architecture, it could have been sitting like that for the last hundred years without being touched.

"This has to be it. Come on." Mackenzie pushed the overgrown grass and weeds aside as she tunneled through to the back.

The stones were breaking apart and falling to the ground around the little stone cottage. The front door had been made of a thick piece of wood, but lay on the ground half in half out of the doorway and was splintered and broken into pieces.

Liam grasped her wrist and pulled her back, kissing her forehead as he moved in front of her. "I know you can handle yourself, but let me go first, okay?" he whispered so low that she could barely hear him.

She nodded her agreement and opened her senses. She couldn't hear anything, but the wind rustling the grass and their heartbeats thumping loudly, and she couldn't smell anything, but old musty wood and the small animals that had taken up residence in the broken down home.

Liam went in, carefully balancing atop the wood fragments in the doorway. She could hear him moving around the small space only to groan in frustration.

"Come on in. There's nothing here. Damn it, we came all this way for nothing!" Mackenzie entered just in time to see Liam grab an old dish off a wooden table and chuck it across the room.

"Maybe there is something here. Something small that will help us." Mackenzie ran her hands along Liam's back then around to his chest, pressing herself into his back. She placed a kiss between his shoulder blades before moving away to search for some kind of clue to prove the last three days hadn't been a waste of time.

Mackenzie looked on shelves that had fallen from the wall to the dirt floor with no luck. All that was there were broken glasses and pottery. Liam moved a rug from the floor and threw it across the room just as he had the dish. When it hit the wall, it fell on top of a large wooden chest. Mackenzie and Liam both moved quickly, hoping that the enclosed box would have preserved something inside of it. Perhaps that is where the clue would be that Nicholi had wanted them to find. Mackenzie, filled with hope, moved the rug and wiped away a thin layer of dust.

With wide eyes, she turned to Liam. "There isn't enough dust here. If it had been sitting untouched as long as the rest of this place, there would be dirt an inch thick on here! This has to be a clue!"

The two studied the carvings in the ancient wood. Ornate markings covered the top, but what stuck out to Mackenzie was the circle high above the rest and the crown carved into what looked to be a representation of a grave. Mackenzie traced her fingers over each piece before lifting the lid. Inside was empty.

"GOD, DAMN IT!" Mackenzie screeched, losing her cool. Everything and everyone depended on them finding the Royal packs. And they were no closer than when they landed in France weeks ago. Letting her own anger pulse through her, she tried to snatch the damned chest from the ground and throw it like Liam would have. Only, it wouldn't move.

"What the hell?" she said after nearly falling on her ass from losing her balance.

"There has to be something here." Liam started checking around the base of the chest, tried pushing to one side or the other, but with no luck.

"What about inside?" Mackenzie asked. She moved back in front of the chest and started feeling around inside the large opening. Maybe there was a hidden compartment or a piece of paper stuck inside.

There were no secret drawers along the side or any papers, but what she did find was a million times better. The bottom of the chest wasn't really there. One minute it looked and felt like the wood the rest of the chest was made out of, and the next, it was gone and before them was stone steps. A lot of stone steps.

"Whoa."

"Yeah."

Mackenzie stood up and gripped the top of the open chest. "Here goes nothing."

Stepping inside slowly, Mackenzie felt for the first step with her foot. If it was some kind of illusion, she wanted to be ready for it. When her foot hit the solid stone, she tapped it a few times before putting more weight on it. After a few solid taps and half her weight, she was a little surer of herself. Slowly, she brought both feet together and smiled over her shoulder at Liam, who watched her hesitantly.

"You sure about this?" he asked.

"All we can do is to go forward. It's too late to turn back."

Without another word, Mackenzie began descending the stairs. Once she had cleared the chest, the walls were lined in the same stone as the outside of the building. The only light came from the sun that was barely peeking through the opening of the chest. When Liam joined her and closed the lid behind him, they were in total darkness.

It was a good thing Werewolves had much better sight than the average human did. Otherwise, they would never have seen the warnings for the missing steps that opened to who knows were, or the few traps that made them duck or climb over random obstacles. Quite simple for them, but if they didn't have the extra abilities that came with the Werewolf DNA they would have been royally screwed. Perhaps that was the purpose, Mackenzie thought and chuckled to herself as she gracefully jumped across an open chasm about 5 foot across to a landing that was only a foot or two wide before the stairs started again.

The stairs came to an end and then opened to a long tunnel lit every so often with fire torches hanging on the walls. Neither Liam nor Mackenzie had yet to say a word. She wasn't sure if it was because she was nervous as hell as to what they were about to find or because filling the silence would feel like yelling in a library. It was as if the passage almost demanded it.

Mackenzie instinctively reached behind her for Liam's hand. She knew connecting with him would help to keep her strong and focused on the task ahead. The fact that they had come down at least a hundred stone steps, and gone through a handful of obstacles most likely meant to kill anyone not a Werewolf and there was still nothing in sight that said it wasn't a great big mouse trap, she needed the added comfort.

When his hand enclosed around hers, his fingers slowly but purposefully trailed along hers as his thumb stroked hers, she felt her heart slow and her fears fade. They could do it together. They would go on and face whatever was at the end of the tunnel together.

Liam leaned over and kissed the top of Mackenzie's head, then took a step forward, tugging her hand a little. She matched his pace, step for step.

Her free hand trailed along the walls, fingering over some etchings that had to be hundreds of years old. There were others that were words written in French and even some in English. Those had to be new. It gave her hope that they weren't about to walk into a battlefield, or worse, a cemetery.

One word stopped her in her tracks.

BEHEADED

The knot in Mackenzie's throat grew bigger, and swallowing it down proved almost impossible. She searched the other words around it to try to find *who* was beheaded, but there were so many names, she wasn't sure what any of it meant.

With his free hand, Liam brushed her hair behind her ear and leaned down. With a whisper as quiet as a breath, he said, "It's okay. We have to keep moving."

Mackenzie nodded her agreement and moved forward, her hand still trailing against the wall feeling the deep grooves and rough crumbling stone left behind by Werewolves of the past.

Mackenzie had no way of knowing what time it was. Neither she nor Liam wore a watch and a cell phone that her father had given her to check in with was turned off in the bottom of her bag to conserve the battery. But with how heavy her eyes were, they had to have been in that tunnel for a very long time.

A loud yawn escaped from Liam, echoing off the stone walls. Mackenzie's eyes went wide, and her head whipped back and forth, searching frantically for whoever was going to pop out of some secret hidden hole and grab them for breaking the silence.

No one came.

"Hey, Mac, does that look like a dead end?" Liam whispered.

"Yeah. Why the hell would there be a dead end?" she replied in a normal voice. If no one came running over his monster yawn, she wasn't going to whisper. She was just about tired of the silence. It was going to drive her crazy if it lasted much longer.

"Maybe there is something carved in it like on the walls at the bottom of the stairs?"

"Only one way to find out." She moved forward until there was nowhere left to go. There hadn't been a turn the entire way. The dead end had to have some sort of clue. Anything to get them out of there and keep them from taking who knows how long to make their way back up and through the chest, if it were even possible. There was magic behind that thing, and she wasn't sure how she made it work to begin with so who knew if she could make it work again to let them out.

The dead end of a stone path was surprisingly not made of stone. It was a very thick wooden door. Only there was no door handle or knob to open it. The only thing there that let her know it was a door was the small sliver of light coming in from around the edges.

Liam dug his fingers into the crack and pulled. With every grunt and groan, the door moved a little more until finally, he was able to get his fingers completely in the opening and yank it hard. The wood flew open, blinding them with the sudden invasion of so much light that their eyes hadn't had time to adjust.

When four large hands grabbed her and yanked her from the cool passage into the hot sun, before she could even see who was doing it, she screamed out. She heard Liam fighting against whoever held him, and as the seconds ticked by, she was able to see. Wherever they were was a Werewolf community complete with buildings, cobblestone paths, and a giant well in the middle of the 'road.' Children ran around practically naked playing in puddles to relieve themselves from the hot, humid air and adults talked and watched, some as humans, others in wolf form. Completely free to be who they truly were.

Mackenzie stopped fighting then. They had found what they were looking for and fighting the people who guarded the entrance to this place would do them no good.

"Liam, stop and look!" she called out. When she stopped fighting, the guards relaxed. When Liam stopped fighting, they all stopped moving.

"How did you find this place, bitten." The guard who held her was large. Larger than even her father and he towered over her and Liam.

"I was sent here to find Evelyn. I am Mackenzie, Daughter of Darren and Great-great-great-granddaughter of Meredith. We mean no one any harm. I bring a message from the United States. Please, does Evelyn still live here?"

"You are no daughter of Royalty. You are a bitten," he spat out.

"I am. My father Darren mated with a human. I was born, and then bitten. I have Royal blood in my veins, and I want nothing more than to use it for good. I came to speak to Evelyn. Is she still here?"

"Who is he?" the guard asked without answering her question or even acknowledging

A smile played at Mackenzie's lips. "My mate."

Mackenzie looked to Liam, love coursing through her at finally calling him her mate. It was the first time she said it aloud, and she could see the fire burning in his eyes. It was love bursting with lust staring at her. Mackenzie could hear a few women who were walking by making the 'awww' sound and one even mention how new the magic radiating off them was. There was even a 'congratulations' yelled out.

Mackenzie had to tear her eyes away from Liam to look back at the guard. "Please, is Evelyn still here? I need to speak with her or anyone else from the Royal line."

"This way," he said gruffly and then proceeded to walk her down the cobblestone street through the middle of town. The guard never let go of her, only forced her to walk while restrained like an animal. She was sure Liam was still being held as well. She tried to look behind her to check, but she couldn't crane her neck far enough. She understood why they needed to take precautions, but it didn't irritate her any less.

The community that was alive and well stopped everything they were doing and stared at the newcomers being lead down the street. The children stopped splashing, the wolves turned and stared with a subtle growl rumbling through their chest, and those still in human form watched with mixed emotions on their faces. Mackenzie didn't know what to think.

"Keep your eyes down. You don't need to know about them. You haven't been granted the right to look at them, bitten." He used the name bitten like a derogatory term. She felt dirty just hearing it. The more he said it, the more it felt like he spat it at her.

"I have a name, you know. Call me Mackenzie, not bitten."

He just let out a huff and tugged her arm a bit harder to make her walk faster. At the end of the road was an old stone building that sat up higher than the rest of the buildings. The steps leading up to the open doorway were large and grand in comparison to the rest of the buildings. Mackenzie counted each one as they passed. One. Two. Three. Four. Five. Six. All the way to twenty-five.

Twenty-five steps above the rest of the town. When Mackenzie looked back over her shoulder, she expected to see a small village that was falling apart, but she didn't. There wasn't one area that looked neglected. There was a small garden to one side and a makeshift playground to the other. She was quickly yanked forward and reminded to keep her eyes down.

"Stop doing that to her! She has done nothing to deserve that," Liam bit out. Mackenzie could hear the anger in his tone and could practically feel the rage bubbling off him. He needed to calm down, or he would lose control and possibly shift into his wolf. Ever since they had figured out how to change when they wanted, they would also sometimes change when they lost control of their emotions without wanting to.

"You two came to our home without invitation. That alone is deserving of our distrust."

"ENOUGH!" Everyone stilled and snapped their gaze up to the open doorway of the stone building. Standing there was a tall woman with dark hair, beautiful curves, and a much younger version of Margret's stunning face.

FIVE

"I'm sorry, Evelyn. These two came through the wall. This... *bitten*... claims to be of your bloodline and demanded to speak to you. That one is her mate, or so she says." The guard who held her arm spoke to Evelyn with almost a reverence. She was most definitely still the leader of this pack, this community. Mackenzie already held a high respect for the woman for keeping her pack so well taken care of. Mackenzie almost huffed to herself when she realized she thought the same thing about Margret not that long before.

That was the thing about assumptions. They were usually wrong. She hoped this was one of the few times it would be right.

"How did you find our village?" Evelyn's voice wasn't harsh or condemning. She stepped forward and waited patiently for Mackenzie to answer.

"Nicholi told us how to find you. We found him and his pack and helped them fight off Alice's pack. He said to tell you he sent us."

"Nicholi?" a soft smile spread on Evelyn's face. "How is he? Still well? How badly did the attack affect his pack?"

"Nicholi is as well as he can be. His mate was killed in the battle. They lost many, but Alice's pack retreated. Their leader was not harmed. He had run with a few guards before too much destruction happened." Mackenzie tried to keep the disappointment from her tone. Just because she would never leave those she considered family behind did not mean that other packs had the same views. In America, if there is an attack, the government gets the president the hell out of dodge. It was the same thing. Or so she kept trying to tell herself.

Evelyn visibly choked up and swallowed hard before regaining her composure. "And the children?"

"They are as fine as they can be for watching their mother killed. But they were not harmed."

Evelyn nodded then turned to the guard holding Mackenzie. "Get Malaki. Let him know his brother has sent visitors."

The second set of hands released her. The gruff guard who kept calling her bitten kept his hands tight on her, not relenting for a second. Mackenzie could feel Liam's calm slipping from him and willed him to trust her and Evelyn. They didn't have much of a choice at that moment.

"You claim to be of Royal blood? But your eyes tell a different story."

"Like I told this one. My father is Darren, descendent of Meredith, daughter of Gwendolynn. He fell in love with a human and had me. In October of last year, I was bitten and forced into this world. Perfect timing with a power hungry psycho bitch on the loose, don't cha think?"

"You knew nothing of our world, though your father was a Royal?"

"Long story short, he took off for my own good when I was a kid. My mother kept it hidden from me, feeding me bullshit about him, so I tried to pretend he didn't exist. I was bit, found Margret, left Margret, and then found my Dad. Fast forward a bit through some bloody battles and backstabbing and here we are."

"I would love to hear the long version one day, but for now, we go inside and have some tea. I hope you do not mind, but I must confirm your blood before we can do much else." Evelyn turned her attention to the guard holding Mackenzie and said, "You may release them. Stand outside the door. If we need you, we will let you know."

Mackenzie smiled at the man even though he was glaring at her. He didn't trust her or Liam, and that was to be expected, but he could have been a little more respectful. As soon as Liam was released, he was by her side, his hands running up and down her arms where the guards had held her.

"You okay?" he whispered low enough for only her ears.

"Mmhmm." She tipped her head up and looked into his eyes, the connection and the closeness of each other helped to settle the nerves in her. She put on a brave front, but the whole trip was terrifying her with every new step.

"This way." Evelyn's words interrupted their moment, but Mackenzie knew time was of the essence. Mackenzie and Liam stepped back from one another but laced their fingers together tightly as they followed Evelyn through the large open doorway.

Inside the walls were the same stone as outside. A large fireplace sat along one wall, and wooden tables and chairs were placed throughout the big open room. Mackenzie could see that there were other doorways leading into halls, but she couldn't see down them. The few windows that were placed around the room let in some light, but candles and oil lamps were the main sources of light in the dark stone dwelling.

"Please, sit. I will have Elsa bring some tea." Evelyn left the room through one of the darkened hallways, leaving Mackenzie and Liam alone.

"How will you prove your bloodline?" Liam whispered worry clear in his eyes. Mackenzie reached out to him with a soft smile and ran her thumb across his furrowed brow and cupped his cheek in her hand.

"I don't know, but I am sure Evelyn has a way. Whatever it is, you have to let me do it, okay?"

Mackenzie watched as Liam struggled with the idea of her in any sort of danger, but when his lips closed into a tight line, and he gave a subtle nod of agreement, she knew he wouldn't interfere.

Footsteps echoed behind them, slowly getting louder as the seconds ticked by letting them know they weren't going to be alone much longer. Liam leaned in and kissed her softly and whispered words of love in her ear.

"Please, sit. We have much to discuss." Evelyn's words broke the quiet in the room, and the three of them moved to the chairs near the empty fireplace. "The tea should be here in just a moment."

"I have seen the destruction Alice is causing here and have been told she is fighting in the name of Margret. Do you know anything about that?" Mackenzie asked.

"Do you know my lineage, Mackenzie?"

"I do not. I have very little knowledge of the Royal bloodline beyond what my own father explained to me and what little I learned from Margret and her son, Geoff."

His name still brought an ache to her chest. She could feel the weight on her lungs and the tears stinging her eyes. She wished that she could simply hate him as Liam did. She wished that his name was like acid on her tongue, but it wasn't, and she knew you couldn't get over that kind of heartbreak, that kind of betrayal, easily.

Evelyn must have noticed her change in tone because her eyes softened, and her head tilted to the side. "Her son, he was important to you."

It wasn't a question, but a statement. Liam stiffened beside her and watched her intently for a response. But no words were needed. Evelyn already knew Geoff was important. So she just nodded.

"Margret had no siblings. She was the sole child of Rosalinda, the Royal Were. She watched her father murder her mother. That changed her from the happy and carefree child she was into a cold and calculating woman who has no respect or tolerance for humans.

When she grew up and no longer had a claim to any type of thrown, she began blaming her own kind for her mother's death as well as the humans. That is when she decided on her plan of forcing the Weres to go back into a single pack with her as the one true leader. Over the years, she bed several males and became impregnated three times. You know Geoff, and then there was Belinda, and then Gregory."

"Where are Belinda and Gregory now?" Liam asked, leaning forward with his elbows on his knees, and his hands clasped together. A soft, sad look passed over Evelyn's face.

"Belinda died many years ago. Before Margret even left for the United States. Gregory passed twenty years ago, leaving this pack to me. His eldest child."

"So, Margret is your grandmother." Mackenzie let out a long breath after that statement. No wonder she looked so similar to Margret. Could this woman be trusted? Had they just walked into another one of Margret's traps? She had trusted Geoff, who claimed to be something he wasn't. What was going to stop Evelyn from doing the same?

"By blood, yes. But that woman will never be family. She is the worst kind of Were out there. Driven by greed, power, blood, and vengeance. Family means little to her unless you bend to her will. Alice fell for her stories of safety and bloodline rights. Margret promised her the world. A life without hiding. A life where everyone fell to her feet in worship. A life where the call of human blood didn't have to be tamed or ignored."

"So who is Alice to you?" Mackenzie asked, chewing on her lip afraid of what the answer might be.

"My sister."

Silence filled the room after the revelation of how much was at stake for Evelyn. She may have claimed that Margret was no longer family, but her sister? That would be hard for anyone no matter how horrible they were.

"Momma, your tea." A small voice filled the space, and all three turned to see a little girl with dark brown hair, brown eyes, and the squared jaw that seemed to be prevalent in Margret's family line. She was the spitting image of her mother.

"Thank you, sweetheart. Come say hello to our guests. This is Mackenzie and her mate Liam. Mackenzie, Liam, this is my daughter, Hannah."

The little girl set the tray of tea on the table between them and moved to her mother's side. She snuggled in close before looking over at Mackenzie and Liam to give a little wave. She reminded Mackenzie so much of her little sister that she had yet to get to know. She hoped she would make it back to spend time with her. Growing up the way she had, constantly moving with her mother and no siblings was lonely. When she found her father and her sister, it was like filling a hole in her heart she hadn't known was there.

"You remind me of my little sister. She's about your age." The girl smiled big, kissed her mother's cheek, and ran off back down the hall. "She is absolutely beautiful."

"Thank you. Have some tea."

Mackenzie picked her cup up and took a deep drink from it. It was bitter on her tongue, but the warmth going down her throat was soothing. She didn't particularly like it, but it wasn't horrible either. As Mackenzie sat the cup down, she saw that Evelyn was smiling at her.

"Thank you."

"No, thank you for what you are doing. Now, tell me how far Margret's reach is in the United States?"

"From what we can tell, she has taken many packs. We traveled all over the north, from the east coast to the west coast, and almost all of the packs have been taken," Liam said, taking a drink of his own tea. Liam hadn't traveled as far as Mackenzie had, but she told him about her change and where Margret found her. It was scary how far Margret's reach really was.

"I know my Father's pack is still intact, and I know of another pack working with him. They are sending out scouts across North America to find packs that are not affiliated in any way with her to build up a defense against Margret."

"So what will you do with this group? Become the aggressors? Find and kill her?"

"I'm not really sure. I know my father has a plan, but my part so far is to find the Royal family and try to get as much help as I can. Rosalinda's sisters stop the hierarchy for a reason. They might want to help keep the Werewolf world how they shaped it."

"I will not force my pack to help in this war. I will tell them the news you bring and of the very real danger that Margret poses. They will be allowed to make their own decisions from there. As for me, I have lived in these woods, in this hidden community for a hundred years. My father left his mother's pack and hid away in these woods two hundred years ago. If he hadn't, Margret would have killed him, either by her own hands or by an order. He built this pack slowly, taking in anyone who wanted to get away from their own packs for whatever reason. Eventually, they had an entire town to care for and keep hidden. And safe.

"Some say that my father was a coward, hiding away from a fight. I say he was brave. Brave enough to hide and take the criticism, instead of killing his own mother in self-defense. Brave enough and strong enough to lead a group of Werewolves that had no allegiance to him other than what he earned. And I too will follow in his footsteps. I will not force them to take on a fight so large that many will not return.

"But I am not my grandmother either. I will not take away their right to choose how to live. Stay tonight. I have guest rooms here you may choose from. Rest well, and tomorrow, I will speak to my pack. I will also replenish your travel bags with food and water for your journey."

"Thank you so much. We really appreciate the hospitality."

"Of course, you are my kin and are always welcome here. Come, our evening meal should be ready."

Evelyn stood and led them back out the door from where they came. Everyone had gathered in the common area and was watching them come down the stairs. Worry laced all of their faces, but one look at their leader walking of her own free will with a smile on her face was enough to calm their nerves. It had to be worrisome to see two strangers stumble through the wall and be practically dragged through their community like criminals.

"Everyone, this is Mackenzie and Liam, our guests! Please treat them as any other member of our home. Let's eat!"

SIX

After Evelyn's statement to the crowd, the silence was broken with cheers and chatter. Many people approached and said hello, introducing themselves. They all walked back through the little town. Mackenzie could smell smoke in the air and a delicious aroma that had her stomach grumbling. The scent became stronger as they entered the trees that surrounded the stone buildings.

After only a few moments, the group came to an open field with wooden picnic like tables and benches surrounding a rather large fire pit that already had three large animals roasting over it. Three men surrounded the fire, turning large pieces of metal that went through the animals being cooked.

"What is that?" she asked Liam, who looked to be salivating at the site before them.

"Bear. Not sure what kind, but those are definitely bears."

"And you know that how?"

"I used to go hunting with my dad. Come on, let's eat."

Liam and Mackenzie were handed plates made from the same clay that formed the pitchers that held the water and the pots that were boiling away with vegetables in them. She smiled and shook her head. They had stepped through the magic portal, literally, and went back in time. This community hadn't aged and grown in technology as the rest of the world had. They all seemed so happy and content. Maybe the rest of the world had it wrong. Maybe the key to a peaceful world was to go back. Forget about technology. Forget about money and barter instead. Forget about being the biggest, strongest, best whatever, and just live.

Mackenzie and Liam sat at a table and were immediately surrounded by a group of women with goofy grins on their faces. Mackenzie smiled at them nervously, unsure of the attention they were receiving but not wanting to be rude.

"How did you know?" one asked with a toothy grin. The others nodded their heads in agreement to the question, and they all leaned in, waiting for an answer.

"Know what?" Liam asked, and then shoved a chunk of bear into his mouth. He moaned in delight and closed his eyes.

"That you were to be mated, of course!" another girl said.

"Oh, um..." Mackenzie trailed off, feeling the heat rush to her face.

"We just knew. We looked at each other, and all of a sudden, this feeling of love and wholeness washed over me. Like I was finally complete. And I knew. I was just glad she felt it, too." Liam took charge of the conversation. With one hand, he rubbed soothing strokes up and down her back. Her embarrassment must have been so clear to everyone and made it even worse.

"Of course, she did! A mating is something magical. If you are to be mated, you will find one another, and you will be connected heart and soul. And the ceremony? How was that?" the first girl asked, glowing.

"We haven't had one yet. We are waiting until we are back in America with her father." Mackenzie thought of Darren, and what he would think when she told them they had been mated. He liked Liam. She wasn't sure what was involved in a mating ceremony, but she knew he would be a part of it somehow.

"He will be so proud. Such a strong Werewolf to take care of his daughter."

Mackenzie smiled up at Liam and knew the woman was right. Her father would be proud and would welcome Liam warmly. They had a long and bright future ahead of them. That is if they could stop Margret.

The rest of the meal wasn't focused on them, but instead, on how their community worked so well and had stayed hidden for so long. Everyone worked in some capacity, or another for the whole group, not just themselves. The hunters provided meat to everyone while the gardeners provided everyone with fruits and vegetables. The teachers taught all the children. The seamstress made clothing for everyone, and the list went on and on. It was truly a community that took care of each other. No one went without, and everyone pitched in.

Finally, as the crescent moon was high above the trees, and the crickets were singing their song, Evelyn stood. The cacophony of voices and laughter subsided almost instantly, and the people listened raptly for Evelyn to speak. She had their full attention and loyalty. It was an amazing sight to see.

"You all know our visitors hail from the United States. The daughter of the Royal Werewolf, Margret, is starting a war among our kind, forcing packs under her rule with the hopes of regaining the title her mother lost. They are targeting humans and having pups bite them without their consent. Mackenzie and Liam came to me to ask for help. I told them I would not order anyone from my pack out of their home to fight in a war that has yet to reach our door. But I do believe if we do not act, it will come knocking sooner than we would like.

"If you wish to help, to be a soldier against a future none of us wants, then tomorrow, speak up during the mandatory pack meeting. But first, really consider everything this entails. Leaving our community, your family, and possibly sacrificing your lives.

"Everyone should go home and talk to a loved one and have a good night's sleep before making any decisions. Goodnight and I love you all."

Evelyn and her guard left the dining area together. As soon as they cleared the tree line, the crowd erupted into nervous chatter again. Liam grabbed

Mackenzie's hand under the table and gave a little tug. When she looked into his eyes, she saw a touch of worry, but he tilted his head in a quick movement toward the tree line where Evelyn had just gone. Mackenzie wanted to get out of there as soon as possible to let the pack talk amongst themselves freely. That and she didn't want to give any more details than Evelyn had. If the pack leader had wanted them to know more, she either would have told them or would have asked Mackenzie to tell them.

With a quick nod, Mackenzie agreed. Liam stood quickly, and Mackenzie followed suit. The two quickly moved to the tree edge, and with one look back at the crowd yelling back and forth about whom the pack needed most to survive, and who the best fighters were, Mackenzie knew that at least some of them would be helping.

The walk back to Evelyn's house was a silent one. Mackenzie just held onto Liam's hand as if it were the only thing keeping her grounded. With the world around them exploding into a million bloody pieces, it was nice to have that one thing that you knew deep down would never leave your side. Liam was her thing.

Inside the stone building was dark with the exception of an oil lamp left on the table by the door with a note that directed them to their room. Liam picked up the lamp and held it high above their heads, casting an orange glow on the walls and floor ahead of them.

Every step echoed, and somewhere in the stone walls must have been a small hole, because the wind whistled through, and a chill coated Mackenzie's sleeveless arms. Even in the summer, the nights can put off a chill, and in a stone building that's sole heat came from a fireplace that wasn't lit, it was rather cold through the hallways.

The room that Evelyn had indicated was theirs was at the end of the hall. The large wooden door was arched and had stunning knots, and details woven into a story that Mackenzie was sure spanned generations upon generations. The door itself could have been a hundred years old and had surely seen its fair share of life behind it.

The door creaked loudly when Mackenzie pushed against it. Inside the walls was the same stonework as the rest of building. There was a large bed in the center of the room and little else.

Mackenzie walked over to the bed and lifted the crocheted blanket to see the mattress wasn't a mattress at all, but a big cloth sack that had been filled with something soft, like a giant pillow.

"Do you think many of them will want to help?" Liam asked as he pulled his shirt over his head.

"Yeah, I think so," Mackenzie said through a heavy breath. Why did he have to start taking his clothing off if he wanted to talk? He should know that would be distracting. A soft laugh, and a crooked grin on Liam's face told her he knew what he was doing.

Instead of giving into him, she rolled her eyes and turned the other way to grab her bag.

"I wish I knew what was going to happen. I wish I could tell everyone willing to help that they would be fine and would come home to their family and live happily ever after. I hate having to ask them to risk their lives. Their lives that so far have been untouched by the craziness."

"Not untouched. Nicholi is something to Evelyn. Remember her reaction? This is personal for them, too. And just because they are hidden for now, doesn't mean anything. Don't you think that after Margret takes as many packs as she can that she isn't going to go after the rest of the Royals? Without their obedience, she is nothing more than a pack leader with a very large pack. If the other Royals don't recognize her as *the* Royal Were, no one else will."

Mackenzie thought about the look of despair that painted Evelyn's face for just a moment before she regained her composure. Liam was right. There was a connection. Of course, there was. How else would Nicholi have known where to send them to find Evelyn?

"Do you trust them?" Mackenzie whispered. She did. But she wanted to know Liam's gut instinct on it. She had been wrong many times before with whom she trusted, but not Liam. So far, he hadn't been wrong once.

"I do."

"You trusted Geoff at one point."

"No, I needed Geoff to help me at one point. I never trusted him." Liam's voice had gone tight, and

Mackenzie knew it was because she had brought up Geoff. She turned to face him and walked up to him, reached out a hand and stroked his cheek, then let her hand fall to his bare chest and rest above his beating heart.

"I should have believed you."

Liam didn't respond. He only bit his lip and watched her. What else was she going to say that she hadn't said before? She chose him. She was his mate. She loved him. Geoff betrayed her, and she was heartbroken by what he did. But not heartbroken in the sense of a lover. No, she had seen him as a best friend, at least in the end. He broke the trust, the love, the loyalty, and recovering from that was just as hard as or harder than recovering from a breakup.

"Did you love him?" he finally asked. They didn't speak much about Geoff and especially not about her almost-relationship with him. There was enough hurt feelings and confusion before when she was unsure of whom she really wanted to be with, but she never felt for Geoff what she felt for Liam. Not even close.

"Not like I love you. You are everything to me. You are my mate. We didn't decide that on our own. The universe did. The magic that we live and breathe did. But if it hadn't, I still picked you. I still would have loved you until my last breath."

He didn't answer with words. Instead, he crashed his lips to hers, encasing her in him completely. His warmth penetrated her skin, and her body hummed in delight. With a fluid grace she had only known since being bitten, she jumped up without breaking their kiss and wrapped her legs around his waist.

Liam guided his hands from her back down to under her ass to hold her against him. Mackenzie grinded against him, telling him without words that she needed him. She needed him in so many ways, but at that moment, she needed his body to ravage hers. She needed to feel the physical connection with him after opening up emotionally.

With three swift steps, Liam had them on the bed. The soft mat below her and Liam's hard body above her sent her senses into overdrive. Liam pulled back and began undressing slowly, like a candlelit strip show. The glow of the fire cast an orange hue across his chiseled chest and now stubble-covered jaw, his yellow-green eyes glowing in the dim light. A small growl built in her chest and Mackenzie reached out to her mate and pulled his naked body down to hers. The feel of his skin under her fingers sent shivers up and down her spine, and when his own growl vibrated under his chest, she was done with the exploration and needed to feel him inside of her, too.

Liam lifted himself off her just long enough for Mackenzie to shed her clothing. As she lay naked before him, she felt that connection, the magic that the told her that this was her mate. This was her Werewolf. Liam was hers and hers alone. And she was his. There was no denying it or fighting it. And she didn't want to. She had chosen Liam long before the magic had.

The small smile on Liam's face and the desire in his eyes told her he felt it, too. When he lowered himself back down on top of her, everywhere their skin touched was alive with fire.

Liam kissed her jaw and nibbled his way to her neck where he licked and sucked right on her pulse point. Mackenzie let her hands find his hard length between them, and she pumped his cock in rhythm with Liam's ministrations on her neck.

Liam moved down her body until her nipples lined up with his roaming mouth, and he enveloped them in the wet warmth. A moan escaped her lips, and Liam grinned against her before he moved farther down.

Mackenzie opened her legs further, begging him to kiss her there, touch her there, and take her there. He traced a single finger along her slit, up and down, barely touching her throbbing clit. Her hips lifted from the bed, hoping to create more friction, only to have him lay an arm across her, pinning her to the bed. Before she could form the words to protest, Liam had plunged two fingers inside of her and lowered his mouth to encase the rest of her pussy. He licked and sucked at her clit as he pumped his fingers into her until she shook with fervor and called out his name in ecstasy.

Liam slowed down his movements as her body calmed. When he crawled back up her body, love shone from his eyes. Mackenzie leaned up to kiss him, tasting her on him. Liam lifted her hips from the bed, lining his length up with her opening and slid in, slowly pumping into her as he looked into Mackenzie's eyes.

She traced his face with her hands, gently stroking his lips, and then caressed his jaw line down to his chiseled chest. When she wrapped her hands around to his back, she whispered, "I love you," then drug her nails down his back urging him to move faster.

Liam didn't disappoint. He pumped his cock into her so fast, and so hard, that she was calling out his name for a second time in a matter of minutes. Her whole body tensed up in a most delightful way. When Liam let out a groan of his own, his body jerked once more as he collapsed on top of her.

With a single kiss to her temple, they fell asleep, still connected in the most intimate of ways.

SEVEN

The next morning was a flurry of activity. The once quiet halls were filled with footsteps echoing off the walls and nervous chatter about the pack meeting to come. Mackenzie dressed quickly and left Liam asleep on the bed. He hadn't slept well in weeks, and she wasn't going to disturb him until it was absolutely necessary.

Slipping out of the room, Mackenzie was greeted by many of the town's people rushing up and down the halls with baskets of food or pitchers of drinks. Some held weapons and others, stacks of paper.

"Good morning, Ms. Mackenzie!" Evelyn's daughter called out as she ran by. Mackenzie smiled at the girl and called back a good morning to Hannah, as well.

"What's going on?" Mackenzie asked the next person that passed by.

"Pack meeting. But you knew that, right?" the woman who carried a stack of linens replied.

"Right, but what is all of this?" Mackenzie motioned to the food and drinks and commotion going on as they walked down the hall toward the main room.

"All of our pack meetings have sustenance and Evelyn provides us with paper and writing utensils to take notes. She expects this to be a longer than normal meeting, so we are making sure everyone has everything they could possibly need."

"Oh, is there something I can do to help?"

"I am sure if you speak with Evelyn she will be able to let you know what still needs to be done."

"Thank you!" Mackenzie said as the woman walked off in a separate direction. Looking around, Mackenzie thought she spotted Evelyn heading down the opposite hallway and followed her. When she realized that she had left the common area, and there was no longer anyone roaming the halls, she knew she had entered Evelyn's private section. She immediately turned around, not wanting to disturb her.

"Mackenzie?"

Mackenzie turned around to see Evelyn standing there with a man. He looked a lot like Nicholi, only older. "I am sorry. I didn't mean to come to your personal space. I hadn't realized I left the common area until it was too late."

"It's all right. This is my mate, Jeremiah," she said motioning to the man beside her. She looked at him with such love and adoration. Did she look at Liam that way? The thought of it made her smile. "Jeremiah, this is Mackenzie."

"You are the one who saved my brother's children. Thank you." Jeremiah came forward and took her hand in his. The gratitude was evident in his voice, and a firm handshake exuded respect. She had earned their trust before she ever met them just for doing exactly what she would have done for anyone.

"Nicholi is your brother? That would explain how he knew where to find you. I was more than happy to help. I only wish I could have helped his mate."

"She did as a mother is meant to and protected her children at all costs. She died bravely. One day, one day you will understand that natural instinct to protect your young." Mackenzie cringed. She wasn't the typical Werewolf on the Royal bloodline. She wasn't a born Were. She was bitten. Because of that, she would never be a mother. She would never have that instinct.

Evelyn sighed and nudged Jeremiah. When he looked to his mate, she shook her head ever so softly. When Jeremiah looked back to Mackenzie, her eye color finally registered with him. "I am so sorry, Mackenzie. I assumed that you were born of Royal blood. I didn't..." He trailed off, looking everywhere but at Mackenzie.

"It's okay. It is what it is. I know I come from Royal blood in quite a strange manner, but I am a bitten Royal. What I don't understand is why being bitten is such a horrible thing to be here. That guard yesterday practically spat the word at me."

"Being bitten is a sign that a born went against the laws of our pack. It is proof that one of our own has strayed. That one of our own has put our entire pack in danger. Humans are off limits. It is the only way our pack has survived hidden away for so long. When humans get brought into the mix, they come with resentment and anger and no knowledge of our life here."

"But that isn't the bitten Werewolf's fault. Shouldn't the anger be toward the born who bit them?"

"It is. They have their own term that is thrown around. Much too vulgar for my taste. But bittens tend to not have the same loyalty, the same values. Most bittens don't have anything in common with our pack. This is no reason, of course, to be hostile simply because of that, but it is common. Animals reject what is different just as humans do. Why does one race of humans act out against another? Why do some men treat women as lesser beings? They are different, and they cannot understand the other."

"Usually, it's because they feel superior." Mackenzie was getting really irritated at the simple accepting of what was described as exactly the same thing as racism.

"Because they do not understand that while different, they are still the same. I wish I could wave a hand and make it go away, but we both know that will never happen. Now, I have a feeling this meeting will be a long one. I will remind everyone of why we called the mandatory meeting, and then let you tell the others in your own words what is going on. After that, we just have to make sure everyone is making the right decision for their family and the pack."

"Making the right decision?"

"Of course. A single father cannot leave his children unattended; the only mid-wife cannot leave without training another in her place when we have two pregnant mothers. We cannot have all the males rushing off to war leaving the pack with little protection. There has to be a balance. But first, we see who wants to fight and go from there."

Mackenzie nodded. She understood that. As much as she wished everyone would help, she knew it wasn't possible. She didn't want to be the reason that even more packs were wiped out completely, even if they volunteered. "Okay, I'm going to go make sure Liam is awake. I will see you in the meeting."

Evelyn and Jeremiah nodded. Mackenzie turned and tried to navigate the way she had come. Somewhere along the way, she made a wrong turn and wound up outside of the kitchen. There were murmurs of voices that she was going to ignore and just find her way back, but then one word caught her attention.

"Alice will be pleased," someone in the kitchen had said.

"Shhh, you are going to get us killed before we even have a chance to tell her," another voice whispered.

Rage boiled through her, and she felt the vibrations in her skin, and the magic take hold of her very being, urging her to let go and let the Wolf out. It took absolutely everything in her power to calm the beast, but she did. She quietly stepped back then ran down the hall, through the den, and into another hall that she hadn't seen before. Thankfully, that one ended in the living room just as the first had and she was able to make her way to her and Liam's room. She had to tell him what she had heard. She had to get him and get back to Evelyn before the meeting started.

Mackenzie flung the heavy wooden door open only to see an empty bed and rumpled sheets. She looked around but saw no sign of Liam. Turning quickly, she headed for the pack meeting room and hoped she would find him before they started. If she was going to tell Evelyn that she had a traitor in her own home, when she wasn't even sure who that was, she needed Liam by her side. Maybe he would have an idea as to how to tell her without her blowing a gasket.

The chairs were filling and the room was full of hushed conversations that echoed off the stone walls in such a way that it made Mackenzie feel like she had walked into a stadium with thousands instead of the hundred that were there. She looked around at first, hoping to spot Liam without looking too worried or upset. She didn't want any of the pack to question her then. Finally, instead of wasting anymore time looking, she closed her eyes and opened her senses. She would breathe deep and just feel for him. She knew his scent like no other, and it was a beacon to her, calling her from the darkest depths to his lighted soul.

When the hints of grass and man tickled her nose, and her heart began to sing, she opened her eyes and turned her head to the left. He stood by the table full of food, talking with a short woman who was placing everything out in large dishes. Mackenzie walked over to them and placed her hand on his shoulder blade. His hand reached up and rested on hers as he looked back at her with a smile.

"Can we talk a minute?" she asked in a serious tone. Liam's eyes went wide, but he nodded and excused himself from his previous conversation. Liam linked his hand with Mackenzie's and led them out of the room into an empty hallway.

"What is it?" he whispered very quietly. She knew that at the level he was speaking that only she could hear him.

"Someone in the kitchen is working for Alice. Two someone's, actually."

"Who? Who would do that... and how would Alice have even found this place?"

"I don't know, but I overheard them talking about pleasing Alice and to not say anything, so they don't get killed before then. We need to tell Evelynn."

"We need to tell her carefully. You don't want to accuse them if for whatever reason, there is another Alice living here."

"Any suggestions?"

"Yeah, don't just come out and say your kitchen people are trying to kill you. I don't think that would go over well."

"No, probably not. Come on."

Mackenzie and Liam entered the meeting room again, this time every seat was full and Evelynn stood in front of the room. It looked as though she was about to start the meeting, but when her eyes met Mackenzie's, she gave Evelynn the slightest shake of her head, hoping she would get the idea.

When Evelynn started down the middle of the room toward her, she knew that she had. Evelynn held her composure, nothing on her face giving away a single worry. She received a few glances from pack members, but nothing that worried them enough to stop their own conversations. When Evelynn stood in front of Mackenzie and Liam, Mackenzie leaned in and whispered ever so quietly that they had a problem.

Evelynn looked back to her mate and with a slight nod of her head, requested that he join them. Once Jeremiah stood beside her, the four of them left the packed room. Jeremiah led them down the hall and through another that put them in a room Mackenzie had yet to see. Not that it was hard to do, as she hadn't seen probably half the large building yet.

"This room is sound proof. I made sure of that years ago when Gregory began to worry about traitors within the pack. Tell us, what is going on," Jeremiah said. Evelynn nodded her agreement, and both waited silently for Mackenzie to begin.

Mackenzie went through the story again making sure to give as many details as possible, even though very few were actually available. She told them how she found herself outside of the kitchen, what the voices sounded like, and exactly what was said.

"Thank you, Mackenzie. Now we must get back. If anyone has already eaten or drank anything, we need to be watchful. Without knowing exactly what their plan is, we have to take all precautions. There were only four in the kitchen today. We shall question them all."

When they returned, the meeting room was so loud that it was nearly impossible to hear one another. As Evelyn moved quickly through the crowd to the front, everyone began to quiet down and take their seats. Mackenzie, Liam, and Jeremiah stood in the back and watched as the pack fell to Evelyn's presence. It was amazing the amount of respect and adoration these people felt for her. If the situation hadn't been so dire, Mackenzie might have even smiled at it. This was a very, very large family.

Scanning the room to see who was where, and if anyone wasn't paying the same kind of undivided attention to Evelyn as the rest, Mackenzie's eyes landed on Evelyn's daughter. She was reaching out to take a piece of food from the table. With the warning echoing in her head from before, Mackenzie yelled out.

"HANNAH! STOP!"

The little girl jumped so far back from the table that Mackenzie felt bad. She felt worse when everyone in the group turned to stare at Hannah and tears streamed down her face. Mackenzie ran over to her at the same time as Evelynn and Jeremiah.

"Shhh. It's okay, baby." Evelynn pulled her daughter into her arms and held her close.

"Hannah, I didn't mean to scare you. I am so sorry. I just didn't want you to eat that, and I yelled out instead of running over. I didn't think. I just did it."

"You guys," Liam whispered, "there are three people trying to leave the room slowly."

Jeremiah looked back over his shoulder, and his eyes narrowed. "DO NOT GO ANYWHERE!" he bellowed. "STOP ANYONE WHO TRIES TO LEAVE!"

Mackenzie saw the asshole guard nod his head and stand a little taller. Three men moved to the doors and blocked them.

The meeting room grew deadly silent. Everyone looked to the other with questioning eyes, but no one said a word. The three people trying to leave attempted to sit back in their chairs. But it was too late. They had been caught.

Evelynn stood, giving her daughter a kiss on the head, and went back to the front of the room.

"We have traitors amongst us. I hadn't wanted to believe it to be true, but running after they realized they had been caught was enough proof for me. Krista, Laney, Chad, come forward and explain yourselves."

Two women wearing chef whites and a young man stepped forward. None of them held a face of remorse. "We have nothing to say."

"You will tell us everything or you will be beheaded right here."

Evelynn's sweet demeanor left in an instant, and what remained was a strong and powerful leader. What she did with this skill was what would place her on the good or evil side. Margret, for example, could be the world's most caring 'mother' and leader one second and be attempting global domination complete with a cult of followers who never questioned a single thing she said the next. She was clearly on the Evil side.

"Margret is our true leader. Alice has shown us the writings that have been hidden from our kind for centuries! If we help her, we will be appointed to Margret's council. We will be furthering our kind and destroying the humans who would only destroy us if they knew we existed," the only male said through gritted teeth.

"What papers?" Mackenzie asked skeptically. "Papers from her mother who died unexpectedly at the hands of her own husband? Papers that unless perfectly preserved would have little chance of being intact or readable after all this time?"

"Yes, papers. It was a family tree and signed papers from Rosalinda's sisters that they renounced the title. According to hierarchy laws, this would leave the next in line to the throne when they are able to take it. And Margret is now able to take it to make the world better. We won't have to hide. The humans will have to hide from us. Why should we be less than they are when we are forever stronger? We are the superior beings. They are weak and meaningless. Why can you not see this?"

"What did you do? You were overheard in the kitchens. What will make Alice proud? Have you already done something to hurt the family you have grown up with or were you only planning to turn your backs on us?"

"I guess you will never know." The man then stopped talking and refused to open his mouth. The two women with him, however, were beginning to fidget, and their eyes were darting around the room at all the angry faces before finally landing on Evelynn and quickly looking back to the ground.

"Krista, do you have something to say?"

The girl said nothing but continued to look to the floor.

"Laney?"

"I... I... I—" Laney began, but Chad shouted out "Say nothing! She is not the one true leader. She cannot make you speak!"

Evelynn nodded her head to the guard who held Chad. Before Mackenzie could look away from her, she heard the distinct crack and cries from the pack watching. It was almost completely unnoticeable, but Evelynn closed her eyes and swallowed thickly. When Mackenzie did look over, Chad was crumbled on the floor, his necked twisted behind him.

It didn't kill him; he was a Werewolf after all, but she knew when a second guard came up and dragged his body away that it was only a matter of time before his head was removed from his body. When Mackenzie turned back to Evelynn, she saw the fearless leader actually wipe a stray tear from her face. When her watery eyes opened, her voice wavered for only a moment.

"We will not tolerate traitors. We will not allow anyone to put our pack, our family in danger. Chad was a traitor. I will grant leniency for whoever speaks first."

"The food! It's in the food! Alice wanted to minimize the pack so when we let her know it was time that she would be able to come in and take the pack!" Krista shouted before Laney could even open her mouth. Tears rolled down both girls faces, and they were drug out of the meeting room wailing.

"It is a sad day for our pack. To lose three members," Evelynn was clearly upset, but the feelings of loss and sadness didn't stop her from what she had to do, "is a shame. To have three members so easily swayed by power and hate. But this proves to you how close Alice and Margret are. Who will stand and fight to not only protect our pack, but every pack out there that hasn't fallen to their will."

Mackenzie watched anxiously as person after person stood from their seats, willing to help, willing to fight. Liam reached out for her, and she folded into his arms, relief washing over her. If they were all willing to help, perhaps they could find more. Perhaps they stood a chance against Margret's growing army.

The meeting went long into the morning after that. Mackenzie had a list of fifty men and women who would be heading to the states to help Darren. She wished she knew more about his plan and what they would be doing, but he had said it was better she didn't know. That it was safer for everyone involved.

"This is my father's contact information. If you can get someone to a town with a phone, you can call this number and speak directly to him. He has access to funds and can help get anyone who is going to help to the United States."

Mackenzie handed Evelynn a piece of paper with Darren's number on it and nothing else. She didn't want to lose it and have it be found by the wrong person with too much information.

"I will make sure we connect soon. I will send someone out today to get traveling supplies and to make the call. Someone I trust completely. You have done us a great service by coming all this way. You alerted us to a threat we hadn't known was so close. You protected my niece and nephew. You protected my daughter. We are in your debt."

Evelynn surprised her by pulling her into a hug. The two women stood, holding each other, for a few moments before stepping back. "By allowing us to ask for your packs' help, we need to thank you. We have a long journey and a hell of a battle to face, but I won't give in. I can promise you that."

"That I am sure of. You are definitely of Royal blood."

"You never gave me the test." Mackenzie had just remembered that Evelynn was to test her blood to prove her story true.

"Yes, I did. The tea was your test. Without Royal blood, the tea would have closed your throat until you turned blue. The Werewolf DNA wouldn't have let it kill you, but you would have blacked out within minutes of drinking it."

"Oh. Okay." Mackenzie didn't know what else to say to that. There really wasn't much else to say. So instead of dwelling on the possibility of choking to the point of blacking out, she moved on. "We need to keep going. We need to find more packs willing to stand against Margret."

"Being secluded here has it benefits and its drawbacks. I do not know where you would find another pack. You have already found the one pack we have relations with, but I can tell you where to find my brother, Edwin. He has no pack. He decided long ago that pack life wasn't for him. He checks in occasionally, for holidays and the like. You can find him in Paris."

"Paris? That's a big city. How will we find him?" Liam asked

"Go to the tourist area and find any pub that allows the public to sing. He enjoys the company of human women and tells me that they love musicians. His name is Edwin. Make sure you let him know I sent you. That should be the first thing you say to him. He travels so he may be able to lead you in some kind of direction. I wish I could tell you more."

"You have given us more than we had before. Thank you, so much. I look forward to seeing you again." Mackenzie felt a lump in her throat. She had grown attached to this pack in such a short time. She feared she wouldn't see them again because Alice would come either after her and Liam or Evelyn's pack before they had a chance to reunite.

"If you ever need a safe haven, or meet a wolf along the way that you trust implicitly that needs a place to go, you may send them here. I will take care of them. You have my word."

After another hug from Evelynn, Mackenzie and Liam crawled back through the magical hole in the wall that lead them back to little stone cottage and the road that would take them to Paris.

EIGHT

As soon as Mackenzie and Liam were deep enough into the woods that they could no longer see the road, they both focused their thoughts on their wolves and let their bodies feel the nature surrounding them. In moments, the pain was gone, and all that remained standing there were their wolves.

Mackenzie and Liam both grabbed their packs in their mouths and took off like a shot. As their paws thundered the ground, and the trees whipped past them, Mackenzie couldn't help but feel like they were being watched, followed even.

Every stray sound made her run faster. She wasn't afraid of a fight, but she also didn't have time for one. They needed to get to Paris as quickly as possible. Edwin was their only lead and finding him was their top priority. If they could just keep running, they could possibly make it to Paris in days instead of weeks. But the longer they ran, the more noises she heard.

When the cracks of branches turned to low growls, she no longer had the option of ignoring whoever was watching her. When two large black wolves jumped out in front of them with teeth bared and fur standing on end, Mackenzie and Liam skidded to a halt.

Liam paced back and forth in front of her, growling and snapping his teeth at the intruders. The two black wolves began circling them, each going in opposite directions, effectively negating Liam's protective stance. Mackenzie didn't need his protection. She could handle her own. She let out a growl of her own and snarled at the wolf closest to her. The color of their fur threw her for just a moment. Geoff's fur was black.

She shook her head to clear the thought that he could be one of the wolves there to hunt her down. Not only did she hope that he couldn't do that, but their smell was all wrong. She knew Geoff's smell almost as well as she knew Liam's.

Her brief moment of distraction was all that the intruder needed to gain the upper hand. Before she knew it, she was on the ground, and the wolf was atop her. With a swift kick of her hind legs to the wolf's stomach, she sent him flying. The ache in her back was only momentary as the muscles and bones healed themselves almost as fast as they had been damaged from her hard fall. Mackenzie wouldn't take another chance. She wouldn't let Margret or her wolves win. She could no longer only be on the defensive. She was strong and powerful, too. She would show them exactly who they were messing with.

Mackenzie lunged at her attacker with teeth bared. She could faintly hear Liam battling the other wolf, but her focus was on the beast in front of her. She knew that Liam could fight better than most. Geoff had been his teacher too, after all.

Mackenzie landed on the wolf and immediately sank her teeth into its flesh. She latched onto its shoulder, hoping to wound it to the point of scaring it. She knew the gaping hole would heal, but she wanted the fear of death in the wolf. She wanted it to tuck tail and run. She wanted it to let the enemy know that she was no longer going to sit back and take it. She wanted everyone to know that she was to be feared by those who were on Margret's side.

The shriek the beast let out as her teeth ripped its muscle from the bone and the blood coated not only its fur, but also hers and the earth beneath them, should have turned her stomach. Months ago, before she had been forced into a war amongst her own kind, it would have made her wretch. But at that moment, she was pleased.

Instead of simply releasing it and hoping it ran before it healed, she ripped the muscle and tissue completely off, spitting a large chunk of the wolf to the ground beside them. The wolf's shoulder would still heal, but it would take much longer to do so.

Mackenzie backed up and growled deep at the black wolf. The fear in its eyes, and the whimper that fell from its muzzle told her what she needed to know. He was afraid. When he limped away into the woods, she turned her attention to Liam's battle, which was no more.

Liam stood over the headless body of the other black wolf. His white fur stained red with the blood of the battle. The dead wolf's head lay a few feet away, and Liam stood on shaking feet staring at the body before him.

Mackenzie padded over to him and ran her muzzle along his and into the crook of his neck. He was a gentle soul, but he did what he felt he had to. He protected himself and her by ending the wolf's life.

After a few moments, the two began their run again. They had to get to Paris more than ever. They no longer ran under the radar. Their presence was known and the only way to finish what they started was to move faster.

Shifting back to their human forms just before the trees disappeared was strange. Mackenzie had never spent a full three days as a wolf before. They did little besides run and sleep, only stopping to eat once. The sunlight fell on their faces as they walked the busy roads leading into the city of Paris. Mackenzie wished she had thought to bring a camera, but then again, what was the likelihood of keeping it in one piece over the course of their trip.

She and Liam may have been in the most romantic city in the world, but they were not there for romance. The thought saddened her. She wished that she and Liam could have started their lives together under happier circumstances. She wished that their future didn't depend on the outcome of the war. She hoped that they had a future. She hoped they would survive long enough to enjoy each other without constantly looking over their shoulders.

The city loomed ahead as they found the iconic river that ran through the city. Following along the flowing water, they finally entered the city of love. Liam squeezed her hand tighter in his and smiled down at her. She could feel his love wrap around her like a blanket, calming her. She looked back to the city and knew they had a hell of a job ahead. Finding Edwin was going to be like finding a needle in a haystack.

"We still have a good six hours of daylight left. We won't find Edwin at any of the places that Evelynn suggested until nightfall. What do you say that we pretend we aren't on the hunt for warriors against the biggest bitch in history, and that we are here as a happy couple in love and looking to take in the sights?" Liam suggested.

Mackenzie knew he had a point. But she also wasn't sure she could just pretend that everything was fine. What if they were attacked when they weren't paying attention? Would innocent people be hurt? Would Alice take the chance of forcing her men to change in public?

"Look, I see that brain of yours spinning through a thousand 'what if's.' Mac, not even Margret would tolerate her wolves turning in public. It would ruin her plan. If I wasn't so against becoming a science experiment, I just might do it myself, but the point is, as long as we stay in the highly populated areas, we will be safe."

Mackenzie let out a sigh of relief. He knew what she was thinking and relieved her worries without her ever having to say a word. "Okay, how about we get something to eat and then find the touristy places and pretend we are just like every other couple in the city? You know, like couples that aren't running for their lives at every turn or who turn into hairy animals whenever the full moon tells them to?"

Liam gave a little laugh and kissed her on the forehead before saying, "Sounds good to me."

Walking hand in hand, Mackenzie watched the people riding their bikes, walking along the water like them, and simply enjoying the day. A few times, they stopped to take pictures for couples and families, and when her stomach grumbled quite loudly, they took a break from the beautiful sightseeing and slipped inside a little cafe.

It felt light and airy inside, which Mackenzie knew was strange, but she had no other way to describe it. The tables weren't so close together that she felt like she was sitting on top of the people next to them, and the windows were large and open, allowing the summer breeze to blow through.

Liam held her hand across the table and looked into her eyes. No words were needed. They could sit together in complete silence and not feel the need to fill the quiet with words. What mattered was that they were together.

Mackenzie heard their server approach before she even spoke. She knew Liam did too, but didn't want to look away. So little of their time together had been calm. So little had been at the moment. Being there, in

Paris, with the man she loved, was like a dream she never knew she would get a chance to have.

Only, the server didn't stop at their table but kept going. When Mackenzie's stomach growled loudly again, the two laughed and began looking around for a waiter. The men in black pants, white shirts, and black vests flowed through the cafe almost rhythmically. It was so fluid how they circled the tables, carried the trays, and never once bumped into each other or any table. Mackenzie could have sworn it was choreographed.

"How do you think we get their attention?" Liam asked with a curious look. Mackenzie wasn't quite sure. She had never been to a restaurant where the waiters ignored a customer looking around like that. They hadn't even approached to let them know who would be their server or to ask for a drink order.

"Maybe say hello the next time someone passes by?" Liam nodded, and they both watched expectantly as server after server floated through the room, but none coming close enough to gain their attention.

"Say Bonjour," the person in the table next to them said after five minutes.

"I'm sorry?" Mackenzie asked. The gentleman was sitting alone, eating cheese and bread, and drinking a glass of wine. He looked up with a smile and repeated himself.

"Say Bonjour. It's the only way to get a French waiter's attention. It took me far longer to figure out than the two of you, but then again, I didn't have someone in the know to help me out. Since I have already been waited on, saying Bonjour would do nothing, but make me look crazy. However, if I want them to come back for any reason, I need to ask for them. Watch," the man looked around like we were. He made it pretty obvious he was done. He even huffed a few times, checked his watch, and began to tap his foot. Then, he looked to them and smiled with a wink. "Monsieur, S'il vous plait," he said. A waiter came right over. Within seconds, the man had the attention of the waiter and was able to ask for his check.

The waiter nodded his head and reached into his apron to retrieve the check. He turned to walk away without another look to Mackenzie and Liam. She quickly called out, "Bonjour!" Many heads turned in their direction. She had said it a little louder than needed, but the waiter stopped his retreat, and they were able to put in an order.

When he walked away, Mackenzie and Liam started to laugh uncontrollably. When they had finally settled down, Liam reached out for her hand once again and said, "I love you."

"I love you, too."

After lunch, Mackenzie and Liam explored the city. But as the sun began to set, Mackenzie was back into full search mode. She kept a running list in her head of every place they had passed by during the day that either had a sign advertising for live music at night or what looked like it might have live music.

"Look," Liam said, pulling her from her own mind. Mackenzie followed his gaze to the tall metal structure that was the epitome of Paris, the Eiffel Tower. With the sun setting behind it, it was absolutely breathtaking. "Come on, let's go up. We can pretend for just a little bit longer."

"But what if we don't find Edwin? What then?"

"An hour isn't going to stop us. If we don't find him tonight, we look again tomorrow night. And if we still don't find him, we keep looking. Look at it, Mac. I bet we can see all of Paris from the top."

She did want to see Paris from the top of the Eiffel Tower. Looking around, the crowd was beginning to thicken. If they didn't get in line right then, they would never make it to the top and back down with enough time to find Edwin.

Biting her lip, she looked around once more before landing her eyes on Liam's. He was watching her with such hope in his eyes that she couldn't say no. Instead, she nodded her agreement, and a thousand watt smile on his face in return was all she needed. The two ran over to the ever-growing line of people and waited their turn to go to the top of romance's most iconic figure.

When they finally got to the top, the sky had grown darker with just a hint of light along the horizon. The city lights glowed in a kaleidoscope of colors, and the city skyline was absolutely stunning. Mackenzie felt Liam move to stand behind her and wrap his arms around her waist. Mackenzie laid her head back to rest against his chest, and they took in the beauty together.

Mackenzie turned in Liam's arms to face him. Running her hands along the hard planes of his chest covered by his shirt, she felt every muscle and scar up to his neck where she wrapped her hands.

"This is exactly what I needed. You are exactly what I need. You and me, we were meant to find each other. You are the one reason that being bitten hasn't completely been for nothing. Liam, you mean everything to me. If I had never been bitten, I would still be at Harvard thinking that werewolves and all that goes with it was folklore."

"You and I would have met even without being what we are. I don't know how, but one thing I have learned in all this is that if the universe wanted it to happen, it would have happened."

Mackenzie didn't let him say another word. She lifted up onto her tiptoes and pressed her lips firmly against his. He pulled her even closer to him. She could feel his heat radiating through their clothes. Her hands that had been softly resting at the back of his neck flexed, gripping him tighter, pulling him closer.

Liam traced his tongue along Mackenzie's lips, sending a shiver of pleasure through her in anticipation. She opened to him, kissing him with as much passion as she ever had.

A snicker of a child's voice pulled Mackenzie and Liam apart in a hurry. They had almost forgotten where they were. Mackenzie could feel her wolf taking over, just as she always did when strong emotions were at play. She wasn't in danger of turning in front of everyone, but her lust could have gotten the better of her and possibly ended up being arrested for public indecency. She tended not to be able to control her lust where Liam was concerned.

Mackenzie looked over toward the voice and saw a little girl blushing and smiling. Mackenzie gave her a little wave and felt an ache in her heart that she was beginning to recognize as a longing for something she would never be able to have. She hoped that in time she would grow to accept that her future held no children for her. She and Liam would have to make the most of their lives together without a family. They were each other's family.

"Come on, our time's about up anyway." Liam led her away from the little girl. With a hand on her back that felt like a lifeline, the two rode the elevator down to the ground. The time for romance was done, and they had to get back to the impending war.

"There was a bar down this way," Mackenzie said, already walking in the direction of the first stop she planned to make.

It had been hours since they had set out down the road in search of the Royal wolf. They had been to at least five different places. Some large, some small, but none held Edwin. Mackenzie hoped they hadn't missed him along the way somewhere, but Evelyn said there would be no missing him. They just had to get close enough to smell him, to feel the magical buzz in the air that alerted her to other Werewolves around her. Until finally at a small university cafe with a sign for open mic night, the musky scent of Wolf wafted on the air, and the musician singing had the distinct facial features of the other Royals they knew. They had finally found him.

NINE

Mackenzie and Liam moved through the small cafe that was jam packed with girls. Excited sighs and many French words were whispered followed by giggles. Most were wearing as little as possible, and their attention was focused solely on the man singing.

Mackenzie didn't understand a single word he sang, but even she could see how easily the girls were fawning over him. A low growl came from Liam's chest, and Mackenzie had to look back at him and smile. He had no reason to be jealous, but the fact that he was made her feel good. Every girl likes knowing that the man she loves also loves her enough not to want to lose her.

The singer's eyes snapped up and locked onto Mackenzie's eyes. For a brief moment, she saw alarm pass over his face, but like a true entertainer, he refocused himself on the song and the stage.

"Let's go by the stage steps so he can't disappear on us." Mackenzie knew the look in Edwin's eyes. He was ready to bolt as soon as he could without disappointing his fans. Mackenzie could feel Edwin as he watched her getting closer. So she looked to the stage and smiled at him. She wasn't there to cause him any trouble, and as soon as she had a chance to talk to him, then he could go back to finding a girl to bed for the night.

The song ended on an impressive note. As Edwin pulled the guitar strap from his neck and told the crowd he was taking a quick break, he walked toward them. His face was serious, and his lips were in a harsh, flat line.

"Before you say anything, Evelynn sent us to find you," Mackenzie whispered urgently.

"Anyone could have told you her name. You better talk fast," Edwin grasped Mackenzie's arm and started to pull her around the corner. A deep growl from Liam and one quick movement put him between her and Edwin. Liam held Edwin's wrist in his hand.

"Keep your hands off her," Liam bit out. He shoved Edwin's hand away and kept his stare directly on the Royal that stood before them.

"I don't know who you think you are, but this conversation is over. Leave. Now." Mackenzie could feel the air around them beginning to shift and saw the ripples in Edwin's muscles under his skin. She had to diffuse the situation and quick.

"Look, we need to talk to you. Evelynn sent us. Alice is working for Margret, who is taking over the entire damn world. We found the pack after days of traveling all off the word of a Were name Nicholi. Then we traveled days more to find you after Evelynn sent us to Paris. We still have a long road ahead of us.

Evelynn seemed to think you would know where to find more of the Royal bloodline."

"If you met Evelynn, you would have to know how to get there. How did you enter the compound?"

"Through a chest in the middle of a rundown cottage in the middle of nowhere. Then when we got through the magical door at the end of an extremely long hallway, after dodging who knows how many booby traps, we were manhandled by a guard who refused to use my name and just kept calling me *bitten*. Then we were dragged through the center of the little town and up the steps to Evelynn's door, which is where we met her. Do I really need to keep going?"

"Come with me." Edwin backed up and turned down a little hallway behind the stage.

"I don't like him," Liam growled, "but we have to follow him. But if he puts his hands on you again..."

"He won't. And we don't have to like him to need his information. If he were dangerous, Evelynn wouldn't have sent us to find him."

Mackenzie leaned up and placed a soft, quick kiss on his cheek, hoping to soothe his nerves. Then she followed the same path Edwin had in hopes of finding out anything she could to stop Margret and get on with her life. A life without people trying to hunt her down and kill her. A life where she and Liam can just be happy together.

Edwin sat in a room that was somewhat closed off from the rest of the cafe. It looked to be some sort of staff lounge, but no staff was in there. A small round table with fold up chairs was all that sat in the room with the exception of a small mini fridge in the corner.

Mackenzie stepped into the room and looked around at the bare walls. It had a very cold feeling to it. This wasn't somewhere you would want to hang out. Perhaps that is exactly what the owners had in mind, to discourage its employees from hanging out instead of working.

"Sit," Edwin said then took a drink of something in a coffee mug. It wasn't coffee, though—that much was for sure. By the smell of it, Edwin had smuggled in some good old fashion whiskey. "I hear a lot. But I stay out of the way and keep to myself. I don't want to deal with packs or the drama that comes along with it. I chose to be on my own to stay out of all of this. I know that my sister is loyal to Margret. I also know that Paris is full of Werewolves at night looking to add to her ranks. Vampires no longer run this place. Alice does. She leaves me alone because I stay out of all of this. I don't know what you think I can tell you."

"It doesn't bother you that Margret and Alice are attacking any pack they can? It doesn't bother you that Alice had spies within your sister's pack trying to poison her? If Alice can attempt to kill one sibling, what makes you think you are safe?"

Edwin's eyes got large, and Mackenzie could hear the beat of his heart increase. The beads of sweat that threatened to roll down his forehead were clear. He didn't know how deceitful Alice could be.

"I have no pack. That means I am of no threat to either of them."

"Margret wants to rule over all Werewolves like her mother. Don't you get it? It doesn't matter that you have no pack now. If Margret gets what she wants, you will be forced to obey her," Liam said.

"Alice has never seen our Grandmother for who she really is. She has always thought the Royal blood was a blessing. She pictured tiaras and fancy dresses, like the princesses in fairy tales. Margret promised her those things were true. It didn't matter that we tried time and again to tell her that it wasn't true. It didn't matter that Margret had killed her own child in her quest for power.

"All that mattered was she was going to rule beside Margret. She would be in line to the throne as long as Geoff never had children." Edwin took another long pull from his glass and set it on the table. He stared into his hands for quite a while.

Mackenzie didn't want to speak and break his thought process. She also knew if she did, her voice might give away how hurt she was. Geoff had lied to her over and over. She should be expecting it after everything he put her through, but with each new revelation, it was like ripping open the wound that had begun to heal. If only Werewolf DNA could knit together hearts like it did skin, it would be a lot easier to move onto hating him.

"So when is the next time Alice will send her Wolves to the city? Maybe we can do something about it."

"I wouldn't. You aren't going to change anything by getting in their way. They already know you're here. Maybe not here in Paris, but in France," he said.

Mackenzie knew they had already been attacked, but she hadn't realized that word would travel so fast. "Like I said, I hear things. You should get out of here before their next hunt. They come once or twice a month, but from the sounds of it, they are really making a push with the war. The full moon is only a week away. You don't want to be here."

"But we don't even know where to go. We need to find others. We need to find the rest of our damn family!" Mackenzie said through gritted teeth. Edwin wasn't helping them to do anything but get more on edge and angrier at all of those involved.

"Our?" he asked with an arched eyebrow.

"Yes, my eyes say bitten, but my blood says Royal. I drank your sister's tea to prove it to her. If you had any here, I would do the same. But Darren is my father, the great-great-grandson of Meredith." She was tired of explaining it. Whether or not she shared, the blood didn't make finding them any less important. If these damn wolves didn't want to be bowing down to Margret, they would help whether she was *just* a bitten, or she had Royal blood.

"I need to go back on. You should stick around for the next song before leaving."

Edwin stood and left the room, leaving Mackenzie and Liam sitting there completely dumbfounded. Why did he want them to stick around? Was it some sort of trap? Was he trying to keep them around for Alice's pack to find?

"Come on, we should probably head out of here," Liam said. Mackenzie nodded her agreement. She wasn't looking to get into another fight so soon or in such a public place.

As they rounded the corner back into the main area of the cafe, Edwin was on stage. The stirrings of music began flowing from his guitar, and the sad tone floated on the air.

"This song is a new one. There is someone who needs to really hear it. Really listen and let the words and the melody sink in. You will know what to do," Edwin spoke into the microphone and looked directly at Mackenzie and Liam before letting his eyes travel the room like a true musician.

Liam pulled her close to his body and wrapped his arms around her waist. She could feel his heart beating faster than normal. The skin on his arms was covered in goose bumps, and there was a slight tremor in his muscles. He was ready for a fight. He was still worried but allowing her presence to calm him long enough to listen to Edwin's song.

Between the mountains covered in grass
Lay the cottage of shattered glass.
The beast within slayed by its love
The blood seeped into the floors
and into her soul, the daughter forgotten
in her father's rage.
The castle stood tall, proud of its kill
King after King found beast after beast

Presenting its body and celebrating with feast after feast

The stone would crumble, but the legends stayed true

Do not step foot in her home,

The forgotten daughter will kill you.

The eerie song came to a close, leaving the entire audience in a somber mood and wondering what had happened to the sexy singer. Edwin slipped off the stage and was gone before anyone could stop him.

"Come on, let's get out of here." Mackenzie grabbed Liam's hand in hers and stepped out of his embrace, leading him to the exit. "We should get a room for the night."

"Yeah, just not in the city."

"Good plan. Let's see about getting a bus or something."

TEN

Mackenzie stepped off the bus into a dark parking lot just outside of Paris. Looking around, Mackenzie spotted a small motel just down the street. Liam led the way, and Mackenzie was more than happy to let him.

Everything was wearing down on her, and she was content to let him make the decisions for the night. She realized that she had never been comfortable with that before, but she knew that Liam wouldn't lead them anywhere that would lead to danger. She knew that if she could trust anyone to keep her safe, it was Liam.

Liam checked them in, paid with the cash that her father had given them, and took the room key from the man behind the counter. Heavy feet padded down the hall, and when Mackenzie saw the bed, she flopped down, clothes, shoes, and all and closed her eyes, letting sleep claim her.

Mackenzie woke to the soft whisper of Liam's voice. She rolled over on the bed and watched him. He sat at the edge in nothing but his boxers, the muscles of his back rippling as he stretched, yet somehow kept the cell phone her father had given them tucked between his ear and his shoulder.

"We're fine," he said then listened quietly for a bit. "Really. Mac did more damage to them than they did to us. I have never been so impressed watching someone fight as I am when I watch her."

A smile crept on her face. The fact that he was telling her father that and didn't even know she was listening meant the world to her. He wasn't complimenting her to make her feel better. He was doing it because he really believed it.

"We found two others so far. Evelyn and her brother Edwin... Yeah, her grandkids... Some riddle. I don't know—something about mountains?"

Mackenzie decided it was time to let Liam know she was awake. She practically memorized that song from the night before. Maybe her father could help them decode it.

"Hey," she whispered. Liam turned to look at her with a smile. She reached her hand out and motioned with her hand for the phone.

"Hold on, Mackenzie's awake. Here," Liam handed over the phone.

She put the phone to her ear and just listened. She could hear her father's pack in the background and his breath over the line. Thousands of miles no longer felt so far. She hadn't realized how much she missed him and his pack until that moment. She was surprised by the tears that brimmed in her eyes. She had just met them only weeks before. She hadn't known growing up that her father was a Werewolf. All she had ever known was what her mother had told her. He was a drug-addled jerk who was in prison. She still held so much anger toward her mother for keeping them apart, but at the same time, she knew the dangers of being near a Werewolf. It was hard to be logical when all your brain wanted to do was be emotional.

"Hello?" Darren's deep voice came through clear over the phone, and Mackenzie smiled. She could picture her father with a smile, sitting on one log by the fire ring talking to her.

"Hey, Dad," she said back. Darren let out a deep breath full of relief. It made Mackenzie smile knowing how much he cared.

"So Edwin gave us this song that was a riddle of sorts. He was trying to tell us how to find another Royal, without actually telling us. Think you can help?"

"Well, I've never done much exploring out there, but maybe we can figure it out together. Let's hear it."

Mackenzie repeated the song slowly, then again. "So, any clue?"

"Let's take it line by line. He started it with 'Between the mountains covered in grass.' So, on the map look for the places between two mountains. Not rocky mountains either, but ones with lots of growth."

"Okay, are we sure he is talking about France, though? There are so many countries out here. This seems almost impossible."

"A few lines of the song are obviously talking about Rosalinda, the Royal Were. Margret's mother. If that place is still standing, you never know what you can find."

"But do you really think it's still there? Wherever this damn riddle actually leads to and after all these years?"

"I don't think Margret would let go of the house that he mother was killed in. It's the reason she is doing all of this. To take back her mother's throne. That house is at the center of everything."

"Okay, so between two mountains covered in grass." Mackenzie dug the map out of her bag and laid it out on the bed. Her father and she talked about each mountain range, either crossing it out completely as not a viable option or circling it as a place to check. "What about the line 'The castle stood tall, proud of its kill'? Is that just part of the story, or another clue? I mean I was told at one point that Rosalinda had an affair with the human king. Wouldn't he want her close?"

"That's a really good point. Is there any way for you to cross-reference the old castles? I can't imagine it would still be used after all this time."

"But hasn't the Royal family used the castle since the 1500s?" Liam interjected. He picked up the room phone, and Mackenzie listened as he asked the front counter about using a computer. "I'll be right back. They said I could use the one in the lobby. I have an idea."

Mackenzie relayed the message to her father and went back to the map. "Do you think it would be far from Paris? I mean, are we going to be traveling another hundred or thousand miles? I just have a feeling that the castle isn't going to be THE castle. I mean if Rosalinda was a mistress, wouldn't he want her away from the main castle?"

"Perhaps, but keep in mind, back in that time, the King had whatever woman he wanted, and no one could say otherwise. He may have kept it quiet to save his Queen from upset feelings, but it wasn't unexpected for the King to have many women."

"Yeah, I guess." Mackenzie had thought she was onto something. The idea of being able to flaunt infidelity was so foreign to her that she hadn't thought about that. "There has to be something else here to help."

Mackenzie and her father spoke about each line. Argued if it had more meaning than the words themselves, and then finally agreed that the only thing of value was the line about the mountains and a stone cottage. At least they would have an idea of what to look for when they happened to find it. After twenty minutes, Liam came back through the door with a large smile on his face and a paper in his hand.

After ending the call with her father, Mackenzie leapt into Liam's arms. She pressed her lips against his and felt him smile. When she pulled back, he looked into her eyes and kissed her again.

"You are a genius. Absolutely, positively, genius!" she said after pulling back again. What could have taken months of travel and searching now would take only weeks or days. The pages that Liam had printed off the computer in the lobby contained locations of castle ruins. They could cross reference the castles to the map that they had already started to narrow down, and cross out even more areas that wouldn't hold anything new for them.

Mackenzie and Liam spent the next hour planning where to go in the morning once they had a good night's sleep.

Mackenzie thought she had heard a noise outside their door once, but when she got up to check there was nothing there. With a final glance out the window before shutting off the light, sleep didn't come as easy as she had hoped. She had a nagging feeling that even though she couldn't see anyone outside their door, someone was watching them.

ELEVEN

Two weeks. It had been two weeks since they left the little hotel outside of Paris. Two weeks of searching and disappointment. As the sun set, Mackenzie looked to the sky. The moon would be at its fullest in just a few hours, and her wolf would demand to come out. She took a deep breath in and thought about the night to come. She thought about her wolf and came to the realization that it wasn't her wolf. It was she. She was a wolf. She had complete control over her time in her other form. She had every memory of every minute spent. It wasn't always that way. But she was damn glad it had changed.

Before she had control of the memory of the nights the full moon shone down, she would awaken the next morning terrified and ashamed of what she might have done. Often, she was covered in blood and once she had to bury what was left of a body. With every full moon after her first, she grew stronger and retained more memories. Then, finally, she was able to make decisions and actually be in control. Since that day, she has never allowed her wolf's thirst for blood to take over. She was able to protect herself as a wolf. She was able to protect those she loved, too. That is what mattered.

"Look at this," Liam said. He had the map that was now covered in angry black Xs and scribbles all over the French countryside. Mackenzie walked over to him and ran a hand up and down his back. His muscles loosened under her touch, and a slight smile that played on his lips from her caress made her heart flutter. "Right here. This has to be it. See, mountains on either side, a valley between them."

Mackenzie looked but wasn't exactly sold. They had said that the mountains had to be green. That the valley between them would be a field of green. The mountains he was pointing out were hardly that. They were rocky with very few trees, and the valley wasn't very large. There would have been no place for Rosalinda's pack to hide or hunt.

"Are you sure? I mean, isn't that more rock than anything?" she said softly, pointing to the map.

"No, I'm not sure. We covered all the obvious ones though. None of those panned out. We keep looking at this damn thing, and it's what it looks like today. But this isn't what the ground was five hundred years ago. Maybe all the mountains with trees and growth were rocky, and the rocky ones were green. Maybe the valleys weren't even there before but now with the shifting plates and earthquakes and shit we are looking at areas that didn't even exist!"

He was frustrated. She could hear the edge to his voice and the constant tugging at his hair and tapping of his fingers against the map made that clear.

"Okay, you are right. Let's just get through tonight. We can run north and maybe by dawn we will be there. You never know, right?"

"Right. Hey... don't let me lose it, okay?"

"Never."

Liam had his share of horror stories from being a wolf, too. But just like Mackenzie, his Tempering period was short. Extremely short. Most newly bitten wolves take years to get to the point that they were at now. Full control and memory. They had both done it in less than six months.

They changed directions again and walked down the quiet country roads. The magic began to hum around them louder and louder with every passing hour. Mackenzie looked to the sky and saw how close the moon was to its highest point in the sky. They had little time to find a place away from the possible passerby before the light of the moon and the magic in their blood made their bodies take on their wolf form.

"This way." Mackenzie pointed to a small copse of trees at the back of an open field the road traveled along. There were houses every mile or so, and farm animals softly snoring into the night. She knew that the smell of the blood through the veins of human and animals alike was going to make it a hard night, but she refused to give in.

When Liam pulled back the branches on one of the trees and used his other arm to gesture her forward, she chuckled. They may not have doors to open, but Liam was ever the gentleman.

"You ready?" she asked with her head turned to the sky. Her skin was covered in goose bumps from the magic buzzing around them, and her hands itched to dig into the ground. She breathed deeply, inhaling the scents of the land around her. The farm animals, the trees, the wind, even the dirt beneath her feet. Mackenzie quickly removed her clothing and placed it into her bag and stood, waiting for the magic and the moon to take her.

The cracks and tearing of her muscles as they transformed from human to wolf no longer felt like years of agony as it once had. She had mastered the skill of changing on command, and since then, even when she was forced to change by the moon's light, it felt like nothing more than embracing her whole self and allowing that magical buzz that had been humming just beneath her skin free.

Mackenzie looked over to Liam whose wolf stood tall and strong watching her. She gave him a nod and picked her pack up by the top strap and motioned for him to do the same. The two moved forward at top speed until the trees would end, and they had to cross farms or fields.

Mackenzie padded out first, sniffing the air. She could smell the warm blood all around her. A deep rumble began in her chest, and her mouth began to salivate. The soft snores of the animals in the barn drew her attention. Her paws took her toward them. She could feel the fur on her back begin to stand up, and her muscles begin to tighten, ready for the attack. They were just animals, after all. There was nothing wrong with feeding on animals.

Liam let out a whimper behind her, and she turned in time to see his struggle. Standing on the porch of the farm house so far away that even for their Werewolf eyesight was a stretch to see was the farmer. Mackenzie drew in a breath and the delicious scent that only humans held filled her nose.

Liam stood completely frozen in place. His furs on end, a growl rumbling in his chest, but his eyes were looking anywhere, but at the man. She could see his internal struggle as if it were painted on his skin. The muscles aching to do what they knew they wanted. His animalistic need urging him forward, but his mind, his consciousness, telling him no. Reminding him that the man had done nothing to deserve this life or death. Mackenzie allowed herself a second breath of the intoxicating scent before moving to place herself between Liam and the farmer. She nudged him with her head until he looked up and locked eyes with her.

Rubbing her muzzle along his, she tried to redirect his attention. Once she knew that he was ready to move, she pushed him backward. After a few steps, he turned on his own and walked away from the man. Mackenzie stayed behind him just in case, but she was proud of him. He fought the urge. He controlled his wolf. And she was just there as backup.

As the sky began to lighten, and the moon fell from its peak, Mackenzie began to feel the pull of sleep. A tall tree with large overgrown roots called to her. There was a hollow between the roots that created the perfect spot to lay and sleep cuddled up with Liam. She moved and stretched until the tree held her snuggly. When Liam came in after her, he wrapped his body around her and laid his head on her side. Their breathing synchronized together, and the warmth between them was better than any blanket she had ever been under before. A distant howl perked her ears, but her eyes were too heavy. Slowly, they began to close and sleep claimed her.

Mackenzie blinked back the bright sunlight and lifted her arm to block her eyes. Her muscles were beginning to tingle and as much as she enjoyed being cuddled up and naked with Liam, she had to move. Once her eyes had adjusted, Mackenzie maneuvered herself out from under Liam gently enough to allow him a few more minutes of sleep.

Stretching her arms above her head, Mackenzie looked around, taking in the surroundings in the light of the day. The dense trees were tall and lush, and the ground was covered in tall grass and wildflowers grew where the trees allowed patches of sunlight to filter through. Mackenzie pulled her clothing from her pack and dressed before waking Liam. As much as a morning lay would be nice, she was ready to get going and to find the next step in their journey.

"What are you doing that for?" Liam asked in his gruff-just-woke-up voice. It always sent shivers down her spine. Exactly the reason she was dressed before he woke.

"Because, as much fun as it would be to roll around with you, we need to keep going. Who knows, maybe tonight we will have something to celebrate."

"Very true." Liam got up and kissed her softly on the lips then stretched his body out as well. Mackenzie couldn't help but watch the way his muscles twisted and turned and flexed. As each piece of Liam's clothing was put on, her disappointment grew. Maybe she should have remained naked under his arm and taken a bit longer to get going. "All right, let's go."

When she didn't move, a knowing smile graced Liam's face. "You wanted to keep moving. I can always take them back off."

A laugh bubbled from within her, and she shook her head. "No, let's go. We will have plenty of time for that later."

Liam moved forward and placed a soft kiss on her forehead and linked his hand with hers. Together, they walked further through the trees, the hot, humid air surrounding them, even so early in the morning. Just when Mackenzie thought the day would be horrid as the sun rose, and the heat grew, the edge of the trees came into view.

As the trees cleared and a large open field appeared, the scene before them was as beautiful as a painting. The tall grass blew subtly in the light wind and shambles of what used to be a small stone cottage sat in the center. Off in the back and almost nestled in the trees, was what used to be a castle. Tall and majestic even in its state of disrepair, it held a sort of majestic quality that kept her captivated.

Mackenzie had only seen this type of beauty a few times. Once in Margret's office on a painting that hung above her desk. The painting held the view back when the castle and cottage were at the peak of perfection, but it was still just as stunning.

"We found it," Liam whispered. Mackenzie nodded her agreement, too stunned to really speak.

TWELVE

Mackenzie dropped Liam's hand and charged forward. The answers had to be in there. They just had to be. Otherwise, they would be nowhere and have no direction to go.

A bird's chirp, the rustle of the overgrown grass, even her own heartbeat was pounding in her ears as she looked around. Margret would definitely have put guards on this place. At least, she would if there was something to be found. What if this house was nothing but horrible memories for her and the secrets that happened there died on the same day that Margret killed her own father? How many others had lived there in the years since? How many years had gone by since anyone had lived there at all? Mackenzie's feet came to an abrupt halt, tumbling her to the ground.

"What's wrong?" Liam asked as he knelt down beside her. He began searching her feet and legs with his eyes, looking for what had caused the fall. "Are you hurt?"

"What if nothing is there?" she whispered. "What if this is all for nothing?"

"It won't be. And if nothing is there, we know we need to keep looking. Mac, you are the strongest person I have ever met. If this is a dead end, I know that you will find another path to take, and I will follow you without as much as a second thought. But we won't know unless we look."

He was right, and she knew it. She had to just go. There wasn't time for freaking out. There wasn't time for her to suddenly doubt all they had done. Lives depended on it. They had to keep moving.

Instead of saying anything, she stood up and nodded to Liam. She didn't trust her voice to be back to the strong one she had been so accustomed to using. While her heart was pounding in her chest, her feet moved forward. She listened carefully and continued to observe her surroundings for any sign of another being, human or wolf.

The cottage was only half standing. Stones lay in the field as far as ten feet away from the ruins that once held Margret's family. Mackenzie felt a wave of unease flow through her, causing goose bumps to cover her skin. It was eerie walking into a building that was known to have been the scene of a brutal murder, no matter how far in the past it was. Every whisper of the wind had her whipping around to see if something was there. She felt as if someone was watching her, and even though she couldn't see a single person, she couldn't shake it.

"Something's not right. It's too quiet here." Mackenzie's voice was just barely above a whisper. If there really was someone out there watching her, odds were they had the same super hearing she did.

"We can come back later." Liam whispered too, even though Mackenzie could see he was only doing it for her. He didn't believe there was anyone out there.

"Later will be dark. No, we should do it now. Just keep an eye out."

Liam nodded and moved forward. With another look at the tree line, Mackenzie followed him into the rubble. Broken furniture lay about covered in dust; overgrown plants had taken over in most of the cracks, and Mackenzie could even see where small animals had turned this into their home. What she couldn't see was any sort of clue that would tell them where to go next.

Anger bubbled inside of her, vibrating her to her very core. Her wolf itching at her skin from the inside, and she wanted out. Mackenzie had to find an outlet for her anger. She had to find her control. She refused to be forced into the change again. She refused to lose herself again.

The old decrepit table lay on its side by Mackenzie's feet. The wooden legs were splintered and rotting, but the table top itself was still a large, thick, solid piece of oak. It took very little strength to kick the legs off the top and send them skittering across the room. Liam looked up from what looked like an old style sink next to the hearth. The stonework matched what was left of the outside of the cottage, but it stood tall and strong. The mouth of the oven held the charred remains of whatever was last burnt so long ago.

The beauty and longevity of the damn fireplace just angered her more. How dare something from Margret's life stand there mocking her? The fireplace has stood for centuries, untouched, still glorious while the world around it crumbled. The fireplace was Margret. Still standing. Still beautiful. And nothing around her mattered as long as she kept standing, above everyone and everything.

If Mackenzie had anything to say about it, her reign would end. A scream billowed out of her as she hefted the large table above her head and through it at the stone work representation of the queen bitch herself. Liam quickly ducked out of the way, as a single stone broke off and crumbled to the floor.

She had marred its beauty. But it wasn't enough. Charging forward, she beat her hands against the wood, over and over until her hands were covered in blood from cuts that had healed before she was even able to strike again. Her feet joined in the battle and eventually, the anger had faded, leaving her only with a blood stained shirt and tears of dread running down her face.

Mackenzie sank to the floor in front of the damn fireplace that refused to crumble. When warm arms wrapped around her, she turned and buried her face into Liam's chest, relishing in the comfort he provided.

"We will find another way. We have to." Mackenzie was sure that Liam was trying to help. The tone of his voice was soft and gentle, but the words sliced her like a knife. There was no other way. They had failed. She had failed.

"How? Where?" Her voice, barely above a whisper, was as sharp as ice wedging between them. Didn't he get it? They had nothing left to go on. As much as she loved him, he didn't understand. So much of this was her fault. She had been the one to trust Margret. She had been the one to turn him. She had been the one too stupid to see who Geoff really was. She had been the one to lead so many packs into danger all the while telling them she was there to help. She had been the one to grow Margret's pack to the point of almost complete national domination. Her. She had to be the one to fix it. But the only hope she had left, sat around her in ruins.

"I don't know. But we keep looking. We don't give up." Liam softly gripped her chin and tilted her head up to look at him. "We won't give up."

Mackenzie pulled her face away from his hands. She knew what he was saying was meant to be soothing and helpful, but at that point, she just couldn't see it. She wasn't quite ready to pick herself up off the floor and move on.

The fireplace loomed above them, mocking them. Tall and strong and indestructible. The only brick that had fallen lay at her feet. Mackenzie looked up to the hole where it had fallen, hoping to gain some kind of guidance from the small bit of damage she had inflicted. If nothing else, it was proof that it could be harmed. That it could be taken down, even if it were one brick at a time.

But instead of seeing an empty hole where the brick should have gone, Mackenzie saw paper. Old, worn paper. With a trembling hand, she reached forward, her hand touching the brittle material as lightly as she possibly could.

With soft hands, Mackenzie brought the papers out of the hole. They were brown from age and folded in a small rectangle to allow it to fit behind the brick. With wide eyes, Mackenzie looked up to Liam and smiled. Maybe it wasn't all for nothing. Maybe, just maybe, the small victory against the fireplace would lead to a victory over all.

"Let's go," Mackenzie said quickly, standing up abruptly.

"What? Let's look at it!"

"Not here. I don't trust it. I don't trust any of this. Let's go." Carefully, Mackenzie opened her bag and placed the papers between the pages of a book she carried with her. It wasn't perfect, but she hoped that it would protect the old paper long enough to get somewhere safe. Not that she had any clue where they actually were or how to get somewhere with any sort of population.

In the minute it took to stand and turn to the opening in the side of the cottage, Mackenzie and Liam were no longer alone. Standing in the field of swaying grass, surrounded by trees and mountains, were at least twenty men and women. They stood silently, unmoving.

Slowly, a figure moved from the back of the group, walking forward. His tall frame, his dark hair, and his smell that wafted on the breeze were like a gentle reminder of all the time she spent in his arms. A lump formed in her throat. She hadn't expected to have to face Geoff so soon.

Liam growled deep and low from behind her. When his arm wrapped around her waist and pulled her flush against him, she turned her head and kissed his jaw, whispering, "Let me handle it. If he gets out of line, do what you need to do."

A stiff nod of his head let her know he agreed, even though he didn't like it.

Mackenzie stepped forward, standing tall and hoping to look full of strength and courage. She knew telling Liam she could handle it was the right thing to do. Even if all she wanted was to run and hide. She had to at least act like seeing him didn't bother her. For both men's sake. She couldn't let Liam see how much it hurt to see Geoff, and she couldn't let Geoff see that his presence did anything but annoy her.

"Following me, Geoff?" she said with a hint of sarcasm in her voice. "Mommy worried about what I will find in Europe?"

Geoff hadn't even gotten close to her, but she knew he could hear her. The few quiet chuckles that sounded out from the group made her smile.

"Mackenzie, just tell me what you found and you can leave. Both of you."

"Right, because I can trust what comes out of your mouth. Besides, I have a feeling that if anything were actually here, your mother would have removed it a long time ago." Her bag felt heavier than a ton of bricks at that moment. But she hoped her lie was as effective as Geoff's were.

"Mac, I may have kept things from you, but I never lied to you. Not really. I didn't lie about the great things a pack can do. I didn't lie about needing to protect our own. And I didn't lie about loving you. Do the same for me and don't lie to me. What did you find?"

Hearing those words, loving you, sent an ache through her she wasn't expecting. Why did it still hurt as much as it did? Why did it feel like a knife in her gut, twisting and pulling and pushing back in? She had Liam. One look at Liam, and she knew without a doubt that she was his mate and that he was hers, so why did it hurt so badly?

She could feel the tears prickling behind her eyes, but she wouldn't let him see her cry. She would push the hurt down and let the pure rage she felt for him, for his mother, for the entire damn war, free.

"Fuck you! Don't you get it? There is nothing here but a hollowed out shell of a nightmare that happened centuries ago. Your bitch of a mother murdered her father right there!" Mackenzie pointed behind her to the ground in front of the sink basin, "Then she took off and probably never looked back. Look at this hell hole! No wonder she turned out insane! Watched her mother be killed then killed her own father. From what I hear, family means nothing to her. She had her own son killed. Your brother. Does that mean nothing to you?" Mackenzie was screaming at that point. She wanted everyone to hear her. Margret had no loyalty. Not to her pack, not to her family.

"Shut up!" Geoff screamed back at her. He took another few steps and brought himself nearly a foot from Mackenzie. Liam's growl behind her grew, letting his presence be known. If it came down to a fight, Mackenzie and Liam would loose, she knew that much. The odds were not in their favor. Not only were they outnumbered by a lot, but also, Geoff had taught them to fight. He would know their cues better than anyone. Mackenzie looked at Liam and urged him to calm down with her eyes. When she turned back around, the look on Geoff's face was as if he had been slapped.

"You've mated. With a bitten." Geoff's voice was only barely above a whisper. Hurt rang through his words as clear as the anger that laced hers.

"Don't forget that thanks to your pack, I am a bitten, too."

"No, you are royalty. You are more than a bitten."

"Maybe, but I wasn't born either. But it doesn't matter. You aren't who I thought you were. And Liam and I are mated. Your mother is a psychopath and your pack is fighting in a war that will be won by those willing to fight for what is right."

"Don't do this, Mackenzie. You know I don't want to see you hurt."

"Funny. You are the one person who hurt me the worst."

Geoff turned to stone in that instant. His features that had been soft as he tried to reason with her hardened, and so did the look in his eyes. He flipped his mental switch to the warrior, and that's all there was to him anymore. "Give me what you found."

"I didn't find anything. What do you think I found?"

"Mackenzie, hand it over."

"There is nothing to hand over." Geoff reached forward but never connected with her. Liam had moved so quickly to intercept him that Mackenzie didn't have a chance to move out of the way, sending her stumbling backward. "Keep your hands off her," Liam bit out.

"Right. Because she's yours now." Geoff turned his eyes to Mackenzie. "How does it feel to belong to someone?"

Before Mackenzie could respond, Liam had shoved Geoff so hard and so quickly that he didn't have a chance to react. Geoff went flying across the field, and the others ran in. Hands were swinging and legs with kicking. Mackenzie even gave into her wolf enough to bite down on one of her captors. But it didn't matter. In a matter of seconds, she was restrained by more hands than she felt like counting. Liam was being held to the ground by four and repeatedly kicked by another two.

Mackenzie cried out for him. She pleaded with Geoff to stop. She pleaded with their captors to stop. She knew that he wouldn't actually be injured after the assault, but that didn't stop it from hurting like a bitch with every kick, cut, or bite they took. Liam wasn't making a sound. She could see his face, strong as steel, staring at each person as they kicked him.

"Enough!" Geoff called out, and the attack stopped. "Don't you see? I could have allowed them to continue. I could have allowed them to kill Liam and you. But I didn't. I don't want you to hurt, Mackenzie. But I still have a job to do. A pack to protect. A kingdom to prepare. Just give me what you found."

"Don't you think I would?" she yelled at him, her voice scratchy. "I would do anything, anything to protect him. But I don't have anything. I didn't find anything. Look at that fucking place! What the hell do you think survived centuries in there? I figured Margret had already cleaned the damn thing out."

"Where are they? The wolves who helped you?"

"I don't know what you are talking about."

"I know you were in a hostel. I know where you were traveling. Then poof. Gone. You were nowhere to be seen until two days ago. Someone helped you. Who was it?"

"Your trackers must have gotten lazy. No one helped us. Maybe they were just too scared to keep perusing us after the last encounter." Mackenzie was smug about it. She knew that the wounded wolf had to have gone back to someone to tell them his partner was dead and as much as the damn pack would gossip while she lived with them in Montana, word had to have gotten around.

Mackenzie looked around. There had to be a way out of there. If she couldn't find it, it was over. And she wouldn't accept that. "We haven't found anything. Just let us go. All we want to do now is enjoy a little time together before we have to go home and deal with the aftermath of your mother. It's a honeymoon of sorts."

"You are still part of our pack. One of ours bit you. And you bit him. You are not truly mated until our pack leader approves it. But you would know that if you ever tried to learn about our ways instead of holding onto the humanity that is no longer yours to claim."

"I never pledged myself to your pack. I left your pack. I am in no one's pack. Neither is Liam. We are two lone wolves who happen to be mated. The magic around us mated us. Or do you not know about that? The entire world stopped, and it was just the two of us. Whatever magic that flows through us to make us what we are, connected me and him together."

The muscles in Geoff's jaw tightened under his stubble covered skin. His fists clenched and unclenched, and she could hear the growl beginning to form in his chest. "Let them go. If I find out you lied to me, I will treat you as any other wolf. This is the last time you get any leeway. Loving you has brought me nothing but trouble. It ends here. Go."

Mackenzie didn't question him or his words. She just ran to Liam and grabbed his arm. The two of them ran as fast as they could into the woods.

Mackenzie and Liam ran for hours, constantly changing directions and courses for fear of being followed. When they finally stopped, neither spoke but listened for any sign that they weren't alone.

"Get the map." Liam was very short when he spoke. He wouldn't look at her, and Mackenzie could feel the anger almost vibrating off him.

"Hey, it's okay. We're fine now." Mackenzie stepped in front of him, placing her hands softly on his arms. Liam pulled away from her, taking a step to further the distance. His rejection was a knife to the heart. "What did I do?" she asked in nearly a whispered, tears lacing her words.

Liam looked over his shoulder at her and his stone expression softened, just a little, when he saw the hurt on her face. "What did I do?" she asked again.

"I know you, Mackenzie. I know your cues. I could hear your heart beating when Geoff talked about loving you. I know you were only pretending to keep your cool. Then you talked about our mating just to hurt him. If you didn't care about him anymore, hurting him wouldn't have mattered. He matters to you. After everything, he still matters."

Mackenzie didn't know what to say. Not because he was right. Not because she held onto feelings for Geoff, but because they had had this same conversation repeatedly. She didn't know how many times she would have to remind him that she chose him.

"Of course, he matters! I wish I could just say I no longer give one God damn shit about him, but I can't. Yes, seeing him was hard. You know why? Because he hurt me. He hurt me in a way that no one ever has in my life. Because he is the son of the woman that we are trying to stop. Because, despite it all, he was my friend," Mackenzie said. Liam was pacing in front of her, agitation growing by the second. "You don't stop caring about someone overnight. You don't stop caring about someone because they hurt you. You stop being their friend. You stop dating them. You stop talking to them, but I don't care who you are, it is almost impossible to stop caring. I bet if I asked you about your first girlfriend, you would still want to know if she were alive or not. If she were hurt or not. Does that mean you still love her? Does that mean you love me less?" Mackenzie watched Liam, waiting for an answer. She wouldn't go on until he acknowledged her. "Well?"

"Of course not. But Geoff is different than my ex."

"How so? Because she isn't trying to kill us? Yeah, I get that. And as for trying to hurt him with our mating? Damn right. I want him to see that I made the right decision. That I chose the right man. I wanted him to get so angry he didn't want to look at me. Maybe I was a bit too trusting, but I knew that he wouldn't actually hurt me. At least not in a permanent way. I had to find a way to get us out. We were outnumbered. Fighting wouldn't have worked."

"But now we will be followed everywhere. It won't be long until they follow our scent and find us here." He was still upset, but at least he was talking to her. They didn't have time to argue. They needed to find somewhere safe to look at whatever those papers held. And they couldn't even talk about them until they knew no one was listening. "Map?"

Mackenzie sighed but pulled the map out. She would let him have his little freak out because there was nothing more she could do. If it had been his ex who should up, she was sure a sure jealousy would pass through her, too. "Here."

She handed him the map and waited as he looked over it. She wasn't sure how he was going to figure out where they were or where to go next. It wasn't as if the middle of the woods had signs saying 'this way to civilization.'

"We're somewhere along here." Mackenzie leaned over and looked to where Liam was pointing on the map. She looked around them then back to the map.

"How do you know?"

"We started here," he pointed to the place on the map where the cottage was, "and then we ran into the woods here, and ran for about twenty minutes before changing direction." He was tracing his finger along the green blob that was supposed to be trees. "We ran at about fifteen miles per hour, so we would have been about there when we turned. Anyway, we went this direction for another ten minutes, and made another sharp turn, and ran for another hour, which would put us about here." His finger was on the original place he pointed out on the map.

"You kept track of all of that?" she asked in awe.

"How else would we know where we were? If you haven't noticed, I am pretty good with directions." His face held a little grin, and she smiled back at him. She should have paid attention to where they were going too, but she didn't. She was so glad that Liam was with her.

"You are incredible, you know that?"

"Well, you manage to talk our way out of and into a million different situations. I might as well be our guide to getting us wherever we need to be."

"Are we okay?" Mackenzie stepped closer. When Liam didn't move away again, she took another step closer. She wanted to wrap her arms around him and kiss him, but she didn't want to push if he needed space. She could give him that.

"Yeah. I just can't stand him." Liam took a step forward, too. When he put his arm around her waist and pulled her to him, she knew they were back. Whatever had passed between them was over, and they could keep moving forward, both as a couple and in their journey to stop the bitch.

"I know." Mackenzie looked up at Liam and stood on her tiptoes to kiss him. It was only a soft peck, but the love that flowed through her was there. "So, Map Master, where to next? We need to move."

It only took three hours of running to find a paved road. Another hour and a half walking to find a little town, and after that, twenty minutes to find a bus station to take them the hell out of there. Liam was ready to grab the first motel they came across, but Mackenzie pointed out that it would be too easy to be found. If they were worried about their scent pointing them out, the best thing to do would be to get rid of the scent trail.

The bus let them off in the city of Yvetot. The old buildings that filled the city were stunning, but Mackenzie didn't have much time to enjoy the sites. They checked into the first motel they came across and didn't plan to leave the room until it was time to move to their next location. She hated that she had to stay in the shadows, but she would do whatever it took to live long enough to give everyone she could a fighting chance.

"I think we are safe for now," Liam said, peeking out from behind the curtains of the brightly colored room. The walls were bright orange, and the bedspread was a matching floral print. Bright would be putting it mildly.

"Are you ready?" she asked in a hoarse whisper. She knew they were alone, but something about what they were about to see made her feel if she spoke too loud, it would disappear.

Liam nodded his head, not saying a word. Mackenzie's hands trembled as she reached into her pack to retrieve the papers. They were brittle beneath her hands, and she worried that one wrong move and they would disintegrate before her.

Slowly, she unfolded them on the bed. The writing was faded but still legible. It was obviously a letter by the way it was structured. If only they were written in English.

"Damn it!" Mackenzie shouted, pushing herself off the bed. She began pacing the room wondering what language the strange words were in. "How the hell is this going to help? How do we even know it's hers?"

"Mac, look," Liam pointed at a word or two throughout the pages. A word she recognized. Loup-garou.

"That's French! Werewolf! I know that one!" she called out with the thrill of hope.

"Which means it's probably all French. Just a very different form from what we've been hearing. We need another computer." Liam folded the letters and placed them back in the book cover where they had been hidden before.

"Of course, we do. I really hadn't wanted to be able to be seen." Mackenzie took a deep breath and prepared herself for the constant over the shoulder checking she knew was to follow. There was no other way. "Let's go."

"I know, but we'll be quick and we won't go down any alleys or go into any dark corners." Mackenzie glared at Liam. She could see the smirk he tried to hide. He thought she was over thinking the whole thing.

"It's not funny! We never know when we are being followed. I used to think I could sense others like us, but apparently, I was so very wrong. Sometimes, I can just tell, but others, apparently not." She had never been more frightened of being out than she was right then. Not when she was a teenager walking home alone in the middle of the night after a late shift at the cafe, not when she was at college for the first time alone. Not even after she had been bitten. The problem wasn't the fear for herself. She was terrified of losing Liam. She knew that he would do anything to protect her, and she could never forgive herself if something happened to him.

"You're right. It's not funny, and Margret's wolves have proven to be good hunters. I hate that we have to be the prey, though."

"You know, I think the prey is these papers. Did you see Geoff? He wanted them. They had to have known about the cottage. Margret lived there, for crying out loud. How had she never found them?"

"Maybe Margret has a weak spot. Both of her parents did die there. Maybe even she has a heart and can't bring herself to go back. Maybe she never knew her mother hid anything."

"How do we know they aren't Margret's?"

"Just a hunch. Margret wouldn't have left them behind. She would have either destroyed them or taken them with her. She is too conniving and forward thinking to leave anything behind." Liam moved to the door and opened it, taking a quick look outside. "Come on, we passed a library on the way here. Maybe we can use their computers."

Mackenzie took a deep breath, pulled up her big girl panties, and headed to the door. Leaning up on her tiptoes, she gave Liam a little kiss. His lips perfectly melded to hers in a way that no one else's would. "I love you, you know that, right?"

"Yeah, I know that. I love you, too. Now, can we go?"

She laughed and swatted at his chest before nodding and following him out. They walked hand in hand, almost completely at ease. If only Mackenzie didn't feel like she had to look over her shoulder every other second, she might be able to enjoy a stroll down the road with her mate.

"Right here. This word means sister." Mackenzie pointed furiously to the screen. They had been in the library for hours poring over the letters, trying to translate them. The librarians shushed them on more than one occasion, and she was sure they were close to being kicked out. "And right here says something about mother. This has to be from one of Rosalinda's sisters. This is exactly what we need!"

"It is. So can we please keep our voices down? Because it's exactly what they need, too." Mackenzie suddenly stopped moving, stopped smiling, and nearly stopped breathing. How could she have been so careless to announce to the world what they had? Hadn't she been the one so concerned with being followed? What if she had just put their lives at risk once again?

"Sorry, you're right," she whispered so low the only reason Liam could hear her was his werewolf side picking up the slack. "Do you see anything else that could tell us where to find her?"

Liam pored over the papers in front of him. He pointed out a few random words like lake and farmer, but back then, those meant nothing. Then, his face lit up. His eyes grew wide, and with every second that passed where he didn't say a word, her heart raced faster. Finally, she could no longer wait for him to speak. She grabbed his shoulder and shook him. With wild eyes, he grinned at her.

"I found it. I know where we have to go."

"Where?" she whispered barely above a breath.

"England. She's talking about a child for a King. That has to be King Henry. Son of Henry the 8th! I think it's time to turn the phone on and call your father."

"I think you're right." Mackenzie and Liam closed out the web page they were using and practically ran back to their hotel room.

Mackenzie dove onto the bed, reaching for her bag. Unzipping and spilling the contents onto the bed, she frantically searched for the cell phone. Finally, under a pile of clothing and toiletries, she found it. Turning it on, she sighed in relief. Things were beginning to go as planned. She just hoped that they weren't too late.

There was static on the line as the call connected. It rang in her ear, once, twice, three times before a deep husky voice answered.

"Hello?" Her father asked with a sense of urgency.

"Dad? Is everything okay?" Mackenzie sat bolt upright on the bed and locked eyes with Liam. Her heart hammered in her chest, and tears formed at her eyes even before he said a thing.

"Oh, thank God. I was worried sick. I hadn't heard from you, and when I tried to call it never even rang. I was beginning to fear the worst. Mackenzie, are you and Liam okay? Where are you?"

"I'm sorry we didn't call sooner, but we wanted to conserve the battery while we were traveling so it was turned off. We didn't want to call until we had something. We're still in France, though. But I'm hoping not for long. It's bad. Margret has wolves here, too. They are spreading and even infiltrating packs to spy. And Geoff was here. What about there? Any progress?"

"Don't worry about that. I need you to stay focused on getting us more warriors and on warning the others, letting them know that if they choose to fight back, they aren't alone. We need the other Royal families on our side. Have you found anything?"

Mackenzie then took the next hour to explain their whole journey to her father. The only thing she held back was her mating to Liam. It was personal and private, and she wanted to tell him in person. She hoped when the war was over, maybe they could do whatever ceremony Werewolves had for that sort of thing. Something to cement the bond between her and Liam and with her new family.

"You have done amazing, Mackenzie. We should be hearing from Evelyn's pack any time now. And you need to get to the airport. There will be a ticket for both of you waiting at the counter to take you to England. Are you ready to start the search all over again?"

"I don't think we have a choice. I am ready for this thing to be over."

"Me too, darlin'. Me, too."

"Dad?"

"Yeah?"

"How bad is it?"

"It's not pretty. Her pack is growing, some by choice, most by force. But our ranks are growing, too. I know what you are doing is going to send a lot more wolves our way."

"Promise me you will stay safe."

"I can promise to try."

"Bye, Dad."

"Bye, Sweetheart."

Mackenzie ended the call and wiped a stray tear that had fallen. She looked up to Liam then back to the phone in her hands and felt another tear roll down her cheek.

"We should go." Mackenzie startled by his words, but his face held more understanding and love than she thought possible. She nodded and repacked her bag.

"Okay, let's go."

THIRTEEN

Mackenzie's eyes were heavy. It had been almost forty-eight hours since she had slept. The flight from France to England wasn't a long one, and Liam managed to take a nap in that time, but her mind was going a mile a minute. Every time she closed her eyes she saw blood. Blood on her hands. Wolves lying on the ground beheaded. Children were crying out for their mother with red painting their faces. She saw Margret's face, smiling as she watched it all happened and kept herself from the battle.

"Could you please take us to a hotel?" Liam was leaning forward to talk to the cab driver through the little window that separated the front from the back. Mackenzie just sat there with her head leaning back against the cushion and closed her eyes, willing the horrific images away. When she felt Liam's hand slide onto her leg and begin rubbing up and down, it wasn't such a hard thing to accomplish.

The move itself was completely innocent. They had touch each other in that way a million times in comfort, she knew he would grab for her hand after the fourth stroke. It was his pattern. She loved that she knew his pattern. But she also loved how the heat radiated from him into her in a primal sort of way. When his hand moved to hold hers, she switched positions, so his hand was now below hers. Then she slowly dragged it from her thigh to her sex.

With a devilish smile and a gleam in her eye, she lifted her head from its resting position and looked at him. The cocky grin on his face, and the stirring she could see in his pants told her all she needed to know. As soon as they got to the hotel, he was hers.

The cab slowed to a stop, and the driver exited the vehicle. Liam leaned over and placed a slow and languid kiss on her lips sending shivers down her spine and straight to her girly bits. Her heart thrummed in anticipation. The strong tug at the back of her head was enough to soak her panties.

"Your stop?" an elderly voice said, pulling them from their moment. Liam chuckled a little when Mackenzie failed to reply only nodded, and a strange sound echoed from her throat. She stood out of the cab and waited for Liam to pay the driver. Her father had not only paid for their flights but had wired more money for them to be able to continue their journey.

"Ready?" he asked, lacing his fingers in hers. Mackenzie looked up at the tall but narrow hotel. It had an old world feel. Perfectly fitting for what they had to do. She nodded her head, and they went in.

Check-in was a breeze, and their room was spectacular. Mackenzie, in all her life, had never stayed anywhere that was so extravagant. She was going to question the cost, being that they were spending her father's money, but Liam placed a finger to her lips.

"Don't worry about it. We haven't spent much of what he gave us to begin with, and surprisingly, this room didn't cost as much as you would think. Can we just relax and enjoy it? Tomorrow we go back to traveling the country in search of wolves that may or may not want to rip our heads off. Tonight, we take advantage of the soft bed, the jetted tub, and the view." Liam pointed over her shoulder. When she turned, she saw the entire city brightly lit against the inky black sky.

"It's breathtaking." But what was really breathtaking was Liam's mouth against her neck leaving a hot wet trail as he moved to her earlobe. Mackenzie sucked in a shallow breath when he encased her lobe and bit down slightly, then swirled his tongue around to soothe the slight sting his teeth left in their wake.

"I want to marry you," he breathed in her ear. She smiled and turned in his arms, looking up and locking eyes with him.

"I'm already your mate."

"I know. But I want to marry you. I want the world to know that you are mine, and I am yours no matter what world we chose to live in. You and me, forever. Will you marry me?"

His words melted her heart, and she whispered a soft yes, before crushing her lips to his. His mouth opened slightly, just enough to slip his tongue out to tease hers. Mackenzie wrapped her arms around his neck and pulled herself closer to him. She wanted to feel every inch of him pressed against her. She wanted to feel his heart beating against her own until she could no longer tell whose was whose. She wanted to be consumed by him.

Liam broke from their kiss, lust clouding his eyes. His fingers grazed the skin of her stomach as he reached for the hem of her shirt. He let his fingers play against her skin, causing goose bumps to erupt and a fire to flame beneath them for a moment before lifting it up and over her head. Mackenzie stepped back and kicked off her shoes, then moved her jeans down her legs. She stood before him in her tattered old bra and unmatched panties waiting to see some laughter in his face. She knew she looked more ridiculous than sexy, but his face never wavered.

His tongue darted out and licked his lips as his eyes traveled the length of her body. Slowly, Mackenzie reached behind her back and unsnapped her bra, letting the material fall from her body to expose her breasts. Her nipples were hard and even the air that brushed them set her nerves on fire.

"Panties, too." Liam's voice was gruff. His tone was commanding. Mackenzie wanted nothing more than to obey his every word. She removed her underwear and stood before him completely nude. She let him eye her body without twitching or trying to cover up. For the first time in her life, she wasn't ashamed to be seen that way. She wasn't worried he would turn in disgust. She wasn't aware of every lump and fold in her skin. She was just Mackenzie, a sexual being about to be ravaged by the man she loved.

"Come here." And she did. She walked straight to him, never letting her eyes leave his. Liam dropped to his knees and lavished her stomach with his tongue and teeth. He moved lower until his nose was nestled in her curls. With a strong hand, he caressed her thigh before lifting it up onto his shoulder, opening her to him. Mackenzie felt his tongue graze her sex, sending spasms of pleasure through her body. The heat from his mouth mixed with the pressure and silk of his tongue drove her mad. When his mouth latched onto her clit, sucking and nibbling, Mackenzie felt the tidal wave brewing. She reached behind her for the wall to hold on to because her single leg wouldn't be able to hold her up the way she wanted. She wanted to stay strong and enjoy every ounce of pleasure and every swipe of his tongue that he was willing to give.

Mackenzie watched in awe at the man before her. She shook from his ministrations, and she never wanted him to stop. He slipped two fingers into her, pumping them in rhythm with the suction he had on her until the wave crested and crashed, sending cries from Mackenzie's lips.

Liam dropped her leg from his shoulder and straightened his back, licking his lips clean of her essence.

"Bed."

Mackenzie wasn't sure her legs would function after such an orgasm. The muscles were still convulsing beneath her skin, but she dared not break the spell. She complied, moving on shaky legs to the bed and sat. Liam stripped before her then approached in all his naked glory. His cock was at full attention and seeped with pre-cum. Mackenzie licked her lips just thinking about tasting him.

"Lay back." Mackenzie swallowed deeply then complied, spreading her legs for him. Liam nestled between them and stared into her eyes. When his lips descended on hers, they were softer, more pliant, less demanding. He pulled back and had a soft smile on his lips and love in his eyes. "Let me make love to you."

Mackenzie felt the unshed tears of happiness as she nodded and ran her hands up his back and into his hair. She pulled him down into another kiss and welcomed his length into her. What had started as a mind-blowing exercise in submitting to her mate was ending in the way they did things best. Full of love and emotion.

Liam's strokes grew stronger, his thrusts deeper. Mackenzie could feel that pull in her stomach all the way to her toes. She was so close to exploding yet again. She gripped his hair and tugged slightly, whispering 'harder.'

Liam listened to her pleas. He lifted his hips slightly higher and thrust into her harder, pulling cries from her body. Her eyes closed, and his movements stayed strong, but sped up with every stroke. Until he let out an animalistic growl and collapsed on top of her, completely spent.

"Does this mean I get to introduce you as my Fiancée now?" he asked between breaths.

Mackenzie couldn't help but laugh. "Yeah, I think so."

It took almost three full days to even find a place to start looking for another pack. Mackenzie and Liam were starting to worry that Darren +had chosen the wrong airport to land in. The airport they had flown into was in the middle of a big city surrounded by other cities and then farmland. But finally, the sight of trees set their minds at ease.

"Ready?" Mackenzie asked as they stood before the tree line.

"As I'll ever be." Liam took her hand in his and stepped through. The forest was much the same as every other one they had been in with trees everywhere, dirt beneath their feet, and animals scampering away from their presence.

"Do you think we should change? We could cover more ground, and then if there were any others around, it would draw their attention more than a couple's excursion through the woods. We could be campers for all they know."

"If you want to, but look around. There is no way campers are a normal thing here. No signs of human activity at all." Liam still hadn't accepted his wolf side like she had. Turning when there was no sign of danger was hard for him. Not physically. He had mastered that before they left her father's pack. But mentally. He still fought against the idea of being a monster. And when he almost attacked a human girl back in the states, it cemented the idea in him.

"You don't have to. What if I change, to bring the attention, but you don't so you can talk to them if they come out?" Mackenzie was trying to be understanding and give him the time to accept himself the way she had. But the truth was, one of them, if not both, had to be a wolf. It was going to be the fastest way to find another pack. If they thought they were being attacked, a pack would come out of hiding to defend itself. Especially if there were only two intruders. Unless, of course, they were like the pack in France whose leader ran, leaving its members to fight.

"No. I have to do this. I have to just do it. I'm not a fucking pussy." His words bit out at her as he pulled his shirt up and over his head. Mackenzie tried to calm her irritation. She knew that he wasn't angry with her. She knew that his clipped tone was irritation with himself. Hell, she knew that she never called him a pussy, and when he calmed down and thought about it, he would, too. All correcting him would do was fuel an argument based on anger and not facts. She knew what it was like to hate herself. All she could do was to be supportive until he got his head out of his ass and stopped taking it out on her.

"Fine." Mackenzie too stripped down. She folded her clothing and placed them in her bag. She watched Liam carefully, looking for any sign that he was struggling. When his eyes shot to hers, they were narrow with irritation.

"I've got it. Stop watching me. You know I can do it." Mackenzie glared right back but turned, allowing him the privacy to shift. When she heard the signature pops and cracks of bones being broken and reformed, she dug deep in herself and found the wolf, waiting patiently to be let out. Mackenzie closed her eyes and took a deep breath in before turning her body over to the wolf.

She no longer felt the pain. All she felt was the peace and freedom of being her whole self. Mackenzie turned to see Liam's white wolf standing there with his pack in his mouth. She nodded to him, but instead of mimicking him, she walked over and nuzzled his neck. She wanted him to know they were okay. Even if he had to be a dick sometimes. When she pulled back to look at him, he made the first move and drug his nose along her face.

Mackenzie picked her pack up and ran. She bounded off trees and boulders, and she howled and chased random small animals that didn't have the intelligence to get the hell out of dodge before their approach. She even marked trees with her claws as they went. Anything she could think of to draw attention if there were anyone there to draw from. Liam just followed behind her, watching the trees surrounding them with his ears perked up. Any noise that sounded be it a bird or a bunny, his head snapped in that direction.

As the sun set on them, Mackenzie's stomach growled. They had run out of packed snacks that morning, so if they were going to eat, they were going to have to hunt. Mackenzie and Liam found a clearing and dropped their packs. It seemed to have enough room for a fire and for them to make camp for the night.

Liam shifted back first. Mackenzie just took a moment to watch him. This man, this wonderful man that she loved, the man she had forced to accept a life he hated. Sadness washed over her. Why did he love her so? She had taken the time to prove her love to him, but how could he love her as strong as she loved him when she had been the one to damn him to this life. How could he not resent her every time he saw her? His hatred for her in the beginning was obvious. He tried to kill her after all. But then he saw firsthand how difficult the tempering was. He changed for the first time and had no memory. No control. She had thought that when they became friends, he had stopped harboring those feelings. But what if he hadn't?

The way he snapped at her when they changed, the way he glared at her, it made her wonder if he still held contempt for her. For her mistake. But without it, they would have never met. She would have gone on with her life as a wolf. Hopefully, she would still have seen Geoff for what and who he was, and she would be alone on their journey. She would have died more than once by then. So, she couldn't say she regretted it. She wouldn't. Maybe that made her selfish, but she would do it again.

"Mackenzie, are you going to change back? We need to make a plan here, and I can't read your mind. I need you to be able to talk to me." Liam's tone had calmed some, but she could still hear a slight clip to it. She sighed and closed her eyes, willing herself back.

Mackenzie could feel the magic swirling under her skin and into her bones and muscles, she heard the cracks and pops, and felt her size change. Finally, when all was calm, she stood on her two legs and faced Liam.

"I need you to talk to me, too." She tried to make her words come out strong, but they were just barely above a whisper and wavered. She had to clear the air. Her heart was heavy with worry of what he would say, but she couldn't keep questioning whether or not he still resented her. Maybe he did love her as much as he said, as much as she loved him, but resentment could eat away at the strongest relationship like a termite in a home. It starts small, but then it festers and grows, until everything comes crumbling down.

"What is it? What's wrong?" Liam stepped toward her, eyes locking on her for a brief moment then scanning the area around them for signs of danger. She reached up, grabbed his chin in her hand, and turned his face back to hers.

"It's not out there. It's right here. You and me. I need to know if you still..." She wasn't sure how to even finish the question. Part of her was afraid that if the words fell from her lips it would be easier for him to agree with them, and the other part of her feeling silly for even questioning it.

"Still what? Mackenzie, you're scaring me here."

"Do you still resent me for turning you?"

"How could you ask that? You know how I feel about you."

"I know how you say you feel, but I also see the pain and torture in your face every time you have to change. I hear the clip in your words and feel the anger as if it were acid on my skin. I just need to know. I need to know that we can talk through it. I need you to know you don't have to hide it. I need us to be okay and strong, and I need to know when all of this is over, I will still have you." A tear slipped from her eye, and she cursed it as she wiped her cheek. It was her turn to try to look away, but he wouldn't let her. His eyes were soft, but his words were firm.

"Mackenzie, I love you. I forgave you a long time ago. But that does not mean that I love the wolf. That does not mean that I don't worry every time it takes over without my consent, every time I let it take over. It does not mean that I despise myself any less when I turn back, and my body rejects my human self because of the lack of freedom, of clarity, than I have as the fucking beast. I will learn to accept this life. I will. And it isn't because you forced me into it. It's because I love you and can't see a life without you. You make this whole existence worth it. You will always have me."

Mackenzie launched herself into his arms and just held him, feeling his heart beat against her skin, feeling his warmth enveloping her.

"I'm sorry I questioned you."

"I'm sorry I gave you a reason to question me."

She pulled back and looked to him, the moment so intense that when her stomach rumbled loudly, they both jumped. Then laughed.

"Okay, so why don't you get the fire going and I will go see what I can hunt down?" he said. Mackenzie looked at him and wondered if she should be the one hunting. He just turned back, and she couldn't ask him to do it again so soon.

"Why don't I do it? I mean, I'm fast, and I can take down a deer without decimating it. Unlike the last time that you tried." She had a smile on her face and so did he.

"Not fair. I was still learning. I'm going. Let me do the manly thing and feed my woman." He pounded his hands on his chest, and she laughed again. "I won't be long."

She gave him a quick kiss before he shifted back and disappeared into the trees. Mackenzie pulled her clothing from her bag and got dressed. She then began to walk around the clearing collecting fallen branches and piling them in the center. She found a dozen or so rocks that she placed around them to create a sort of ring and then dug through her bag for the lighter. After many failed attempts, she growled in frustration, throwing the damn lighter across the clearing.

"Fucking hell," she said aloud and stood, stomping off in the direction she chucked the useless thing. Without it, and a lot more patience, it didn't matter what Liam caught, it would be raw, and the idea nauseated her.

"You should have brought a newspaper." The voice startled her from behind. She whipped around to see a group of four men surrounding her wannabe fire pit. One took a few pieces of paper from his back pocket and shoved them into the wood pile and another leaned over with his own lighter and provided the flame. The paper lit up, hot and bright, and caught the small twig on fire, then another.

"I guess so," she said keeping her voice as steady as she could.

"You and your friend were not making a secret of you being here. I have a feeling that was on purpose. But I need to tell you that these woods are claimed. You can keep moving."

The man was tall and extremely muscular. His blond hair was long and pulled back into a ponytail at the base of his neck. Blue eyes penetrated her in an uneasy way. So much so that she wasn't sure if she should approach him as if she were stronger than all four of them combined or to stay put and show her fear.

"We aren't looking to stay. We like to make ourselves known. That way people don't think that we're being sneaky. We're traveling. Looking for some people. Some wolves. Our home is in America."

"That's a long way to look for someone. Tell us who you're looking for, and maybe we can help you get on your way a little faster."

Mackenzie took a deep breath and stepped forward. She wouldn't cower. She couldn't. "I'm looking for the Royal family, my family."

The men all stared at her, their chests puffing out. The silence that hung between them was thick with tension. "You are not Royal. You are bitten. Leave. Now."

"No. My mate and I will stay the night. If your pack has no Royal connection, we will be on our way. But we will give you the same warning we give everyone. Not for ourselves, but for you. Margret is coming. She already has taken most of the United

States and has begun her war in France. Whether you believe it or not, I am of Royal blood. I am a descendant of Meredith. Thank you for your kind welcome and starting our fire."

It sounded like a dismissal. And it was. She just hoped that they would listen. If they didn't, she was in serious trouble. She knew she could hold her own against one of the giant men, but there was no way she could take on four.

"You will leave now. Mate or no mate. How do we know you are not part of Margret's plan to find and take the Royal packs? How do we know you are not with her?"

"So you know of Margret?"

"Leave. Now." Mackenzie could see the spittle that left his mouth as he bit out the words. His whole body was trembling, and his eyes flashed greenish-yellow for a split second before fading back to blue.

His pack brothers stood at his side, watching, waiting for the command to take her, she just knew it.

"No." She was playing with fire, but she had no choice but to wait for Liam. She wouldn't leave because they demanded it, and she wouldn't leave without him.

"We will leave in the morning. You are more than welcome to come back and make sure we are gone."

The man let out a deafening roar, and the other three approached her as if capturing a young woman was second nature to them. Not an ounce of feeling crossed their faces. It was just another order.

Just before they managed to grab her, Liam's white wolf bounded from the trees and placed himself between her and the pack. The growl that emanated from his lips made even her skin crawl.

"What are you doing here?" One pack brother asked the wolf. The leader elbowed him and shook his head.

"That is not William. The fur is not right. That is her mate. Turn back, or I will have her beheaded before you can blink."

"Do it, Liam. We will be okay," she urged. And for some reason, she knew that deep down they would be. The pack had been cordial until she defied them at every turn. Now that Liam was back, she would gladly pack up and leave. She delivered the message. If they chose not to listen, then that was on them.

Liam huffed and shook his head, but Mackenzie nodded to him.

"Listen to your mate. Change back now."

So he did. Mackenzie watched as his body contorted and shifted from beautiful wolf to stunning man. When he stood tall and faced the pack, their faces went white as a ghost.

"How can this be?" the man whispered. "Who are you?"

"How can what be?" Liam asked, confused.

"Get dressed. You are coming with us."

Mackenzie followed the men in silence, taking in as many details as she could. She huffed to herself a little. They had been in the same situation time and again, but something was different this time. This time, the new pack didn't march them through the woods, asserting their dominance. They simply walked beside them, making small talk with Liam. They asked where he came from, how he met Mackenzie, how he got caught up in the whole Margret debacle.

Liam was careful with his words. She could see where he held back and where he felt confident that the full answer wasn't going to do them any harm. He tried asking questions of his own. Why had they been so shocked to see him? Where were they going? How much longer until they reached their destination. All they would say was 'you'll see.'

"So you claim to be Royal, Mackenzie. Care to explain your eyes?" the man walking next to her asked.

"My mother is human. You would think after hundreds and hundreds of years that another royal would have slept with a human. My father can't be the first. I don't understand how this is such a hard concept." She was tired of constantly having to explain herself. She lost track of how many times she had to explain away her eyes. Perhaps she should get contacts...

"And him?" he asked, motioning to Liam.

"He is my mate. I turned him on my third moon cycle."

"Hmm."

"Through here," the leader of the group said as he pushed apart some branches and stepped in. Taking a deep breath, Mackenzie followed. What made him 'hmmm' at her? There were so many unanswered questions that it made her restless.

What lay before her reminded her of full moon nights in Montana. A large group of people sitting around campfires with tents set up randomly and laughter all around. Liam moved next to her and gripped her hand in his. "Stay by me?"

"Always," she replied in a whisper.

As they walked through the camp, it seemed like everyone stopped and stared at them. Or maybe just Liam. It was a strange feeling being the one with the center of attention. She rather liked not having the spotlight on her.

"I wish they would stop staring," Liam said under his breath, refusing to look at anyone in particular.

"Welcome to the club," Mackenzie said with a slight chuckle.

The closer they got to the largest of the fires, the denser the pack stood. They parted to allow them through, though quickly closing the gap after they passed. As they reached the front of the group, a large man stood with his back to them, poking at the fire.

"William, sir. I think you need to meet the two you sent us to follow."

As William turned around, Mackenzie gasped. His blond hair, his blue eyes, his single dimple, and chiseled jaw. All of it was an older version of Liam. It was as if Liam had aged thirty years. The man was gorgeous. Mackenzie turned her head slowly to look at her mate.

Liam stood stock still with eyes wide and mouth slightly open. Quickly, he closed it, but licked his lips and tried to say something, but stopped. He tried again and failed again.

"My name is William, and you son, look like you could be my blood. Is this magic or are you my blood?"

"I... I don't know, sir." Liam stood up tall and presented himself as confident and calm, but Mackenzie could hear the hesitation in his words and the slight waver in her voice.

"Well, are you a warlock? Or do you know a witch to have spelled you?" William seemed to be entertained with the turn of events. Was it possible that he had others showing up looking like a younger version of himself?

"No, sir. I came here with Mackenzie, looking for packs to warn them of Margret. Looking for those willing to stand against her. Looking for the Royal family in hopes that they would stand against her. I do not know why we look so similar."

Mackenzie thought about Liam. How quickly he learned, like her. How strong he was, even for a werewolf. How Margret had found her on purpose, because of her special blood. Margret knew Mackenzie was a relative. She had to have. This meant that her coming across Liam was no accident either.

"Oh, my God, Liam. He's your grandfather," Mackenzie whispered. All heads whipped around to stare at her. "It makes sense. She said she found me because of my special blood. She knew I was a Royal descendant. She had to have. She wanted more royalty in her pack. Think of how fast you were able to control it. Think of how little time it actually took for your Tempering. Damn it, think about the fact that I happened to come across you while out with one of the largest packs in the area, and they just happened to not be able to stop me from turning you. It all makes sense. She fucking planned it this way."

Murmurs turned to an uproar around them. Apparently, talking so freely about Margret wasn't such a good idea. But Mackenzie didn't take her eyes off Liam to take in the scene. She watched as his jaw hardened, and his eyes iced over. He almost crushed her hand inside of his and swallowed thickly.

"ENOUGH!" William yelled out. The entire area became silent. "Now, you will explain to me," he said to Mackenzie.

Mackenzie took the next half an hour telling the tale that had been her insane life since she was bitten. William listened intently, and when she began to speak of Liam's abilities, William smiled that proud smile that only can come from a parent.

"I had a son, who liked to leave the pack from time to time. He could very well have procreated with a human. Do your parents know their parents? How can a Werewolf hide his life from a family? I do not understand."

"My father was adopted. We have never been able to find his parents. He looked. He looked everywhere as soon as he was old enough. There were no records of his birth or his parents. He was simply dropped off at the police station."

"We will do a test. If you pass, then we know Royal blood runs through you. And I have no doubt that you are mine."

"The tea?" Mackenzie asked softly, not wanting to step in on their moment, but not to be able to help herself.

"Yes, how did you know?"

"I drank it for Evelyn in France to prove my heritage."

"Then you will not mind drinking again for my pack."

"Not at all."

As soon as the words left her mouth, a woman raced forward with two steaming mugs of tea. Mackenzie took a long drink, remembering the same tones and flavors on her tongue. She looked to Liam, and he looked confused.

"It tastes the same as the one from Evelynn."

William laughed. "Ah, she tested you, too. But she said nothing because you were not yet aware, I assume. I have never had the pleasure of meeting her, but if she was a friend to you, I would honor her as a friend to us. Who is she descended from?"

Mackenzie wasn't sure how to answer. She didn't want to give him a reason not to trust them, but she didn't want to lie.

"Margret is her grandmother. But she does not follow, nor does she wish to submit to her. Her pack has joined the fight."

"I see. For now, we do not talk war or politics. Tonight, we feast in celebration of my grandson coming home!" William called out, and then pulled Liam into a manly half embrace before turning him to the pack. "Welcome Liam!"

"Welcome Liam!" The whole pack shouted together.

FOURTEEN

Hours had passed in William's tent. Mackenzie and Liam sat surrounded by his closest and most trusted pack members. They had been by his side for over one hundred years. They spoke very tactically. Mackenzie's brain whirled with the numbers and maneuvers they had planned.

"So basically, you want to fight over here. You plan on taking out Margret's growing pack in Europe. Right?" Mackenzie asked, fighting a headache.

"Right. I will send out teams to find other smaller packs that while not members of my own are still loyal to me. We will band them together and attack Alice and all of the wolves she has collected. You and Liam will go to Spain. I will let them know you are coming and meeting you at the private airport. You, Mackenzie, will get to meet your great-grandmother. You will speak with Meredith and my mother, Ingrid."

"That simple? You know where they are? They are actually together?" Mackenzie wanted to cry. After traveling so far and fighting so many battles, it was almost over. They had almost completed their task, and they could return to the states. They were going to be one step closer to ending the war.

"Yes, they are together. You forget that I am Margret's cousin, not a distant relative. Her mother, my aunt. It takes more than time to lose touch amongst family unless it is wanted. My mother and I are very close. She only left the pack to me, because she is very old and wanted to live her final days with her sister by her side. I visit them once a year. She will love you."

"That settles it. It was so wonderful to meet you, William. I hope that when everything is over, I can come back and get to know you more. I would love to know my family history. You have another grandson, by the way. My brother. He's still young and human, so I don't know how much he will ever get to know, but I thought you would like to know."

"When the time comes, send word for me, and I will let you know where the pack is. We are a traveling group, never staying in one place for too long."

"I figured. Tents and all," Liam said then stood and embraced his grandfather. Mackenzie stood back and watched with a smile on her face. Maybe things were finally looking up.

"Jameson can take you to the private airstrip. There will be a plane waiting for you. When you land, you will be greeted by members of Meredith's pack, and they will take you to her and my mother. Good luck and we will be rooting for American wolves."

"Thank you. Good luck to you, too. Please keep in touch and let us know how things go on your end,"

Mackenzie said before leaving the tent. Liam took another moment then joined her. Jameson led them to a small Jeep about three miles from camp and drove them to the middle of nowhere that just so happened to have an airplane.

As the tiny plane flew through the air, Mackenzie watched out the window. So much that she had always wanted to see, so much she had always wanted to do. She would have to come back some day. When the wolves were no longer at war, when she and Liam were married. Perhaps they could travel the world in comfort, after saving up enough money to do so. When they got back to the states, she swore she would only sleep in a bed, in a house ever again. She had enough of tents and sleeping bags.

But then again, maybe not. She knew when the moon called that the only place she could be was outdoors. But damn it, she would be taking hot showers every night. She missed showers. She missed shaved legs and clean hair. She never was a girly girl, but she was clean.

"What are you thinking about over there?" Liam asked through a yawn. He had fallen asleep again. She didn't know how he could manage to sleep so easily or so often. When her mind was going there was no stopping it, no matter how tired or safe she was.

"Hot showers."

Liam laughed but agreed that he too could use one. The pilot took that minute to call over his shoulder that they would be landing in just a few moments. Mackenzie darted her eyes back to the window to watch the dissent.

When the field came into view that they would be landing on, she was shocked. William had said they would send a few pack members to take them to Meredith, but there were more like a few hundred.

"Do you see that?" Liam asked his face practically pressed against the glass.

"Yeah. Incredible."

The plane touched down and bounced Mackenzie in her seat until her butt felt numb. When they came to a complete stop, Mackenzie stayed sitting, just watching out the window. She saw so many people. Some with blue eyes, brown eyes, hazel eyes. And then she saw them. Yellow-green eyes. And not just one set, but many. This pack had a mix of bittens in their ranks. None of the others so far had besides Margret. The rest treated bittens like a problem, like dirt.

"Come on. They're waiting," Liam said and stood, holding a hand out for her to take. Mackenzie placed her hand in his and laced their fingers together. She stood on shaky feet and followed Liam out of the plane, down the metal stairs, and up to the mass of werewolves.

"Um, hello?" Mackenzie said in an uncertain voice. She hated wavering. She hated feeling or looking weak. And it had been happening more and more frequently. So she took a deep breath and tried again. "My name is Mackenzie. This is Liam, grandson of William. We were sent here to speak with Meredith and Ingrid."

The reassuring squeeze that Liam gave her hand was enough to tell her she sounded as strong as she had intended. The pack slowly stepped back, leaving two graying women. They stood tall, but what Mackenzie assumed was once a strong frame was very thin. Their skin was wrinkling, but their eyes still shone with life.

"Welcome. How amazing that you two found one another. Both Royal blood from such distance to come together to create the strongest union our kind will have ever seen. My girl, if I were five hundred years younger it would be like looking in a mirror. Come, come," the one elder said. Mackenzie assumed that was Meredith, because the other woman, whose white hair could have easily been blonde in her time, kept her eyes trained on Liam with one hand over her mouth in awe.

"I am so pleased to meet you, but William said that we would be meeting a few pack members at the airport. Is something wrong?"

"Not at all, my dear. When word spread of long lost Royal blood coming to visit, they wanted to welcome you. I know of what my niece is doing as do they. To see someone so young and so new to our world fighting so hard to stop her is nothing short of a miracle."

"A miracle?" Mackenzie wasn't sure she liked that reference. She had enough on her shoulders. She didn't think she could handle hundreds and hundreds of wolves expecting miracles from her. She was just one girl who got caught up in some bullshit and decided to fight back.

"Yes, my dear. A human. A human girl who knew nothing of our world is forced into it by, I hate to say, the worst werewolf in our history to say no and to fight back. And to make so much change and cause so much damage to Margret's plan in less than a year's time when no one else, not a single born or bitten, Royal or not, has done so is a miracle. You, my dear, were the inspiration we all needed to fight back instead of hiding in the shadows or waiting for her to come to us. And Liam? He was your inspiration. He was your miracle."

"Shall we go home?" Ingrid finally managed to say. She stepped forward and took Liam's other hand in her old one and led them back through the crowd to the first of fifty cars.

"Cars?" Liam asked. He slid into the back seat next to Ingrid, and Mackenzie slid in next to him. A man that looked almost as old as the sisters did took the driver's seat, and Meredith sat in the front. The closing of car doors sounded from all around, and as they faded to nothing but engine motors, the man put the car in drive and pulled off the field onto an old dirt road.

"Yes, of course. We do not live hidden away in the woods. We have a castle off the beaten path and visitors think it is a home for the insane. It keeps the tourists away and keeps the locals from asking too many questions. I rather enjoy having a house with things like electricity and running water. Seeing the world change, seeing technology be born, it is amazing. I know and have lived a life without it for many years. I know how hard it used to be. Why would I choose that? Just so that I can change to my wolf in the middle of the woods? We have over one hundred acres in the middle of nowhere. We can change all we want!" Ingrid twinkled with laughter. It was so happy and infectious that soon everyone was laughing along.

The drive was short, only fifteen minutes or so from where the plane landed, which Mackenzie was beginning to realize wasn't an airport at all, but simply a landing strip the packs used exclusively.

The castle that stood before them was made of stone in various shades of grey. Along the sides, ivy grew almost to the top. The entryway was arched, and large stone statues of wolves stood on either side standing proud and howling. There were four stories of windows, then what looked like little cone rooms at the top of each corner. It was as if the castle had been ripped right out of her fairy tale book from when she was a little girl.

"It's so pretty!" Mackenzie said in a single breath. She could feel her excitement growing.

"Yes, dear. It is. It absolutely is. Welcome to Lycanthrope Manor." Meredith held her hand out before her in a grand sweeping motion with a smile a mile wide on her face.

"Really?" Mackenzie asked with a chuckle to her voice.

"Well, yes. None of us were very creative. The locals call it Thrope Asylum for the Mentally Ill."

"Okay then. Let's go."

As they walked up the long stone path to the door, the other vehicles began to empty. Mackenzie tried to look at every one that passed her, really look at them. There were so many, how could Meredith and Ingrid be sure that they didn't have any spies among them? Evelyn was sure she could trust her own too, but that had proved almost fatal.

Once they entered the house, the pack members began going their own way in all different directions. Their footsteps echoed through the stone hallways until they were left alone in the foyer, just the four of them.

"I am sure you are exhausted. Why don't I show you to your room and give you two some time to rest and clean up before dinner. I will have May, my granddaughter, bring you some fresh clothing and take all of yours to be washed."

"Granddaughter? How closely are she and I related?" Mackenzie asked with a slight excitement to her voice. For a girl who grew up with just her mother, all of a sudden a big family was exciting.

"You, my dear, are my great-great-great-granddaughter. You are two generations removed, but still cousins. But I think you two will get along as if no time spanned between you at all. Come on, this way."

"Liam, what is your favorite dish to eat? I will have the kitchen cook it special just for you," Ingrid said. Liam lit up like a little boy on Christmas. Mackenzie could practically see him salivating.

"Oh. That is such a hard question! Pizza. Loaded with pepperoni and bacon and sausage and mushrooms. Or fried chicken! Made super crispy and served with mashed potatoes and gravy! NO! I know. Lasagna with loads of cheese and meat sauce."

Ingrid laughed then patted him on the cheek. "Whatever you like, my darling. I will have the kitchen prepare it for you."

Ingrid walked off, and Meredith motioned for them to follow her up the old staircase. Pictures lined the walls; most were paintings, but one photograph caught her eye.

"How did you get this? I don't even have one. I've never seen it before," Mackenzie asked in a hushed tone. She stood before a framed portrait of her and her father from when she was about two. She sat on his shoulders smiling away in the middle of the woods. She didn't even remember it. They looked so happy. She didn't remember many happy moments from before he was locked up—before he left. She had to remind herself that he never was locked up, but had left to keep her and her mother safe.

"It was sent to me. I have known about you since the moment you were born. I was surprised to hear you had been bitten, but I knew about you. Most of the Royals have all lost their way. They don't know how to reconnect to their past. Your father's mother sent that picture to her mother, who copied it and sent it to her mother, and that is when I saw it. When Emily died, I inherited the photo and hung it on the wall with the rest of our family."

"But my father didn't know how to find you. Why would it be so hard for him if you keep in touch with your line?" She wasn't trying to be a smart-ass, but she honestly wanted to know if her father sent her overseas with no real information to see what she could do or if he really had none to give.

"Unfortunately, my dear, we have lost many over the years. I have my own thoughts on how that came to be, which we can discuss later, but when Darren's mother died, and her mother died, he lost his ties to me. I know his mother never wrote down any information that could be used against us, including our location or her own. I never knew where your pack had moved. All I knew was the United States. That is a big country to search."

"So is the entire European continent," Mackenzie mumbled.

"Touché. Come. Your room is this way." Meredith led them up a second flight of stairs then down a long hall adorned with gold and red accents. The door on the end, far from any other door, stood open. "Here you are. There is a bath and are fresh towels as well as a bed to rest. May should be up soon." Meredith leaned in and kissed Mackenzie on the cheek, leaving her and Liam standing in the doorway.

"Hmm," Liam mumbled as they walked into the room and closed the door behind them.

"What?" she asked as she watched him closely. She couldn't tell if he was about to joke with her or if something was actually bothering him. It was odd for her to not be able to read him.

"It's just, well, I'm pretty sure we are related now."

Mackenzie couldn't help but laugh. A full on belly laugh that had her sides hurting.

"It's not funny! I'm serious. Does this change anything between us?" Once she heard the hurt in his voice she wiped the tears from her eyes and steadied her breath. She hadn't meant to upset him, but the amount of relative between them was minimal.

"I'm sorry, babe. I didn't mean to laugh. I thought you were kidding. Yes, if we are both of the Royal line, we are related. But distantly. We don't even know how far from Ingrid you are. It could be three or four generations. And we already know I'm four from Meredith and THEY are sisters. That's like a million times removed cousins. That's like telling two strangers they can't be together because Adam and Eve were their million-times grandparents, and they were the same ones. We're talking relatives that were siblings HUNDREDS of years ago. I love you," she moved closer to him, "and I am your mate," she reached out and grabbed his shirt in her fist, "and I am going to marry you," she pulled him closer, "so you can't get rid of me now."

Mackenzie could feel his heart beating wildly beneath his shirt and could feel his deep breaths against her skin when she pulled him the rest of the way and crashed her lips to his. His warmth penetrated her skin, making her sigh against him. When his arms wrapped around her waist and lifted her from the ground, she smiled into the kiss. She lifted her legs and wrapped them around his muscular frame and pulled back from their kiss, her hair falling down, shielding their faces like a curtain. She leaned in and placed a kiss on the tip of his nose, soft and sweet.

"We okay?"

"Better than okay. We're getting married. I guess the sides of the aisle might get a little confusing though."

"Oh, shut up!" She laughed and tried to get away, but instead of letting her down gently, he began tickling her and threw her to the bed. Mackenzie landed with a soft bounce and suddenly, all the joking was left by the wayside. She lay back, resting on her forearms and watched him approach her as if he were stalking his prey. Her heart sped up, but she kept her breath even. She wanted him to work for it. But that didn't stop her body from wetting her between the legs. Liam took a deep breath in as he climbed onto the bed, a growl rumbling in his chest. Moving on his hands and knees, he positioned himself above her the inches between them alight with invisible flames, setting her skin ablaze.

Liam lowered himself slowly until he was damn near touching her from head to toe. When his lips touched hers, their bedroom door opened, startling them both. Mackenzie gave his chest a slightly stronger shove than she had intended, sending Liam crashing to the floor.

"OH! I am so sorry! I can come back later," a young woman said quickly. Her face was turning a brilliant shade of red, and she was looking anywhere, but at Mackenzie and Liam.

"No, I'm sorry! You must be May. I'm Mackenzie." Mackenzie climbed from the bed and walked across the room to her distant cousin. May had dark hair and eyes like she did, but her face was beautifully angular, and she was tall and muscular in a way that Mackenzie never was—not even since being bitten. Mac straightened her blouse along the way and hoped that she wasn't turning as red from embarrassment as May was.

"Yes, I am. Welcome to our home. Here is some fresh clothing for you and your mate. Grandmother said to tell you dinner would be at six-thirty. I'll just leave you to, uh, rest." The little grin on May's face and a lilt to her voice made Mackenzie's hope for not turning as red as a tomato become nonexistent.

"Thanks," she squeaked as May slipped back out the door.

"She thinks we're going to have sex," Mackenzie said, hanging her head in embarrassment.

"Because we are," Liam said, and he approached from behind, positioning himself to begin kissing her neck.

"Not anymore. Did you hear her? Six-thirty is dinner. I for one need a long—very, very long bath. Then a nap while you take a bath. Sex can wait. We have hundreds and hundreds of years to have sex." Mackenzie turned around to face him and placed a hand on his chest and pushed him away a little.

"Or we have right now because we never know what's going to happen tomorrow," he said with a grin. Mackenzie shook her head and walked toward the bathroom.

"Later. Bath now." She stepped into the bathroom and closed the door behind her. As she filled the tub with hot water, she realized that with the way their world was working, Liam might be right. She didn't know when the next attack would be or if they would survive. She opened the door back up and called out to him.

"Liam?"

"Yeah?"

"Want to take a bath?"

He didn't give her a verbal answer. The man running to her while stripping off his clothing was answer enough.

FIFTEEN

Mackenzie wasn't sure what to expect when they sat down to dinner, but a massive dining hall with fifteen tables that stretched the entire room, side by side, wasn't it. Everyone that had met them on the airstrip was present—at least, she assumed so when hundreds of wolves were sitting down to eat. The tables were covered with an assortment of meals, three of which were pizza, lasagna, and fried chicken.

Liam sat beside her, and she could hear his stomach growling as he looked at the food before them. Mackenzie leaned over to Meredith who sat on the other side of her and whispered, "How on earth does your kitchen cook this much food in such a short amount of time? Do you have a full wait staff on board?"

"I employ five witches in my kitchen. They are paid well, don't have to hide their magic, and we eat well. It's a win-win, shall we say?"

"Witches? Like magic and spells and potions?"

"Yes, dear, did you think we were the only beings from the story books?" No, she hadn't. But she didn't think she would ever meet anyone that was anything, but a werewolf either. Geoff had explained that witches were very real, and so were vampires, in one of their early heart to heart talks. Just thinking about him drove ice through her chest.

"I've just never actually met one before."

"You probably have and just didn't know. They are everywhere, surprisingly. Most don't know they have powers and others just know how to blend in. Eat, eat." She motioned to the food before serving a heaping spoonful of mashed potatoes onto her plate.

Mackenzie turned to Liam and whispered in his ear, "Did you know witches made this food? Pretty cool, huh?"

His response was a grunt and a nod through a mouth full of cheesy, meat-covered pizza. Mackenzie laughed a little to herself and dug in. She hadn't realized how hungry she really was until that moment. She put away four platefuls before pushing away from the table. She hadn't been able to indulge her werewolf appetite since the feast with her father's pack before they left for France.

As chairs started to scratch across the floor, and people started to leave the dining room, Mackenzie stood, too. While she didn't leave the room, she did leave the table to walk around the massive hall and take in all the artwork and architecture. She could hear Liam talking to Ingrid. It was obvious the two were already taken with each other, and she smiled to herself. She was so glad he had found a little light in their dark journey.

"Now that it's just us, we should probably talk," Meredith said, pulling Mackenzie's attention from a painting of three young girls.

She turned and walked back over to the table. Sitting there was Meredith, an older man, May, Ingrid, and Liam. When she sat, she knew that all of the light-hearted atmosphere was about to fly right out the window.

"This is my son, Gavin." Meredith motioned to the man sitting with them. "May is his daughter. Your great-great-grandmother was his sister."

"It's nice to meet you," Mackenzie said. She felt slightly awkward as Gavin watched her with such intensity that she didn't know what to make of it.

"You look like her. At least, I can see the resemblance. The eyes and the nose. It's nice to meet you, too." Gavin finally looked away, and she could see the slight shudder in his chest. After a moment, he returned his gaze to the group and all signs of unrest was gone.

"What was her name? What were all of their names?" Mackenzie pulled her self-made family tree out of her pocket and unfolded it, showing the names that had been filled in. Mostly, she knew how many generations were between her and Meredith, and she had Margret's line filled in a little from speaking with Evelynn, but she wanted the whole picture. The more information she had, the better.

"You have been working hard on this. I do not think any of us has a complete tree, but it would be a nice addition. When you have completed this, and your journey is done, I would love to have a copy. You can bring it when you visit again."

Mackenzie smiled at her grandmother before agreeing. "Okay, so I know my father's mother was Henrietta, and I know that I have two uncles, Dylan and Marcus. My great-grandmother was Glenda, but that's all I have for this side."

"Glenda had two children, Henrietta and Florence. After the colonies were formed, and the great war between them and England, both Henrietta and Florence left to make their home in the new world, America. They were the first of our kind to step foot on American soil."

"Wow," Mackenzie said in a soft breath. She knew her family had history, being royal and all, but there was something amazing about her family being the first in her home country.

"Florence never mated nor had children. She has appointed her successor should the time come and set up a stable and strong pack. They will be good allies for you. If your father is not aware, you will find them in the south. Their pack controls from Texas through Louisiana, as long as Margret hasn't taken them. I haven't heard from Florence in six months, which is not unusual, but she should be able to hold her own against an attack."

"So who was Glenda's mother? Or was it her father that was from the Royal line?" Liam asked just as wrapped up in the story as she was. Ingrid sat beside him, beaming at him. The wrinkles around her eyes did little to hinder the sparkle that shone when her grandson spoke.

"Her mother, my daughter, was Emily." There was a distant sadness to her eyes when she said her name, but a soft smile graced her lips anyway. "Emily would have been so proud of you, Mackenzie. Just as I am."

"You should be proud of Darren, too. He is organizing everything in America. He wants Margret stopped as much as I do, if not more. Many of his friends have lost their lives to her, to their packs."

"I am. If I could leave here, I would travel to the states and assist anyway I could there. But I cannot. We will do everything we can here, and I will send help to the states. But I must stay here." Meredith looked to her son and said "Gavin, put together two groups. One to travel the North and to the east, informing as many packs as they find of the imminent war and taking out as many of Margret's wolves as they come across, and the other to go to the states with Mackenzie and Liam to help with the battle there. Where Margret is needs the most power. She needs to be stopped."

"Yes, Mother. Mackenzie, will a hundred wolves be enough?' Gavin stood and placed a hand on his mother's shoulder, but looked to Mackenzie and Liam.

"Any wolves you could send would be enough. We do not take asking them to risk their lives lightly. Any that will volunteer to help are appreciated."

"All of my wolves would volunteer to keep their pack as it is, under my rule, and as strong as it stands now and has stood for seven hundred years."

"I wish I had known about my family growing up. But then again, I was a human, and probably wouldn't have known what to do with you all then," Mackenzie said with a slight chuckle. She joked, but it was true. She wished she had known them longer. She just hoped that she would have a chance to get to know them in the future.

"But we cannot change the past, only prepare for the future. Now, Ingrid and I have something to attend to, but we want you to meet us back here in an hour. Can you do that?"

"Absolutely." Liam and Mackenzie stood from the table and hugged their grandmothers before watching them walk out of the large dining hall.

Mackenzie lay on her bed with a phone pressed to her ear. The static crackled through the ringing as her father's deep voice answered.

"Mackenzie? Are you all right?" Darren's voice was frantic, and Mackenzie could hear loud shouts and growls coming from the background.

"I'm fine, what is going on?"

"Don't worry about that, but we have to make this quick."

"We found the family in England, and they sent us to Spain. Dad, we found Meredith and Ingrid. Rosalinda's sisters. We're with them now. They are sending you a hundred more wolves to help the fight."

"Good job, Mackenzie. We need them. Margret has taken another three packs in the last week. Her numbers are growing rapidly, and the amount of pups we have encountered is scary. Mackenzie, I love you. Remember that."

A loud cry sounded through the phone and a crash. The phone hung up on her. Mackenzie's hands were shaking, and she swallowed thickly before sitting up and turning to Liam.

"Something went wrong. A battle. I have a really bad feeling, Liam." Her voice wavered, and tears pricked at her eyes. She knew in her gut that wherever her father was, he was in trouble. His pack was in trouble. She just hoped that the help Evelynn had sent would get there in time.

"He will be okay. Your dad is a strong man, a strong leader." Liam moved over to her and sat down on the bed. The mattress dipped beneath her with his weight, and she leaned into his side, hiding her face. Her breath heaved as she tried to control the emotional storm that had been brewing inside of her for weeks. His lips brushing across her hair, and his whispered words of encouragement broke the dam that had been building inside of her and the salty tears coated her cheeks.

"What if he isn't?" she whispered through her sobs. Mackenzie sat up and wiped at her eyes furiously, trying to stop the tears. "I shouldn't be sad. I need to be angry. I need to be fucking furious. If anything happens to my father, Margret will pay. I will kill her myself."

Liam watched her, not saying a word. It was almost as if he knew that she didn't want his coddling, even if being in his arms was the only thing that felt right anymore. "Okay. Let's get angry. Let's finish up here, and tomorrow we go home. Tomorrow we join the fight."

Mackenzie smiled at her mate. He understood her better than anyone did, and she knew that together they could face anyone.

Mackenzie and Liam stood in the empty dining hall waiting for Meredith and Ingrid. They had already been there for half an hour, and they themselves had been ten minutes late. Mackenzie shuffled from foot to foot. Liam leaned against the wall by the door with arms crossed.

"Do you think they were on time, and since we were late they left?" she asked. She was more than ready to find out what her Grandmother's grand plan was. Because as soon as she knew, she could get ready for their departure. It was time to go home.

"No, they would have waited. Something is going on." Her heart stammered in her chest. Surely, their quiet respite wasn't over. Had she led Margret's wolves to even more packs? Had they fallen because she was too careless to cover her tracks?

"Do you think Geoff was able to follow us? To William? To here?"

Mackenzie watched as Liam's muscles tightened, and his chest rose and fell deeply before he replied. "No, I don't think about Geoff. I hadn't even considered that. It would be impossible to track us between the cars and airplanes we took."

"I don't try to think of him either, but when I think of something going wrong, he is at the forefront of my mind. Right now, something going wrong means that Margret's wolves have taken another pack. It wouldn't be the first time I led them to fresh blood. All those packs back in the states? Every one of them that fell because we saw them while I was stupid enough to trust him? Their blood is on my hands. I don't think I can handle more."

"I'm sorry—" before he could finish his sentence Ingrid came racing through the door.

"My darlings, please come with me. Quickly now," Ingrid said and motioned them to follow her. She was back out of the dining hall as quickly as she had entered. Mackenzie and Liam had to run to catch up to her before they lost her in the maze that was the castle.

"Ingrid, what is going on?" Mackenzie said as she got close enough not to raise her voice. Speaking privately was hard enough with other werewolves around, she didn't need the echo of the stone walls to make her words travel to even more ears.

"We don't have much time. Come, come." Ingrid slipped down a narrow corridor and as soon as both Mackenzie and Liam had followed, a loud bang sounded from behind them, and they were submerged into pitch black.

A small scrape followed by a snap echoed around them, and a small orb of light was shining from Ingrid's hand. She put the match to a torch and the orange glow that it cast on her face was eerie.

"What is going on?" Liam asked, his eyes darting all around them. Mackenzie followed his lead, hoping to see a way out. Their eyes adjusted quickly to darkness to the point where they could see almost as clearly as they could in solid daylight.

"You are fighting for our future. We thought you deserved to know the history. The real history."

"What do you mean?" Mackenzie asked in a hushed voice, still worried about being overheard.

"What I mean is that it's time to meet my mother."

SIXTEEN

Ingrid pushed open a stone door that Mackenzie hadn't seen. The seams lined up perfectly with the edges of the stone that the door itself was impossible to notice unless you knew it existed.

Ingrid stepped through first, crouching low to make it through the small doorway. Liam followed her and with a deep breath, Mackenzie trailed behind. Before her stood Ingrid and Meredith on opposite sides of a bed.

A woman with paper thin skin that was nearly translucent and hair so thin and so white, Mackenzie was sure that if she blew hard enough the gentle breeze would make it fall from her head.

"Come, come," she said in a hoarse whisper, then turned her head to the side to cough. Mackenzie and Liam stepped closer, their hands finding each other without intention. His fingers laced through hers brought calmness to her that she only experienced with Liam.

"Ah, yes. The magic between you two is strong. So strong. I have only seen a love like this once before. You must fight for each other. Fight for your future before evil takes it from you as it did before."

"Who? Whose love was taken by evil?" Liam asked worry clouding his eyes. Mackenzie ran her thumb across the back of his hand, hoping to ease his mind.

"Mine, my sweet child. Sit, listen." Gwendolynn patted the bed beside her. Ingrid moved back, allowing Mackenzie and Liam to get closer to sit next to the first werewolf. Mackenzie sat slowly and with great care. She was terrified of hurting her and ruining any chance she had of learning more about their race from anyone outside of this room.

"Percival and I," she paused, with a faint smile on her lips and a hand over her heart, "he and I were madly in love. We met as children, grew up together, and shared our first kiss together. We were inseparable. Unfortunately, my family was below his station, and at that time, I had no choice in anything. I was considered a harlot simply for holding his hand. If they had known we had kissed, I would have been stoned. My father arranged my marriage to another man when I was just fourteen. I was considered old, and since no one had asked for me, I wasn't deemed worthy of more than a goat in trade. I was devastated. And when my husband tried to bed me, I cried the whole time. It hurt, and he wasn't the man I was in love with. Percival was so angry with my father. His father married him off, too. To a young woman whose family was very prominent in the area. Her family ran a farm that produced herbs and vegetables like no other. Morgan his wife, created soaps and medicines that worked in ways no one understood.

"One day, my husband grew angry as I cried through our nightly encounter, and he hit me until I stopped. When I awoke, my womanly area was so raw and sore that I couldn't walk. After two days, I left. I knew if I were ever to be found, my husband would beat me until my last breath, but I hated him. I couldn't stand the sight of him. So I left knowing that I was leaving everything behind. My family, my home, my Percival.

"After three months, I had found a small building that had been abandoned and turned it into my own home. I had a garden in the back where I grew what vegetables I could, and I taught myself to hunt. I was learning how to make it on my own. Something unheard of for women at that time.

"Then, there was a knock on my door. Never before had anyone knocked on my door. Never before had I even seen a single person within a half a kilometer from my home. With my heart in my chest, I slowly opened the door, expecting to see my husband or my father there ready to drag me back. But it wasn't. It was Percival.

"He didn't say a single word. He just pulled me into his arms and held me. I didn't know what to say, so I just buried my face in his neck and embraced him. It had been so long since he had held me that I didn't dare say anything to make him stop. What we were doing, even just holding one another, was so wrong.

We were both married, but not to the one person we loved. Not to each other.

"When he finally pulled back, I could see tears in his eyes. He told me that he had been looking for me ever since I had disappeared. He feared the worst. He thought my husband had killed me. When my father and my husband gave up looking for me after just a month, he didn't. His wife thought he was going hunting whenever he searched for me. He always made sure to bring something home with him. Then he kissed me. And it was like no time had passed without one another.

"Soon, he was visiting me every few days. Then, it became almost every day. When I finally gave my body to him, he came to me every day. I asked him what he was telling his wife. He didn't like to talk about her. He said not to worry and that it was handled. He told her to be happy he came home with food for the table and money to keep her in fine things.

"One day, we had fallen into bed together. We made love often, and when my door opened slowly, quietly, we never even noticed. It wasn't until I heard her scream that we knew we were being watched. That was the last day of my human life.

"His wife was a witch. Her whole family had magic. She was so hurt, so angry that she tapped into her family's magic to produce a spell so strong and so vile. She had to spill blood to do it. She sacrificed her own brother to punish us. Her spell turned me into a werewolf, ruled by the moon and with a thirst for blood and him into a vampire. Destined only to live at night and crave blood. But together? We could see each other. We would crave each other. But we could no longer have each other. She made us practically immortal. The only thing more powerful than ripping our heads off was the bite of the other. Her magic flows through all of us. It is destined to curse my line for as long as we live. At least Vampires cannot be born. She showed leniency with Percival. She did not curse his family, only him. The problem came when more werewolves and vampires were being created. It was an unintended transfer of her magic.

"She never intended for our species to gain a real population. But it has, and now it must be managed. My daughters were right in allowing packs control of their own. No one person, or werewolf, should control an entire species. Percival had created many vampires before he knew what he was doing. Just as I did. Eventually, when I could remember and control what I was doing as a wolf, I was devastated. I went and found as many of my victims as I could. I explained what was happening. I offered them a place to live. I offered them a new family and they followed me.

"Even though I had stopped creating new wolves, my pack had not. I instituted rules against human blood. I put together a guard of sorts to enforce the rules. I did it all to protect them, and to protect those still with their humanity. Eventually, after many, many years, I mated. It was more of a magical draw that I am not sure I can explain as my love for him was strong, but it was never as it was with Percival. We had three beautiful daughters, and then while they were still young, a small faction of my pack decided we had too much power. They killed him to get me to step down. I was too stubborn. I had them taken care of.

"When my girls were old enough to lead on their own, I had preparations in place to step down. To divide our pack amongst them to be run separately as each saw fit. I sent them to three distinct areas and sent wolves with each of them.

"Then, I was attacked. I was nearly beheaded, and if it weren't for Ingrid coming back for something she had left behind, I am sure another of the rebels would have come to check to make sure I was gone." The frail woman finally took a moment to take a breath, and she coughed and wheezed into a napkin while her two daughters stood by her side, watching on worriedly. Mackenzie looked to Ingrid to see her reaction to the story, to being named as her mother's savior.

When Gwendolynn's coughing subsided, she returned her glistening eyes to Mackenzie and Liam. "After that, I went into hiding. I let them all think I was dead. When Rosalinda took over so quickly and so easily, I knew my own daughter had plotted my demise. She wanted the power. She changed the rules. She allowed the killing of humans, just not the turning. Her only rule was to keep out of sight. Do not let the humans become suspicious. When the wolves became less than discreet with their hunting, she executed them for disobeying her.

"Eventually, ruling the werewolves was not enough. She found a way to the humans, too. She married a human close to the king and managed to get herself into the Royal bed as well. Our kind didn't take well to her new plan for the future, and another coup was created. Her human husband was part of the Royal guard and was in charge of finding the beasts that had been terrorizing their kingdom. What he didn't know was that two of his men were werewolves themselves and planned the whole thing. They had been the wolves to destroy entire villages in a single night just to get the Kings attention. Just to make him declare a hunting party. And when they found their queen, they took her hand and gave it to her husband. They knew that her husband would kill her himself."

"But why did you stay hidden for so long? The entire world thinks you are dead. You could have stopped this before it ever started. You could have stopped Rosalinda," Liam said with a hint of anger to his voice. She could feel his agitation radiating off him in waves.

"To do that would have meant to kill my eldest daughter. No matter what she did to me, I could not kill her. Even if it meant hiding for nearly eight hundred years. But had it not been her, it would have been someone else. Werewolves are no different from humans. The hunger for power runs deep. You two must stay strong. Do you feel the magic that connects you? Do you feel the hum beneath your skin that calls to you?"

Mackenzie could only nod. When she and Liam mated, it was like nothing else. Whenever they touched, she could feel him under her skin. She just had never thought it was magic. She had thought it was love. "So, my biting him? Is that..."

Mackenzie couldn't bring herself to say the words. She had heard from some that the sire link is what made them close, and her father said that it had nothing to do with it. That her love was hers and hers alone, and the magic that connected them through her bite wouldn't make her fall in love with him.

"That, my dear, makes it stronger, but it doesn't make it so. The connection from your bite amplifies feelings. It does not create them. Why your mating is so much stronger than that of others, I am not sure. Perhaps it has to do with you both being of my direct bloodline. Or perhaps..."

Gwendolynn stopped talking and stared at Liam. She sat up and placed a hand along his cheek and turned his head one way then the other. Her breath hitched in her throat, and she lay back, clearly spent from the amount of energy that took her.

"What? Perhaps what?" Mackenzie asked almost in a panic. She had to know. Gwendolynn was sharing so much with them. She wanted to know it all. She had a deep gut feeling that by the time they made it back to Lycanthrope Manner, her great-great-great-great-grandmother, mother of all werewolves, would be gone.

"Liam, tell me, what is your mother's maiden name?"

"Atherton."

The gasps in the room told Mackenzie that his mother was a key to the puzzle. His Royal blood, his mother's name, and her. It all added up to create their special bond, but she didn't understand why.

"Gwendolynn, is Percival still alive?"

"Yes, my dear. Percival Atherton is still alive."
And suddenly, it all made sense.

"I would like a word alone with Mackenzie,"
Gwendolynn said. Meredith and Ingrid looked to their
mother in shock before standing and heading toward
the door. Liam squeezed her hand and kissed her
cheek and followed them.

"The magic in you is strong. Stronger than any
other from your generation. The fact that human blood
mingles with your own does not diminish your
powers, but intensifies them. The power to love and to
feel a connection with humanity is what will keep you
from becoming like her. Margret has great strength
and power of her own, but she lost the ability to truly
love over time. To truly care about anyone. When her
son died, it wrecked her. She loves Geoff. In a way.
But she sees him more as a tool of power."

Gwendolynn began to cough, and Mackenzie
could see the color drain from her face with every
wheeze and cough. She looked around for some water
or a tissue or anything to offer this woman to help, but
she saw nothing. "Do you want me to get Ingrid or
Meredith?"

"No, no. I'll be all right. My time is coming to an
end." Mackenzie felt her heart seize in her chest. She
didn't know this woman, but knowing they shared a
bloodline, and a destiny made it hard to listen to her
talk about death so easily.

"Okay," she said above a whisper.

"I wish I was able to help with Margret, but you can see that this old woman would be no better in battle than an infant. The infant may have a better chance than I would. The cute and innocent thing could possibly get them spared. But I can help you. I can give you the tools you need to distract Margret long enough to finish the war once and for all."

Mackenzie leaned forward as her voice began to trail off. If Meredith knew of a way to help, Mackenzie needed it. She needed every ounce of help she could get. Gwendolynn reached up and placed her hands on Mackenzie's shoulders and pulled her closer. When her shallow breath brushed across the skin of Mackenzie's neck, she whispered, "This will only hurt for a second."

Before her words registered, Mackenzie felt the searing hot stab of teeth in her neck. She tried to pull away, but all that did was to tear at her skin more. Gwendolynn's fingers dug into her shoulders, and her teeth latched tighter. Mackenzie could feel the blood dripping down her neck in warm waves and her head becoming light with the blood loss.

Mackenzie's eyes had fluttered open and closed for a minute or two before Gwendolynn released her, licking the wound and then pulling back to look Mackenzie in the eyes. "That bite will heal, like every other injury you will occur in your very long life. But this bite will scar. Most do not know this, but a bite from me, the original, bears a mark. My daughters and my granddaughter do. They know of the mark. They know that with every bite I give, I release a little of my own magic into the bearers blood. Let her see your scar and tell her that you met Edwin, the grandson who resembles her dead son inextricably. How he helped you in your fight against her. Her son is her weak spot. Remind her of him, and show her that I live, that she will never truly be the all-powerful queen. It will cause her to lose focus. You must strike then."

Mackenzie reached up to her neck and felt the skin knitting itself together, and instead of the smooth skin she was accustomed to, there were two rigid raised crescents. As her skin healed, she could feel a buzz within her. It was almost the same as when the full moon was approaching, and her body begged to be one with nature, but different. The energy was there, but she could focus it. She wasn't being compelled to do anything. Instead, she felt like she could control every cell within her body to do as she wished.

"The power is strange when it first enters you. Do not expect more than can be done. But stronger, faster, and more focus. You will run like the wind and move mountains as if they were nothing but a pebble. And you will be able to see the world in your head two steps ahead of everyone else." With every word that Gwendolynn spoke, her voice grew more tired, and her eyes began to droop. "I must rest now, my child. Please, do not let her destroy our way of life. Do not let her-"

Before she could finish, her eyes closed and she fell asleep. Mackenzie stood, fingers still at her neck and walked toward the door. With a final glance back at the woman who started it all, she walked out the door.

SEVENTEEN

The plane was cramped. Every seat was filled, and the leg room was a joke. It didn't help that Liam was glued to her side and kept pawing at her like a horny teenage boy on prom night. Ever since she walked out of the room with Gwendolynn, Liam had been obsessed with her neck. Staring at it, licking it, kissing it. At first, she enjoyed the attention. But after eighteen hours, she was more than over it.

"Seriously, Liam. Can you please just give me a little space? I really need to sleep a bit before we land. We have what? Four hours left of our flight? You should rest too. We have a lot ahead of us. We don't know the next time we are going to get to just sit and relax."

"Sorry, I don't know what it is, but—" a growl rumbled from his chest, soft but noticeable. The woman across the aisle turned and stared with a slightly scared look on her face.

"You are causing a scene. Just rest. Please." Mackenzie closed her eyes and turned her head so that the scar was being hidden by the seat. Finally, she felt Liam shift and the heat from his body ease.

The plane landed on the tarmac without a hitch. It was early, and Mackenzie was ready to depart and get to work. She was tired of traveling and tired of small confined spaces. What she really wanted was a bed of her own. Only, she didn't have one. She had nowhere to actually call home.

"When all of this is over, we need a house. A place of our own."

"I like that idea. After all, a married couple needs a place to call theirs." The tone of his voice left little to the imagination. The deep penetrating look in his eyes dashed what little was left. She knew exactly what he was thinking, and the tingle spreading through her body was onboard.

"Mackenzie!" A deep voice called out through the crowd mingling around the luggage carousels. Her head whipped around and saw her father, standing tall and as big as ever. He charged forward, a weary smile on his face. Mackenzie ran to him, thankful to see him alive after their last conversation. Liam followed behind with a smile on his face.

She threw herself into his arms, and he hugged her furiously for a minute... then he stiffened, breathing in deeply. He set her down and looked at her with questioning eyes. "You smell different. You have your scent, but more."

His eyes scanned her and landed on her neck. With wide eyes, his mouth slacked open. Self-consciously, Mackenzie's hand flitted to her neck and traced the scar. Darren closed his mouth and pulled his eyes from his daughter's neck to her eyes. "I have heard stories. The only way to gain a scar is from the original. Gwendolynn. But it's impossible."

"Not impossible," she said dropping her hand.

"We have much to discuss. But not here, come." Darren said and shook Liam's hand before pulling him into a hug. They walked out of the busy airport together and to Darren's Jeep. The pack planes were useful for small distances, but the entire ocean wasn't a possibility.

Once they were in the confines of the Jeep, Darren looked at Mackenzie who sat beside him in the front seat. When he didn't start the engine, she knew the conversation would be done then and there. At least she was only telling her father and not the entire pack-army-whatever they all were calling themselves.

When she finished, Darren didn't say a word. When he reached up and traced the scar with his own fingertips, Liam growled in the back seat causing Mackenzie to glare at him. "I can't believe she still lives. You have her magic in your blood. You and Liam. Together, you will be strong. Stronger than any others."

"Yeah, that's what Gwendolynn said."

"I have only seen one with the scar. The Elder One. He bears the mark on his leg and his neck. He was turned by the Original. He will know your mark. he will recognize your scent. She chose you." Mackenzie felt like her father was rambling, but she didn't stop him. She didn't know what to say even if she did.

"Should we get back?" Liam asked. Darren nodded his agreement and started the Jeep. By the time they pulled onto the highway, Liam's fingers had found her neck again.

"Is this normal?" Mackenzie asked her father, gesturing at her neck and Liam's hands.

"Yes. Anyone who does not share a direct bloodline will be more attracted to you. Liam is more so because, apparently you two have mated. I can feel the magical bond between you. It is stronger than it was when you left. And stronger even than I feel between the most loving mates within my pack. Liam, you must not let your anger or jealousy loose within our ranks. She will gain attention, even more than she would on her own. You must stay strong and calm with the knowledge that your mate bond is strong. So strong that nothing will break it. No one will break it."

"Yes, sir." Mackenzie turned in her chair and could already see the jealousy dangerously balancing on the edge of his control just thinking about another wolf looking her way. With a sigh, Mackenzie rested her forehead against the glass pane of the window. Her life was already going to be difficult in the coming days, weeks, months. While Gwendolynn gave her a tool to make the final battle easier, she sure as hell made the journey to that battle a lot more difficult.

The Jeep bounced and shook from side to side as they left the main road and drove on the mostly hidden trail that lead back to Darren's pack in the middle of the woods. They had set up deep in the forest where no campers dared to travel. With enough little cabins to house a pack of at least fifty, the area was well developed. Mackenzie wondered how they kept from being found, but decided that was a question for another day. She wasn't sure she could handle much more information on magic and secrets.

The pack was all gathered around the meeting area. They were talking over one another to the point where Mackenzie couldn't make out one person's statement from another. Although, when she saw Analise, she tuned it all out anyway.

"ANALISE!" Mackenzie yelled and ran. She barreled through two large men and darted around two small children to practically jump into her best girlfriend's arms. She and Analise had joined Margret's pack at the same time. And both had left as soon as they realized the evil that she was capable of committing. Not to mention the time Analise saved her life.

"Oh, thank God, you're back!" Analise squeezed her tight then pulled back, worry in her eyes. "Mac, I want to hear about everything, but first, you and Darren need to get this pack under order and hear what's going on."

Worry flooded Mackenzie's heart. She whipped her head around to see Darren watching his pack and Liam standing beside him, speaking softly. So softly, she couldn't hear him. The fact that he whispered, the only way he could have spoken without her hearing at least a murmur of his voice, scared her even more. Liam lifted his eyes and locked them on her as a sad smile crested his face.

"Enough!" boomed Darren's voice. The pack silenced immediately, and he took his place at the front of the meeting area. "Mackenzie, come here, please."

Mackenzie moved quickly to her father's side. She wasn't sure what was going on, but if he wanted her next to him, she would be. She had a lot to tell the pack that would soon be growing with wolves from all over the world. Most of the male member's stared at her, their eyes ghosting to her neck briefly before Darren cleared his throat, throwing out a challenge with his eyes. He didn't speak the words, but Mackenzie knew the look he gave them was that of a protective father. She had seen it on many fathers of her old schoolmates whenever a boy would get too close. She had always been so jealous of that look. Now she knew what it was like, and she was so grateful to him for it.

"Now, tell me. Who was scouting? I left explicit instructions to guard that house!" Mackenzie looked to her father confused. She didn't know what house he was referring to, and the fact that he was so upset scared her even more. Could the house in town where the children stay be in danger? Would Margret stoop so low as to attack defenseless babies? Mackenzie almost scoffed to herself. Of course, she would.

"It was Matt, sir. He has not returned." Someone from the group answered.

"What house?" Mackenzie asked, looking to her father for an answer.

"Your mother's."

Mackenzie's heart sank into her stomach just as the meal she had on the flight was coming up. She turned and ran for the tree line, expelling the contents of her stomach the moment the trees hid her from view.

Her mother. Margret was after her mother. She hadn't spoken to her mother in nearly a year, not since leaving for Harvard the previous fall. She hadn't wanted to after she found out the lies she had been told about her father. But now? It was all she could do to stop herself from screaming bloody murder and crumbling into a pile of tears.

She heard him approach before she felt his hands on her back, caressing up her spine to hold her hair back. "Get it out. We'll go get her. We will make sure she is safe."

Mackenzie straightened her back, wiping her mouth with the back of her hand. She turned and looked the love of her life in the eyes and said, "If she isn't, I will kill that bitch with my bare hands."

Mackenzie's fear was beginning to be clouded with rage. She stormed off toward her father and the pack. "We leave now. We can't wait. What if Margret already has her? That has to be why Matt didn't come back. No one from your pack would betray you, would they?"

It was strange giving her father orders, but she had become used to calling the shots in her time away.

Liam helped keep her safe and sane, but he allowed her to make the calls.

"No. I suspect that he is no longer with us. Matt would not turn his back on this pack. He was born into it and has been loyal for the last 300 years. You are right; we must leave now."

The pack broke out into murmurs again, but a single raised hand by Darren hushed them. "Do not fear. You know what to do. Those of you assigned to protect the pack land do so by all means necessary. Those of you back from scouting, return. If you find anything useful, send one back, and two keep watch. Remember, we will be having many new wolves joining our ranks in the coming days. Ask where they come from and who sent them. If it is anyone besides William, Meredith, Ingrid, or Evelyn—then turn them away. Let them know it is only temporary until we can verify who they are. If they are truly on our side, they will understand the need for added security.

"Liam will train everyone who stays here to fight. He has learned both from me and from Geoff. If you all learn the way that our enemy fights, you will be better able to fight against him and his men. You will listen to him as if you were listening to me. You will work hard. You will not waver. The battle is coming to us, and we must be ready."

"No, I need to go with Mackenzie!" Liam shouted across the crowd. Anger flashed in Darren's eyes, but Mackenzie placed a soft hand on his arm, and then walked to Liam.

"You can't. Darren is right. This is something he and I need to do. We put her in danger. My Dad and me. If it weren't for us, Margret would have no interest in her. I need you to teach this pack everything you know. Not just about fighting, but also about the maps and everything you did to keep us alive and to move forward over there. I need you to do this. If you are here, then I can trust that they will be prepared. I can trust that we will be ready to finish this fucking war once and for all, and you and I can get on with our happily ever after."

"Does the Big Bad Wolf get a happily ever after," he whispered with a roughness to his voice she hadn't heard before. He linked his fingers with hers and caressed the back of her hand with his thumb. "Promise me you will come back to me. Don't take any stupid risks. You have to come back to me."

"I promise," she whispered before kissing him soundly. The hoots and hollers from the pack reminded her they were not alone, and she pulled back to stare into his moist eyes. She would do everything she could to keep her promise. She still had a lot of life to live with Liam. He deserved happiness, and she never wanted to be the reason he didn't get it.

Mackenzie turned to look for her father, and saw him in the arms of Nadia, his mate. They were so in the moment that she felt like she was invading this personal private moment for them to say their goodbyes. Nadia moved her hand to her face and wiped under her eyes. Darren leaned down and kissed her forehead, and then his eyes scanned the crowd and landed on Mackenzie. With a nod, he let go of Nadia and moved toward her. Mackenzie gave Liam a hug goodbye as well, and stepped away, forcing herself not to look back.

She knew if she did, she might change her mind about him staying behind, and she couldn't. Her need to have him by her side didn't match the need of him to stay and train everyone to protect themselves, the pack and their very way of life.

EIGHTEEN

Between the Jeep and running in wolf form, Mackenzie and Darren made it to her mother's house within a day. Speed limits didn't matter when her mother's life was on the line. It wasn't like they could really get hurt anyway.

When Mackenzie knew they were just a block away from her mother's house, they changed back. Once dressed, they ran. When they saw the flashing blue and red lights, they ran as fast as they could while still looking human. There were people everywhere. A few recognized Mackenzie and stared at her with worried looks.

The house was in shambles. Windows were broken, and the door was nothing more than shards of wood barely hanging from the hinges. A sob escaped her lips as she ran forward, stumbling over her own two feet. Her father's arms wrapped around her waist to hold her up just as the sheriff was coming toward her.

"Mackenzie Duncan?" he asked in a gentle tone. All she could do was nod her reply. "And you are?" he asked, looking to Darren.

"Her father."

"I wasn't aware Mrs. Duncan was married."

"Haven't been for a long time. Doesn't mean I'm not her father. What's going on? What are we going to find in there?"

Mackenzie listened to her father take charge. While he was getting the small details that the police actually knew, she opened her senses up to try to find anything they would have missed. Blood. She smelled blood and a lot of it. She also smelled the rank fur of whoever had done this. If she wasn't mistaken, they had to have been in wolf form for a long time to leave such an intense smell behind.

"Mackenzie? I asked if you knew of anyone who would want to abduct your mother?"

"She isn't in there? You mean she isn't—" Mackenzie couldn't bring herself to say the word dead. She refused.

"We don't know. There is a lot of evidence of a violent attack. But she isn't here. Her clothing, purse, phone, keys, are all here and look to be where she would normally place them. The couches are torn to shreds, as are the carpeting and blinds. I don't know what happened in there, but it looks like someone let loose a bunch of wild animals."

"Can we go in?" Darren asked. Mackenzie was thinking the same thing. They needed some kind of clue. Margret wouldn't have taken her mother unless she wanted Mackenzie to follow. If she were just trying to mess with her head, she would have killed her immediately.

"I'm afraid not. But, Ms. Duncan, you can head on down to the station, and as soon as we know anything, we will send someone to talk to you."

"Do I have to go?"

"You aren't being ordered to, but why wouldn't you want to be in the one place that can answer any questions you might have?" His voice had gone from concerned to distrusting. His eyes narrowed, and she could see the small twitch in his mustache.

"I just need some time alone. Can I at least go into the backyard?"

"I suppose that will be all right. Mr. Duncan, can I ask you a few more questions?"

Mackenzie didn't wait to hear the answer. She practically sprinted around the house, looking into the windows as she did so. There were claw marks on just about every item she could see, and it was as if they used her mother's blood to mark every single piece. It wasn't just blood pooling on the ground or a spatter across the wall, but almost strategically placed on pieces of furniture that led to the back door. How the police hadn't noticed, she wasn't sure.

Her mother's house had a good sized yard. Her favorite part had always been the grove of trees that backed up to her property with running trails twisting and turning for miles. With a deep breath in through her nose, Mackenzie locked onto the scent of the blood. Her body vibrated with the need to run. To follow the scent to her mother. To destroy those that dared to lay a single claw on her.

"Go no. If we don't clear the trees and get out of sight in the next two minutes, the Sheriff will be back here." Her father's voice was barely a whisper as he approached from behind. The hairs on the back of her neck stood on end, alerting her to the fact that she was being watched.

When Darren's heavy arm rested across her shoulders, he led her toward an old swing set that had been there when she and her mother had first moved in. She had never really used it. She was much too old at the time, but it served as a place to sit and get away from the constant nagging of her mother.

She felt a tear slip thinking of her that way. Her mother used to drive her crazy with wanting her to be normal. To act like every other teenager out there. Whenever Mackenzie would do something extraordinary, her mother would flinch. When she joined the track team and won matches, instead of boasting about her daughter, she would ask why she wasn't more concerned with makeup and dates than getting all sweaty. Mackenzie never knew why her mother acted that way, but it became clear then. She hadn't wanted Mackenzie to show any signs of being more. Of being the daughter of a werewolf.

She wiped at the tears angrily. She loved her mother dearly, but that didn't change the fact that she had kept her father away, or that she had lied for years and years, or that she treated her as if she were less of a person because of her true self. She loved her all right, but she didn't like her much.

"He stopped looking, let's go," Mackenzie ground out through her teeth before darting into the trees and getting off the running path as soon as possible. Darren ran beside her, stride for stride. When they could no longer see any remnant of the destroyed house behind, they slowed just long enough to pack their clothing into a small pack and change, allowing their wolves to take the lead on the hunt.

Blood drops and the scent of fear fueled her. She had run fast before. She had pushed herself to the point of near exhaustion before. But never had she ran with such a speed that her heart pounded so fast and so hard in her chest that she nearly passed out mid-stride.

A growl erupted from her chest at her weakness. She slowed slightly, just enough to clear her head of the darkness that was threatening to take her under. A scream penetrated the air around her, and all common sense was lost as she pushed herself back to the breaking point.

Darren's wolf flew past her, letting out a mighty roar, warning anyone in their path to move or die. The trees cleared leaving an open field and a small warehouse that used to hold grain for all the livestock in the area. Mackenzie had explored it on many occasions when she needed to get farther than the swing set. She could smell her mother's blood and could hear her faint heartbeat. She was alive.

Two wolves charged out of the door, teeth snarling, eyes glowing wild and green. Their moves were awkward and disjointed. They snapped their jaws before being in the position to make contact and as such, opened themselves up to an easy counterattack.

One thing was finally in their favor. With Geoff traipsing all over the world looking for her, he had no time to train the new ranks.

With one quick dodge and attack, Mackenzie had her teeth sunk deep into one of the wolves' throats. She could feel the vibration of its mangled cry as the blood coated her fur. When his heart stopped pumping, she wretched her head to the side, fully separating the wolf into two pieces.

Mackenzie heard her father's distinct roar and turned to see the other wolf had already been disposed of, and the door to the cabin flung open. Darren had three wolves attacking at once. She ran in, momentarily stunned to see her mother tied to a bed, bloodied and beaten, and watching the scene with horrified eyes.

"Behind you," she hoarsely whispered just before a sharp seething pain sank itself into her back. Mackenzie howled and rolled, flinging her body just right in order to dislodge her attacker. Only, he didn't let go, and a piece of her flesh went with him as he flew from her into the wall.

The wolf spit out a wad of blood and fur and lunged again. Mackenzie fought with everything she had. She kicked hard, moved swiftly, and bit without remorse. But so did he.

A gurgled cry from another wolf distracted her attacker just long enough for Mackenzie to finish it. With the last bit of strength she had, she pushed off bitten and broken legs to lunge forward and grasp his neck in her razor sharp teeth. The claws on her paws dug in deep to whatever flesh they could find, and she bit down hard. When her teeth grazed bone, she released and quickly clamped back down severing the spinal cord. The beast went limp beneath her just before her own body gave into her own injuries.

Before her eyes fluttered closed, she heard her mother's soft cries proving she was alive, saw her father's wolf limping toward her, and dismembered wolves all around. Six wolves against her and her father. They had done it. A smile graced her lips as her body took the needed rest to heal.

NINETEEN

Mackenzie woke to hushed voices. While their words were quiet, the anger in them was obvious.

"You were supposed to leave and never come back. You were supposed to have nothing to do with her. Now look at what you have done! What your kind did!"

"She found me. She had already been bitten. Don't you see? This is her destiny. She is meant to be a wolf. She is meant to stop the biggest threat our kind has ever had. Hell, if it were up to Margret, humans would turn into nothing more than a source of food or pack growth. Mackenzie is trying to stop that. We all are."

"I knew I should never have let her go. If I had kept her with me at the community college, she would have been fine. No one would have ever found her. She had to go to Harvard. She had to go and show how much more she was. Drawing attention. Running faster than everyone even though no doctor could figure out how or why with how heavy she was."

"Margret would have found her anyway. All that would have done would make her hate you."

"Better to hate me when I am doing what's right for her than this. I remember your anger. I remember the broken walls and doors and that boy. I remember it all. I also remember the tears and the sadness when I had to tell her you were gone for good. You weren't there when I saw things start. When she started the running and not a single person in our whole town could top her? When every full moon she found a reason to be out at night, but could never explain to me why it was so important to break curfew. When I had heard a growl rumble from her chest as she was sleeping that I swore sounded exactly like you did the day you destroyed our house. If you had been honest with me, I never would have slept with you, married you, and my daughter wouldn't be a goddamn wolf!"

"You wouldn't have a daughter without me! You would be a lonely old woman who was just as lost and alone as when I found you. You wouldn't have had a roof over your head for the last twenty years or money in the bank to feed her. Have you ever stopped to wonder what your life would look like without the money I put in there every month?"

Mackenzie had heard enough. She needed to eat, and they needed to hide her mother away somewhere safe and get back to work. It was time to stop being on the defensive and go on the offensive. It was time to find the bitch and take her down once and for all.

"Can you two please stop arguing over my very existence or your heart break from more than ten years ago? I mean, really. Mom, you lied to me. You lied every single day. And the letter? Don't even get me started. But this? This arguing and this betrayal? That can wait. We saved your life, and now we have to take you somewhere to keep you safe."

"I'm not going anywhere with Darren. It won't happen. Why can't you stay with me? We can hide out together."

"Didn't you hear a word he said? This whole thing, this whole damn war, depends on me somehow." Mackenzie pulled the collar of her shirt to the side to show the mark from Gwendolynn. "This right here is from the very first werewolf ever. She thinks it's up to me. After no one knowing she was alive for almost a thousand years, she showed herself to Liam and me. If it weren't up to us, why would she waste her time? You are going even if I have to knock you out and drag you there."

"No. How do I know I will be safe surrounded by other werewolves? Your father couldn't even control his anger around his own child. How do I know that these strangers won't take one whiff of my blood and think I'm lunch?"

"Because, I have never done anything to break your trust. That's all you, remember?" Mackenzie knew she was being harsh, but she had no intention of backing down or forgiving her mother so easily.

"Fine. But when this is all over, you and I need to talk. I'm not the only one at fault here. Or do you not remember leaving for college almost a year ago and forgetting I even exist?"

"Fine." Mackenzie ground the word out between her teeth. She knew her mother was right about that. She meant to call a hundred times, but never knew how to say the things she needed to say. She didn't know how to tell her mother that she was right about Harvard, that she would never make it through the first year. Only, it wasn't the school that stopped her. It was the wolf that bit her.

The three sat in silence and ate something out of a can that her father heated up on the stove. The label had worn off long ago, and Mackenzie's best guess was that it was supposed to be chili.

"It's going to take longer to get back. We can't run with her. We should call the pack to let them know that we found her and that we are safe."

Darren tossed a small cell phone from his pocket to her with a wink. He knew that she wanted to speak with Liam, and she was grateful. "Don't you want to talk to Nadia?"

"Nadia and I have been together for many years. I miss her dearly, but I remember what it is like to be newly mated."

"Thank you." Mackenzie felt the smile creep onto her face and the heat hit her cheeks. Mackenzie left the little cottage, already dialing the phone. She heard her mother practically screeching about mating and boys and no-good-werewolf-assholes. But when Liam's voice echoed through the phone, it didn't matter.

"Hello? Mackenzie?" he asked hurriedly, in a worried whisper.

"Liam," she said back. Her heart racing and her eyes stinging with tears. She missed him, and the drama with her mother was getting the better of her.

"What's wrong? What happened? Is it Darren?"

"Nothing is wrong. We got here in time. Mom is safe, beaten up and sore, but okay. Can't say that she and I are okay. But that can come later."

"Did you get hurt?"

"Nothing that didn't heal. We took out six of them. Six wolves that no longer fight for Margret. Is it wrong of me to be glad for that? I mean I killed someone. I've lost count of how many wolves have died because of me, but all I can think is thank God because now they won't be trying to kill me anymore. They can't hurt anyone anymore."

"It's not wrong. They would have kept hurting people, and you stopped them."

"I miss you," she said. Liam always knew what to say to make everything better, and the only other thing she could possibly need at that moment was he there with her.

"I miss you, too. You guys heading back?"

"Yeah, but Mom will be with us, so it's going to take a while. But we should be back in a day or so."

"Good. Two of the packs from Europe arrived. We have another hundred wolves ready to fight."

"Liam. Send at least ten wolves to your old house. Have them keep an eye out, but stay out of sight. If Margret knew you were Royal, she knows your brother is, too. And we know she isn't above torturing our family to get to us. My mother is proof of that."

Mackenzie heard his breath hitch as he barked out orders to someone in the background about collecting a team and meeting him to go over directions. "I love you, but I need to handle this. I won't be here when you get back. I have to go, too. What if I'm too late?"

Mackenzie didn't want him to go, but understood why he had to. "Be careful and be fierce. I love you, too."

Mackenzie and Liam both hung up, dread filling the pit of her stomach.

"Can we slow down?" her mother panted out after an hour of trudging through the trees. They had decided against using the trail as they had to find the little cabin, worried that it would make them an easy target for not only more wolves, but the police as well.

Leaving her mother's house after ignoring the police request for questioning wasn't exactly a smart idea, but she didn't have a choice if she wanted to find her mother alive.

"Yeah, sorry." Mackenzie thought they were going slow, but with her mother not being used to traveling on foot, her injuries, and the simple fact that humans just weren't as fast and able as wolves, she realized that she wasn't going as slow as she thought they were. "We just have to get back as soon as possible."

"Liam won't be there whether we get back tonight, tomorrow night or the night after. He is going to protect his brother. You just have to believe that he and the rest of the pack will be safe," Darren said, his voice full of faux confidence.

"I know. We need a plan. Something better than wait and see who dies next. I'm tired of always looking over my shoulder. It's time to turn the tables," Mackenzie responded. She decided to ignore the obvious fact that no matter how careful the pack or Liam were, Margaret was powerful. They all took a chance of not coming back.

"You want to go on the offensive? We have less than a hundred wolves on our side. And we are spread out all over the country. It's damn near sucicide." Her father's voice raised with each sentence. A quick glare from both her and her mother and he quieted down again.

"No, the others from Europe arrived. Close to a hundred of them. They are there and waiting for us. This is the only way I can see this working. If we want to end this war sooner rather than later, we have to stop running. We have to stop being afraid of what's next. We need to strike. We need to have her looking over her shoulder for once."

"So how do we do that?" he asked.

"We use our resources. Analise has knowledge into the California pack. I happen to know where they keep all of their born young pack members and their mothers."

Mackenzie's mother gasped, and the look on her face was that of pure disgust. "No, Mother. The point wouldn't be to hurt the children. Only commandeer the building with them inside, not only to protect them from the fighting, but also to prove a point. To prove that we are strong, and we will do what it takes. By the end, those children will need a new pack anyway. We will just replace their current caretakers."

The fact that her mother could think she would actually harm a child almost killed her. The way her mother looked at her now, full of distrust and disgust kept her away.

"That could work. Do you have anyone from Montana you can talk to? Maybe someone who wasn't thrilled with what was going on but wasn't ready to leave?"Her father was finally seeing that her plan had merit. That it could really work.

"Maybe. I can try. I'm not sure how I will get in touch with her though." Mackenzie kept moving forward, leaving her father behind with her mother. She needed to think, and the constant feeling of being watched by her mother made that hard.

By the time they got back to the Jeep, police were swarming the area. Hiding in the trees would only last so long. She knew she needed to speak with the sheriff to clear her name, but she didn't have the time to waste or the patience to deal with it. The people responsible for her mother's attack and disappearance were no longer an issue. But she couldn't exactly tell them that either.

"What are we going to do?" Mackenzie said under her breath. It was meant more for herself than the others, but Darren heard her none the less.

"Well, you can go out there and deal with them, getting taken to the station for a few hours of questioning, and then meet us back at the pack. They have nothing to detain you over, but if you don't answer questions, you will look even guiltier than you did running yesterday."

A sigh slipped from between her lips, and she closed her eyes, tipping her head up to the sky. The sun had set long ago, and they were approaching another full moon in the coming days. She could feel the magic even more than she ever had before. She had a feeling it was because of the new scar that adorned her neck.

Mackenzie looked at her mother then back to her father. She was about to give in and take the day of questioning when her mother spoke up. "Or I could be found. I could stumble out of the woods, and let them find me. I can describe some crazy man that was drunk and passed out, giving me a chance to escape. The police will take me into custody to keep me safe and you two can go back to fighting whatever battle you've got going on. Just make sure to let me know that you are okay when it's all over."

Mackenzie had to admit that her mother's plan would work. As long as Margret didn't send anyone else after her. A cop wouldn't be able to do shit against a wolf. "Dad? What do you think?"

"I think I lost the right to tell her what to do or not to do long time ago, kiddo. This one is between the two of you."

"Okay, but you have to promise to demand protection. I will make sure to send a few scouts to keep an eye on you. Give me that," Mackenzie gestured toward her mother's handkerchief that had blood on it. "This will let the guys find you, no matter where the police take you. They will keep you safe."

"Okay." Her mother handed over the garment and awkwardly leaned in to hug her daughter. "I do love you, pretty girl."

"I love you too, Mom." Mackenzie finally embraced the gesture and hugged her mother back tightly. Until she squealed, and Mackenzie had to let go. She had forgotten the extent of the injuries and how her mother didn't heal as she did.

When her mother backed away, Mackenzie and Darren stepped farther from the tree line and watched as her mother performed with the grace and skill of an Academy award winner. She stumbled more than she had through the root-filled forest and cried out as if she had a knife in her gut. Police came running from three different directions. An ambulance was there within five minutes, and the area was cleared out in ten.

Mackenzie and Darren ran for the Jeep. As soon as the doors closed, the engine was started, and they flew down the road.

TWENTY

The pack land was full. Mackenzie had only seen more wolves in one place once before, and that was at Lycanthrope Manner. People were shoulder to shoulder, but everyone was making it work. The cooks were working round the clock, and tents were being set up side by side between every cabin. Liam had said another hundred had arrived on the phone, but the wolves standing before her were many more than that.

When their presence was noticed, cheers rang out at their return, and Nadia ran to Darren, throwing her arms around him and kissing him soundly. Mackenzie smiled but looked away. Instinctively, her eyes scanned the group for Liam, before reminding herself that he wasn't there.

"You ready?" Darren asked startling her. She had been lost in her own thoughts of Liam and had zoned out completely.

"As I'll ever be." The entire drive back, Mackenzie and her father had been figuring out the best course of action. First, they needed intel. Then they needed to scare the living shit out of Margret.

"Thank you all for coming. If you could all gather around. We have decided on a better course of action. Please, get close, and Mackenzie will explain everything to you and answer questions as best as she can at the moment."

Murmurs filled the area, which, of course, ended up sounding like a room full of people shouting. More wolves must have shown up since she had spoken with Liam. There were easily three hundred people before her. All ready to fight and follow her lead. She was grateful. And terrified.

"I also want to thank every single one of you. You believed me when no one else would. You see how bad Margret truly is, and you know that the world she wants to create is not a good one. Some of you I know, others I have seen in passing, and even more, I have never met before yet here you stand. I hope to get to know each one of you before you head back home with news of our victory. With news that our way of life will not change because of one woman who is hell-bent on reliving a past that so many of our kind renounced hundreds of years ago.

"I say we are done looking over our shoulder. We are done waiting for the next attack. It is time to fight. It is time to go after Margret and every single thing she holds dear."

Mackenzie waited to continue speaking as the crowd cheered her words and the power of the mass of people all working toward the same goal flowed through the group.

"First, I need a group of five to take this," Mackenzie held up her mother's handkerchief, "and trace the scent back to my mother. Stay out of sight. She should be in police protection, but you and I both know how much good that will do her if Margret really does send her wolves after her again.

Hands raised, and Mackenzie beckoned them forward. She handed the kerchief to the first man that got to her. With three men and two women, who Mackenzie knew were good warriors as she had seen them fight in Europe, she felt her chest ease a little knowing her mother would be safe.

"Thank you. Analise?" Mackenzie called out. She couldn't see her friend, but she hoped that she had stayed behind when Liam had gone back to Montana.

"Back here, Mac! You think I would have left? Look at this place! You all need my help now more than ever." Mackenzie smiled. She couldn't see her, but she would recognize that voice anywhere.

"Absolutely. Contact your informant from California. Find out as much as you can. Where they are, where they are going, and any information on Margret herself."

Murmurs echoed back and forth until Mackenzie raised a hand waiting for the crowd to quiet again. "How many of you are willing to attack? Not wait for the fight to come to us, but to go and end it once and for all." Every wolf before her stood taller and raised their hands high in the air. "No matter what happens in the coming days, know that I am proud to fight next to you. Proud to call you all friends and family. I need a group of fifty. I need at least ten women. No offense guys, but children feel more comfortable with women and where we are going, there will be a lot of kids.

"If you want to be part of the fifty and go with me, meet me after the meeting, and I will go over all the details. Next, I need someone good at tracking. I need a member of Margret's pack found. Not just any member, but someone I hold dear to me. I need to get a message to her. If she sends one back, I need you to find me. This could be the most important task of all. Before you volunteer, please know that this is dangerous. Hell, everything we are doing is dangerous.

"I... can... go," a small voice said from the group. Mackenzie searched the crowd, looking for the body of which it belonged.

"I cannot see you, please come forward."

Slowly, the group parted to allow a young boy to come through. Mackenzie recognized him almost immediately. Alarms rang out in her head, and she nearly growled at him. "How did you find us? What happened after we left you in the woods in France?" she demanded. The group quieted down, and those closest to Christophe grabbed him by the arms and held him.

"Please... I help. You... helped. My... turn." His words were slow and thick with his accent. He had to think about each word before saying it. Mackenzie looked into his eyes and opened her ears to hear his heartbeat. Only, there were too many others around to really know whose was whose and be able to tell if a racing heart meant a liar, or just someone terrified because there was a group of almost two hundred standing there staring at him like he was their next meal.

"How did you find us?"

"He found our pack," a woman said, moving forward quickly. She too had an accent, but her English was clear. "He found us a few weeks before the scouts came to spread the word about what you were doing here. He remembered you. Told the pack how you tried to help him. That you were good people. He insisted on coming, even though he is still Tempering."

"If you have yet to gain control, I am not sure you will do well in battle. Perhaps this is a mission meant for someone who cannot help fight physically. Can you be fast and discreet?" Mackenzie said, turning her attention back to Christophe.

The woman who had vouched for him translated and Christophe nodded emphatically. With doubt still creeping in the back of her mind, she agreed to allow him to go, but asked that another go with him just in case he didn't return before the full moon.

After assigning her father the job of continuing to train those who would remain behind, Mackenzie left the overcrowded area to find a minute to herself before putting together her own special team. Taking the pup house in Alaska was a bold move. But she also knew that Margret once said only pups and their mother's live there. The fathers tended to travel and to be used where needed. She just had to hope that they arrived on a day when the adult population was limited to half the parents.

"Mackenzie?" a soft voice said from behind her. Mackenzie turned quickly, hitting her knee against the wall, wincing as the pain radiated in pulses down her leg. "Sorry."

"It's okay, Nadia," she said to her step-mother once she was able to open her eyes and look at the person talking to her. "What's up?"

"I want to go with you. And there are many others ready to go as well. I just wanted you to know that I have as much faith in you as your father does. I want to help."

"I would be grateful. I know you will be a great asset in Alaska," Mackenzie reached out and squeezed Nadia's hand. "I need to give Christophe and Hector the message for Natalie."

"Who is Natalie?"

"My old roommate. We were really close before I left."

"Why didn't she leave with you?"

"She had already pledged to Margret. And she was in love."

"Pledge? Does she make them pledge? What witch does she have under her employ to create that kind of magical bond?"

"That isn't natural for our kind?" Mackenzie didn't know why she was shocked. Everything else out of Margret's mouth had been a lie, too.

"No. It was used long ago during the first pack wars. It made sure the members would remain loyal and trustworthy. After the wars had ended, the practice did, too. Or so I had thought."

"Apparently not. Would that bond keep Natalie from helping us? It's my best chance at getting real insight into what the hell is going to happen next."

"It could. But if there is a seed of doubt already planted in her mind about Margret, you might be able to get the help you need without the bond interfering. The best thing to do is to try."

"Thanks, Nadia." Mackenzie watched Nadia turn and walk back toward the group. With a heavy sigh, Mackenzie walked into her father's house to begin to write a letter.

Natalie,

I know I should have written sooner, but when you have someone following your every move and sending assassins after you, writing a letter seems to be forgotten. I don't know what you know about the war happening all around us, but there is a war. Basically, Margret's pack, which has grown to more than half the packs in the United States and even across the world against everyone else.

I don't know how to say this, but I need your help. I need to know where Margret is. I need to know where she is going to be. I know you don't believe in what she is doing. I know you pledged your loyalty to her, but you know she is wrong. Even if you can't tell me where she is, can you tell me where she isn't?

Please know that even if you don't help, I still love you. I still miss you. You and Teresa are the best, and one day we will see each other again. Take care.

~M

Mackenzie folded the letter and went to find Christophe and Hector. It didn't take long as they had already packed their bags and were waiting by the fire pit for her. She handed Christophe the letter and told the men how to find the Montana house and what Natalie looked like. They ran off toward the trees, but Mackenzie knew they would be flying. With Christophe not able to actually turn on command, running wouldn't be an option.

With a deep breath, Mackenzie turned to go and face the next phase of the plan.

"Wait, so we are attacking a house full of children?" One woman screamed out in horror. The rest of the group called out, some encouraging the move while others outright forbidding it.

"No! Listen to me. We go and create a distraction. Something to draw the adults out of the house. Then, when only the children are inside, we go in. When we have secured the house, we let the adults go tell Margret what has happened. We will not be touching a single child. We will not be harming a single child. We are simply using them to hopefully draw out some of Margret's wolves to take them out and thin her rank. She will send her best fighters to regain control of the Alaska house. That is why the wolves we let go will only think we have ten. When Margret sends her men to take the house back, we surprise them with our numbers and take them all out."

"I don't like it. Using children as pawns. I can't. I would rather stay here and protect our own children. You know she is going to retaliate. I will find someone else to take my place." The woman stood and glared at Mackenzie before leaving the cabin. Mackenzie knew that her plan wouldn't go over well with everyone. But it was the only plan she had besides sit and wait for shit to fall in her lap.

"Does anyone else want to leave? I will understand, and I am sure Darren will be able to use you elsewhere."

Two more stood and apologized before leaving. No sooner had they left three more came in. "Heard you needed a few more?"

"Absolutely. Take a seat."

Mackenzie sat outside on a log by the crackling fire and watched the path that lead in and out of the pack land. She had never felt such longing as she did at that moment for Liam. She needed to feel his arms around her and hear him tell her everything was going to be all right. To tell her that she wasn't leading the pack to certain death, but to a victory to give all werewolves a better future.

More and more of the men were approaching her to ask questions, both about the plan of attack and about seemingly nothing at all. When one of them tried to trace the scar on her neck, she hit him hard, making an example out of him. Then she made her way to the log and glared at anyone who came within ten feet of her. And in such a small space, with so many people, she was glaring an awful lot.

Her heart ached to know that she had to leave soon. Knowing that she didn't know when the next time she would hear his voice or feel the calluses on his hands caressing hers would be. But she had to be strong. Everyone else was leaving their mates behind for the greater good. She just had to believe when she returned from Alaska that he would be there waiting for her.

Footsteps behind her followed by the low and steady heartbeat she had come to recognize as her father to let her know it was time. She stood and turned with glassy eyes, yet refusing to allow them to shed a single tear, and nodded.

"Nadia will be right back. She went to say goodbye to Lyla. I placed another ten wolves at the house in town. Are you sure about this, Mackenzie? Do you know how many guardians the pups have in Alaska?"

"No. I'm not sure of anything except that we can't keep waiting for her to strike. When we don't know it's coming, we aren't prepared, and we lose more people. I would like to finish this with as few casualties as possible. I already have too many deaths on my hands."

The Jeep pulled up, and Nadia climbed out, walking toward them. Mackenzie excused herself to allow them a private moment and went to gather her team.

"We leave in ten minutes!"

TWENTY ONE

Mackenzie had never been to Alaska before. She had thought that most of the year it was covered in snow, but as she and fifty other wolves hid amongst the trees, the ground beneath her feet was not covered in snow, but instead, vibrant with life.

They had been watching the house for almost two full days. Waiting to see who all was there, what their routines were, and to make sure that not a single child was hurt in the crossfire. Mackenzie looked to Nadia and nodded. It was time.

Standing from her position, Mackenzie stepped forward. With every step that brought her closer to the edge of the trees and being in sight of the house, her heart beat faster. The light was brighter just before her. She knew that in two more steps, she would be exposed. She would have to hold her head high and walk straight up to the door. Perhaps they didn't know what she looked like. Maybe they did, and they would invite her in to hold her captive. Either way, for their plan to work, she had to get into that house.

She could hear children screaming and playing in the house as she took the steps up the porch. Then, nothing. The house went silent. They knew someone was there. Her hand had never felt as heavy as when she lifted it to knock on the door.

The solid wood door let out three loud *thunks*.

Mackenzie stood and waited. With every second that passed where it didn't open, she thought of just as many ways they would fail. Finally, the wooden door before her swung open to reveal a young woman, who looked only a few years older than Mackenzie. Although, that told her absolutely nothing. Most likely, the woman was over 200 years old.

"Can I help you?" the woman asked eyeing Mackenzie before locking eyes with her.

"I think you can. My name is Mackenzie Duncan. Margret has been looking for me. This is the closest of her pack locations to where I was and I am tired of running from her."

"I am not sure I understand what you are talking about. Pack? What is a pack? And who is this Margret? If you are in danger, perhaps you should be calling the police."

"Please, don't play that game with me. I can hear your heartbeat, feel the magical pulse that flows through our kind strong in this house, and as I used to be in Margret's pack, I know for a fact this is the Alaska house. Now, are you going to invite me in or should I just push past you and call her myself? You do have her on speed dial, right?"

It was a bold statement. But she didn't know what else to do. She HAD to get into the house. Had to.

Then ten of the wolves outside had to draw out the twelve adults from in the house. When they did that, the others would enter the house and stay out of sight. That way, they would still have an element of surprise when Margret sent her wolves to take the house back.

Mackenzie took a step forward, preparing to shove her way past the woman, but in the end, she didn't have to. She nodded her head and stepped back allowing her to enter. The woman looked outside and scanned the trees. Mackenzie hoped that her team remembered to stay back for the full five minutes they had planned.

When the door closed behind her, Mackenzie swallowed thickly. Five of the other adults in the house came into the room and stood in a circle around her, their arms crossed over their chests, and hatred in their eyes. Seven others were out in the house somewhere.

"So, are we calling Margret or what?" How she managed to ask without a tremor to her voice she wasn't sure. This was the plan from the beginning, and she was glad to be doing it, but that didn't mean standing alone with six werewolves surrounding her didn't scare the living shit right out of her.

"I think first you need to tell us what you are really doing here. Why are you trying to destroy our pack? Our way of life?"

Mackenzie couldn't help but shake her head and let out a little laugh. "I'm sorry, what?"

"You. Why are you getting other packs to attack us? Why are you telling everyone that Margret is in a league with the vampires? Do you hate your own kind so bad as to have us killed?"

"That is insane. Margret is taking over packs and killing anyone who doesn't agree with her. I am out there warning everyone I can that she is coming after them. And I don't know a single vampire!"

"She lies. Just tie her to the chair and call Margret." The only man in the room was irritated, and his gruff voice felt like sandpaper in her ears.

"Fine, tie me to the chair. I told you that I want to face Margret and I will wait here for her." Mackenzie moved to the chair sitting in the middle of the room and sat. With her arms flat against the chair, she waited for someone to move forward with a rope or tape of some kind.

A loud bang echoed through the house, shaking the walls and floor beneath her feet at the same time. Two of the adults looked to her with accusation while the rest ran from the room and out onto the porch. The two women who stayed behind hurriedly tied Mackenzie to the chair with jump ropes that happened to be lying on the floor next to a huge pile of toys before yelling that everyone was to stay in their rooms. Mackenzie wanted to laugh at the idea of jump ropes holding her down, but kept quiet.

A flutter of footsteps sounded above her. She could picture all the children running to their windows to look out and see what was going on. Mackenzie only hoped whatever had exploded was far enough that they didn't have to see the battle that was about to take place. The five more adults ran past her in a blur. That meant two were still inside. Unless they slipped out another door, but Mackenzie wasn't going to be taking any chances. The first thing they would do would be to search the house.

Mackenzie closed her eyes and tried to listen. She could hear the frantic heartbeats above her and the water dripping in a sink somewhere, but she couldn't find any signs of the group that was supposed to come in after her.

She gnawed on her lip as the deep-seated feeling in her gut grew from confidence with a hint of fear to downright worry that she had led fifty wolves to their death. Did the Alaska house have more members than they had seen? Had the team that was meant to come in after her been caught somehow?

Mackenzie pulled on her restraints. The rope burned into her skin slightly, before healing just as quickly and within seconds, she had freed herself. Slowly, she tiptoed around the room, looking out windows and listening at the door.

A bang from behind her made her jump and turn, ready to fight. But it was her team barreling in through the back door. They had another man with them, being drug by the arms, his eyes closed and his head drooping off to the side.

"He was outside the door. One quick knock to the side of the head and he was out," Brian said.

"One knock put a werewolf out?" Mackenzie asked incredulously.

"Well, I said quick, not soft. Pressure points are a very useful thing." Brian grinned big before dumping the man on the floor.

"Can we at least put him on the couch? These people have no idea what is really going on. They are under the impression I have vampires working for me!"

The whole group laughed until they were interrupted by a tiny voice that broke Mackenzie's heart. "Daddy?"

The group whipped around to see a child that looked no older than five standing on the stairs with wide eyes staring at the unconscious man. Mackenzie moved toward her and saw her flinch, taking another step back up the stairs.

"Daddy is just sleeping. He will be okay. Why don't you go back to your room as you were told, okay? I promise I won't tell that you came out of your room."

"Who are you?"

"Just someone trying to help."

The little girl didn't press for any more details. she just turned and ran up the stairs.

"I think I need to go see what's going on out there. You guys stay here. Keep the kids in their rooms, but be nice. And if this one wakes up before I'm back, try to talk to him without sending him back into La-La land."

"You got it."

Mackenzie could hear the howls and cries of battle long before she could see it. She knew what she was about to see would be bloody, and it scared her more than life itself that it could be her own wolves. It hurt her heart even more to know that the wolves they were attacking didn't know who Margret really was. But they were fighting in her name all the same.

When she approached, what she saw devastated her. Bodies were strewn about, some still alive and healing, others completely gone from this life.

"ENOUGH!" she yelled loudly with a slight growl to her voice. The fighting around her subsided with her members subduing the few remaining of Margret's pack. "You will leave this place. You will leave, and you will tell Margret that she has lost the Alaska pack and the pups are now under my command until we can place them with a pack that can care for them. Margret will not take this land over. She will not take Europe. She will not grow her pack any larger, and we will never bow to her as the Royal Were."

"You will never take our children!" one woman called out.

"I believe we just did. It saddens me to do so, but Margret left us no choice. Please know that not a single finger will be laid on them. We are not cruel people. We do not kill for power like your leader. We do not kill for revenge. We do not wish to have every wolf in this world bow to us over ancient history. We wish to live in a peaceful world, in our own packs, by our own rules. To do that, we have to minimize your pack. We have to have these children grow up in a pack that teaches them right from wrong. And your pack isn't it. Take them away from here."

Mackenzie motioned for five of her group to lead the three remaining members of Margret's pack away.

They began to struggle and fight until they were knocked unconscious and dragged away. Margret would send more than they had hoped. Because their numbers were greater than they had anticipated, it took more of her own to keep them at bay. By Mackenzie's guess, the three they had let go would tell her of 15-20 wolves keeping the Alaska house instead of just ten. She would have to get more wolves there and quick to be able to outnumber them again.

"Mackenzie, we lost a few of our own," a man by the name of Gregory said. He was a member of her father's pack. Mackenzie approached him, hearing the waver in his voice. He was kneeling on the blood soaked ground in front a body.

She didn't want to look. She hadn't wanted to lose a single member of her own team. She had hoped that with an element of surprise, they would be safe. With the training they all had, they would be stronger. They were overall, but not without losses of their own.

When silence fell amongst the group, Mackenzie knew it was bad. She kept her eyes averted, but moved closer. She wasn't prepared for the scene that lay before her.

Mackenzie placed a hand on Gregory's shoulder in condolence, but when her eyes landed on the lost life before her, a scream erupted from deep within her, echoing off the trees. The stabbing pain in her chest brought her to her knees, the impact with the blood soaked earth forcing much-needed air into her lungs.

Nadia's lifeless body, bloody and broken, was resting on the ground beside her head. The world around Mackenzie all but disappeared, all except for

Nadia. Mackenzie's stomach twisted and expelled what little was in it, and sobs choked her until she was red in the face.

Two large hands landed on her shoulders, and the sadness and rage that flowed through her body lashed out, knocking Gregory to the ground. Mackenzie screamed and cried and wailed her fists against him until all the energy had left her body a shuddering mess against his chest.

He held her close, rubbing her back before scooping her into his arms and carrying her into the house, all thirty-three other wolves, both from the battle and of those still hiding in the shadows, followed behind.

When Mackenzie finally calmed down enough to breathe without sobbing, she noted that the living was much smaller with forty-five wolves inside than it was with ten. Slowly, she sat up from the couch that Gregory had placed her on and took a sip of the water that someone had placed beside her.

Nadia was gone. So were four others. She had failed to keep them alive. Her plan had failed. She had failed her father. She should have kept her safe. He was going to hate her. It was her plan that killed his mate. How could he not?

"Who else?" she asked barely above a whisper.

"Jenna, Dean, Malik, and Donte`," someone said from the back of the group. Mackenzie nodded her head. She needed Liam. She needed someone to hold her close and to tell her that even if they lost five wolves, forty-five still lived, and they accomplished what they set out to do.

"The children?"

"Have been fed and given things to do in their rooms. A few of the older ones I think have caught on. I think the oldest is thirteen. We had to lock him in his room. Luckily, his window already has bars on it. I bet he was already a handful for them," a wolf named Ashley said.

"Okay," Mackenzie stood on shaky feet and began pacing the room, "I need to tell my father what has happened. I had planned to send a few back with the news of how things went, but Nadia..."

"Mackenzie, you have two men running full speed through the yard toward us," a young man standing by the window said. The whole group made way for her to get to the glass pane to see who the visitors were.

"It's Christophe and Hector," she said then ran to the door, flinging it open. Mackenzie took the porch steps in a single leap and met them half way through the yard.

"Well?" she asked frantically, looking for some kind of clue in their eyes as to whether or not Natalie was helpful.

"She wrote this for you. She wished for me to hug you for her, but I told her that was probably best conveyed with words as Liam would have my head," Christophe said with a slight smile. Only his comment made her think of the head she just saw.

Mackenzie took a deep breath, willing herself not to break down again. These wolves needed a strong leader while they were away from Darren. It was her plan that got them killed, but they all came along willingly knowing the risks. She would feel that guilt for the rest of her days, but in the end, they had to take the house. She couldn't second guess herself. The plan would work. It had to.

Hector handed Mackenzie a piece of paper. When she unfolded it, she saw that it was the letter she sent to Natalie, but with Natalie's own response written at the bottom.

Mac,

I am so sorry that I didn't leave when you did. I should have believed that it would be better with you than staying here. Teresa left the Montana house for the California house on Margret's orders shortly after you left. The more I see here, the more I listen, the more I know it isn't right. Margret is keeping the other houses completely in the dark about what is really going on. You have a huge price tag on your head, and I am glad to see that it hasn't been cashed in yet.

Margret has plans to bring a soon-to-be mother to the Alaska house next week. Please be careful and find me when you can.

~N

Mackenzie folded the note up and put it calmly in her pocket. She wanted to do nothing more than scream. That was not in the plan. The plan had given them weeks before actually facing Margret. First, make the pack smaller, then the final fight. Mackenzie began to pace, her thoughts racing. Were they strong enough to survive? Were they big enough to put up a fight? It no longer mattered. Margret was coming, and now she would come with everything she had. She would make a statement, taking out any and every pack in their path to reclaiming their house. Margret was a go big or go home type of woman. And she refused to go home.

"I will be heading out tonight to return to my father's pack. We will return with as many wolves as we can while still protecting his land and the young pups here. Please, keep those children safe and happy. We need their trust in us, and stay alert. It's almost time."

TWENTY TWO

Mackenzie and the five wolves that insisted on accompanying her back to Darren ran. Mackenzie pushed herself faster than she thought possible. Her chest stung with the exertion, but she didn't stop. She didn't stop to eat. She didn't stop to sleep. The crescent moon grew larger with each night that passed.

Mackenzie knew they had a matter of days before the full moon hit. She could feel it. This cycle was going to be different. Stronger. More magical than any other she had felt before.

They all ran straight into camp without stopping to change back. Mackenzie looked for Darren with heaving breaths and found him training the others to fight. He stood in human form yelling out commands to the wolves. They must have all been quite mature as they did exactly what they were told, showing they were in complete control of themselves.

All eyes turned to them, Darren quickly looking through them, and his face falling when he didn't see Nadia. Mackenzie looked away, too ashamed to look her father in the eye. She padded forward and into his house to shift back to her human form. She dressed quickly and within a minute her father walked in behind her.

"Did you succeed?"

"We took the house. The children are all safe. Only three of Margret's wolves were allowed to leave. One is being held in the house. The rest died in the battle."

Mackenzie spoke softly, still refusing to look her father in the eye. She could hear his heart racing and knew that he was aware something was off with her tone. "And of our side? How many did we lose?" his voice was just a whisper.

"Five. Jenna, Dean, Malik, Donte, and..." Mackenzie couldn't say it. She couldn't tell her father that she got his mate killed. The tears that she had tried so hard to hold back fell, and a sob wracked her chest before she lifted her eyes to her father's face.

"And who? Tell me. Tell me who?" his words were hurried, and the strain in his voice told her he knew exactly who, but he had to hear it from her.

"And Nadia."

Darren let out a roar and fell to his knees, sobbing. Mackenzie tried to move toward him, but the glare in his eyes told her to leave.

"I'm so sorry," she whispered before slipping out the door. Darren needed time to process. He needed to grieve. She only hoped that when he came out of the cabin, he didn't hate her. Mackenzie walked over to the cabin that had become hers and Liam's since their return from Europe.

She just needed to close her eyes for a minute. Just lie down and close her eyes and pretend that her world wasn't chaos and war and death. One minute to pretend that Liam would be there to hold her, to love her.

One minute to just be.

As she strolled through the house, she peeled her dirty clothes off and let them drop to the floor, not caring enough to pick them up or carry them to the small bedroom. She was dirty and tired and wanted something she didn't have to care about.

Mackenzie climbed into the bed, her eyes already closing when she felt a warm body next to her. His scent had infiltrated her very being before she had a moment to scream and latched onto Liam tightly. He turned to her, a smile on his face and his arms open.

The minute his eyes landed on her red-rimmed eyes and disheveled look, his smile fell. "Come here," he said. And she did. She fell into his arms and cried against his chest. She finally felt safe and at home enough to let it all out. She knew that Liam would never judge her or think she was weak for her tears.

"What happened?" he asked after a few minutes.

"Nadia."

"Oh, Mackenzie."

Liam held her, as she cried never letting go even when her sobs became so violent the whole bed shook. Slowly, she calmed and looked into his eyes. "Your brother?" she asked afraid to hear the answer.

"Fine. We left enough wolves watching the house. I knew you needed me and was worried he would see me."

Mackenzie hugged him close.

"PACK MEETING! PACK MEETING! PACK MEETING!" A deep voice boomed from outside over and over. Mackenzie stood and dressed, then held Liam's hand until the front door.

"I don't want Darren hurt anymore and seeing us holding each other might do that."

"I understand." Liam leaned in and kissed Mackenzie soundly on the lips before pulling back and opening the door. They gathered with the group to see Darren at the front, pain clearly etched on his face and sobs filtering through the crowd.

"I call this meeting to order. Mackenzie, get up here and fill us in on what happened," Darren said with anger clearly lacing every word. Mackenzie moved forward and stood where her father had just stood moments before.

"We took the Alaska house. We know where Margret is. We were successful in every aspect except keeping every member of our side alive. I am sorry to say we lost five of our own. Jenna, Dean, Malik, Donte, and Nadia."

Her words were clear, but her sorrow-filled each word spoken. She allowed the crowd their moment of shock. Some cheered their victory while others cried with grief.

"Analise, have you heard from your person in California?"

"Just a moment ago. That's why the meeting was called. Margret is heading to Alaska. With everyone."

Panic filled the air, but Mackenzie knew it was coming. She already knew Margret was going to be heading to Alaska and with the news that her three members brought, there was no other option she would take. If she had been on other business, she would have sent people to take care of the problem for her. But this way, this way Margret would think she was ending everything once and for all.

"PACK YOUR SHIT!" Darren bellowed. "WE LEAVE IN TEN MINUTES! WE WILL HAVE HER HEAD!"

TWENTY THREE

Nearly two hundred wolves were pacing the Alaska ground, looking for any sign of Margret or her wolves. The sky glowed red from the blood moon on the rise. When it hit the highest point in the sky, they would all change.

She had a feeling that even the moon seemed to know that by the time morning came, everything would be covered in blood. She only hoped that amongst it, was Margret's body.

Mackenzie could feel every beat of her heart vibrating in her chest. She could feel everyone's anxious steps under her feet. Everyone was ready for the morning to come and with it, the end of Margret's power play. Life could continue on without fear of war and death and psychotic women who believed in some hundreds of year old royal claim to rule the world.

A subtle crack sounded from behind. Mackenzie turned just in time to see her old friend standing there with a finger to her lips. Mackenzie wanted to rush forward and hug her, but wasn't sure if Teresa would be accepting of that. She stayed with Margret, after all.

So instead, she stood silently, waiting for Teresa's next move. She stepped forward, and Mackenzie tensed, but didn't move. Slowly, Teresa's hand outstretched with a piece of paper in it. Mackenzie took it and read.

You have five minutes. She is coming from the North. They went around in hopes of surprising you. I am sorry I didn't believe you. Good Luck.

Mackenzie smiled at her and nodded. She couldn't speak the words, but she hoped Teresa knew just how grateful she was for the heads up and that she knew she wasn't mad. Mackenzie looked down to the phone in her hand and sent a quick text to Hector, who had placed himself to the north. They had groups in all directions, but their largest force sat to the south, expecting Margret to come barreling through.

Next, she sent one to Darren to move half of his men to join Hector's group. When she looked up to say goodbye to Teresa, she was already gone. With a quick whisper, she took three others and headed to the north. If Margret was going to sneak in, she was going to be met with a large force of opposition.

Mackenzie was expecting Margret and her wolves to come at them already in fighting mode. But they didn't. When Margret showed up, she walked forward with her hundreds of wolves behind her. From what Mackenzie could see, Margret's numbers were only slightly larger than their own.

"Why do you hide? You have shown no fear in attacking me or mine before. You ran away like a petulant child when you learned the rules of our kind. Now you hide in fear after killing and taking the one house that should be sacred to all of our kind?" Margret's voice boomed. It was obvious she would continue her lies to keep her pack fighting for her.

"I am not hiding. I am right here. Along with hundreds of wolves who know the truth. Know that you feel your mother's reign should belong to you. We are your opposition. We agree with the others of the Royal line that packs should rule amongst themselves. Complete power is a thing of the past."

Mackenzie had come out of the tree line into the opening to face Margret and her pack. It must have looked ridiculous to any watching to see a single girl standing up to hundreds ready to tear her bit by bit.

"It is no secret who my mother is. My question is why you hate the original family so much. Did Geoff break your heart so badly that this is your revenge? You are willing to lose countless lives over a lust filled few months?"

Mackenzie could hear the snickers from Margret's side and the growl from deep in the woods that belonged to Liam.

"For those of you who don't know, Geoff is Margret's son. I don't know why they like to hide it, but it is the truth. Not 'like a son' but her actual blood related child. I made him leave when I found out that he was keeping in contact with Mommy dearest and was telling her where every pack we came across was located. Within a matter of days, your pack attacked them. Was I hurt by his betrayal? Of course, but my heart lies with my mate. This has nothing to do with Geoff."

Whispers of son and lies flew through her group, and Mackenzie was glad to see worry flash in Margret's eyes. Finally, the group behind Margret parted, and Geoff moved through the group. He stood tall, and his body square, but his eyes showed the fear that truly lay within him. Geoff knew her well enough to know she wouldn't stand their alone.

Mackenzie moved forward, and so did Margret. With a raised hand and matching eyebrow, Mackenzie warned Margret not to take another step. Margret stopped but cast her eyes to the sky.

"A full moon is upon us. A blood moon, the most magical of nights. It is said that the first blood moon came when Gwendolynn changed for the first time. I hope you are prepared for the strength of a Royal wolf on a blood moon."

Mackenzie scoffed. Slowly, she moved her hair from her neck exposing the bite that Gwendolynn left on her. As she did so, the wolves moved forward from the trees. Darren, Liam, and the other wolves of Royal decent moved forward to stand beside her.

Margret's heart skipped a beat, and her hand flashed to her own neck exactly where Mackenzie's scar was. "We know the power of a Royal were. Did you honestly think I wouldn't find out about my lineage? Or did Geoff fail to mention that fact?"

Margret cut her eyes to Geoff suddenly and then back to Mackenzie. "Are you sure you are prepared to take on the granddaughter of the original? Are you willing to risk all of their lives?"

"The original chose me—" before she could speak any longer, the moon hit its highest point in the sky and bathed them all in its red light. Their wolves begged for freedom, and with a speed like never before, Mackenzie turned.

Howls filled the air before the blood-curdling screams of war. Mackenzie wasn't sure which side jumped first, but when she stood on all four paws, the world around her was chaos. It was a sea of wolves, all different colors and sizes battling for a future they believed in. Mackenzie looked around to find Margret's wolf and charged forward.

She was hit from the side and knocked to the ground. A golden colored wolf was atop her snapping and clawing. Mackenzie used all of her force and kicked the wolf from her. A crack echoed off the tree it hit, and the wolf hit the ground with a thud.

Two more came after her. She continually lost her focus as she was trying to keep an eye on Margret, who sat in the middle of the field with five wolves surrounding her. Standing there, guarding her. She had so much confidence in her victory that it pissed Mackenzie off even more. With two fast and hard snaps of her jaw, a brown wolf had fallen, his head falling to the side and his blood running in rivers to her paws.

With a growl, she turned on the grey wolf that was nearby and baring teeth at her. With two quick movements, he was down and wouldn't be getting back up. Mackenzie pushed forward, until she stood before Margret and her guards. She let out a deafening roar but instead of Margret standing to the challenge, three of her guards sprang forward.

Mackenzie could usually hold her own, but when her eyes locked on the black wolf who she knew so well, she lost concentration for a single moment. She had hoped that Geoff would have stepped in, but the way he just watched and never left his position by his mother's side showed how little power he actually had. Not only over the pack, but his own choices and decisions.

Mackenzie felt teeth sink into her hind quarter at the same time as she tried to fend off the wolf in front her. With a yelp, Mackenzie fell to the ground and waited for the final blow that would end her. Three against one, she had no chance. She just wished to see Liam one last time and hoped like hell that her father would take Margret's head in the end.

As if he had heard her thoughts, a white wolf, her white wolf, charged over, knocking her attackers to the ground with his body. The energy within her grew with his presence. The wounds on her side and neck knitted together quicker. And she stood with more power and more grace than she should have had just moments after facing death.

Refusing to look anywhere but at the single battle raging between her mate and the two remaining guard wolves, Mackenzie joined in the fight. She could feel a strength pulsing through her that she hadn't known before. She was faster and more prepared for every move her opponents made and most importantly, she knew that Liam was safe. Her mind no longer wandered, and she focused.

Mackenzie latched her teeth onto the shoulder of the wolf that had attempted to leap at Liam. The flesh cut away, and blood filled her mouth. The wolf cried out, which only caused her to bite harder, until she felt its arm completely separate from the rest of its body. Crumbling to the floor, Mackenzie stood atop the wolf and put it out of its misery.

Liam stood from his kill and limped toward Mackenzie. She immediately took in his injuries, glad to see they were already healing. With a nuzzle of love to her mate, she pressed forward. She had to get to Margret.

As she approached, she could see the fear and surprise in Margret's eyes that she survived her guards. Geoff moved forward hesitantly. His eyes never leaving Mackenzie. Slowly, they circled one another neither making the first move.

Mackenzie didn't want to fight Geoff. Not only did she doubt her skills against his, but also she doubted her ability to kill him to save herself. He wasn't just anyone. He wasn't just one of Margret's wolves. He was Geoff. Asshole or not, Geoff was different. He used to be her friend. He used to be more than her friend.

A growl from Margret ended the little dance between her and Geoff. He winced but answered her command none the less. The black of his fur came barreling at her at a speed she wasn't expecting. His body collided with hers sending them both to the ground. Snarls and snaps erupted from them both as claws and teeth sliced skin and muscle.

Mackenzie refused to look him in the eye. She tried to focus on the feel of his claws against her skin to fuel her rage and desire to end the fight. She tried to let her inner animal take over and make survival her top priority. But she couldn't.

Mackenzie lunged toward Geoff after having kicked him away, only to have him dart under her and then to stand, knocking her body to the ground. Geoff pounced, placing both paws on her shoulders, pressing her into the ground. A snarl fell from his mouth as he bore his razor sharp teeth and brought himself closer to her neck.

Mackenzie allowed herself to look into his eyes. If he was going to be the one to kill her, she wanted to look him in the eyes as he did it. She said a silent goodbye to her father and Liam, grateful that he knew how much she truly loved him. Geoff's eyes seemed vacant. There was nothing but a wild animal present in his eyes.

That wasn't the Geoff she knew. He had always been in such control. Slowly, she raised her head as far as his weight would let her, and she licked the side of his face. When she lowered herself to the ground, she turned her head, closed her eyes, and waited for the inevitable.

She heard the sounds of war and the cries of death all around her. She could smell every drop of blood that was covering the earth. And she could feel the vibrations beneath her of hundreds of battling wolves fighting for their lives. What she didn't feel any longer was Geoff's weight pressing down on her. Slowly, she opened her eyes to see the black wolf sitting next to her. He leaned in, nuzzled her neck, and then turned and ran.

No one stopped him, probably because they were busy with their own battles. It was then that Mackenzie saw the carnage that surrounded her. Bodies and blood as far as she could see. She had to stop it. It had to end, or there would be more dead than living, and that was not what she wanted.

Turning, she locked eyes with Margret, who had been watching her entire altercation with Geoff. Margret was finally showing emotion. Pure rage filled her as she watched her son abandon her. And Mackenzie wanted to gloat. She gave Margret what she hoped looked like a smile and padded forward. She didn't run. She felt like she was almost sauntering. She wanted Margret to anticipate her approach. She wanted to see her squirm.

A very large brindle wolf charged past her, pushing right through Margret's last few guards and attacked her. She fell backward, not expecting the impact.

When the remaining guards got their footing and defended their 'queen,' it didn't matter how fast Mackenzie ran—it was too late. It was as if time stopped moving when the three wolves held her father down. Margret's first move since the battle had begun, and it was to run to Darren and latch her teeth onto his throat and rip his esophagus out in a single move. She spat the bloody bits of flesh in Mackenzie's direction before returning for a final blow, severing his head completely.

She stood triumphant, and howled. Many wolves stopped fighting and watched in horror as their pack leader lay in a puddle of his own blood. Pain seared through Mackenzie's heart like a hot knife twisting and carved a permanent scar.

Margret had to die. She had to pay for what she had done. Mackenzie would not let her take Darren's pack. Could not let her. Her sister would not grow up in a world where Margret controlled her every move.

Without thinking twice, Mackenzie lunged taking everyone by surprise. Black rage clouded her eyes as she clawed and bit any piece of flesh she came into contact with. She was hit and bit from all sides, but she continued her attack until the light in Margret's eyes went out. Mackenzie didn't want to bite through her spinal cord to end Margret's life once and for all— she wanted to feel the life pulse ending beneath her paws. She wanted to watch as her father's killer died. With a strong slash, she cut through her neck, letting her head roll away through the puddles of blood.

Before she even had a chance to howl in victory, a body crashed into her and teeth punctured her neck. The world went dark around her, and all she could think was that at least she died after Margret.

TWENTY FOUR

Mackenzie blinked and groaned as light spilled into her eyes, blinding her. Silence surrounded her. She sat up quickly, taking in the room. She let a bubble of laughter escape. She was alive. She thought for sure that she was a goner.

Liam. Where was Liam? She jumped up out of the bed and ran to the wooden door, flinging it open. She heard his footsteps and smelled his unique scent before she saw him.

Liam bounded up the stairs at the end of the hall that led to the room they had placed her in and ran to her, scooping her up in a hug and burrowing his face in her neck. Mackenzie let the tears fall freely. She couldn't tell if they were from happiness that Liam was still alive and with her or from the ache that was like a hundred pound weight on her chest when she thought of her father.

"You did it, Mackenzie. She is gone. Margret is gone."

"So is my dad," she whispered through the tears. Sobs wracked her chest until she was gasping for breath. Liam just held her close, letting her cry and being there for her. He didn't tell her it would be okay. He didn't tell her everything was all right. He just told her to go ahead and cry for him. It was as if he knew that she couldn't hear the words that everything would be okay. Because as far as she knew, it would never be okay. She had just gotten to know her father and he was taken from her.

Mackenzie pulled back and stepped away, wiping the tears from her eyes. "What about the rest? How many survived? What happened after I almost..."

"I killed him. No one would take you from me." Liam's voice was hoarse, and he choked up a bit at the end. Mackenzie looked to him and moved back to hold his hand and bring it to her cheek.

"No one will take me from you. It's impossible. Thank you for helping me." Liam's hand slid from her cheek to the back of her head and pulled her forward, locking his lips on hers.

His kiss was passionate and fierce, as if he were proving to himself that she was still there. When he pulled back, Mackenzie could see the glisten in his eyes that he quickly wiped away.

"How many? How many wolves do we have left?" she asked again.

"You have almost three hundred wolves outside waiting for your command."

"Three hundred? That's all? There had to have been nearly six hundred fighting! That's half! We lost half the wolves?"

"Between both sides, yes. Now we are all one side. Your side."

"Why my side?"

"You killed Margret. All of her pack is now technically yours. She had killed... so his pack was hers. Until you took her head. The packs from Europe are only waiting to make sure you are okay before returning home and spreading the news of Margret's fall."

"I wonder what Alice will do?"

"I have a feeling William will take care of her."

"I don't want to lead hundreds of wolves. Hell, she could technically have thousands with all the packs she took over. What do I do?" Mackenzie was pacing the room, worry filling her more than it had in a long time. Not only was everyone relying on her, but also there were wolves out there that were only still there because of the fact that she killed their leader. They probably hated her but felt compelled to stay because of stupid werewolf politics.

"Tell them to go back to their packs and elect a new leader. Or whoever would have been next in line anyway. Tell them to spread the word that Margret is gone. Tell them whatever you want. But we have to go out there."

"I need to talk to Analise. Where is she?" Mackenzie needed a girlfriend. She didn't know that she would say anything different than Liam had, but she needed her anyway.

When Liam didn't answer her, she turned abruptly, the silence as deafening as if he had spoken the words. Liam's eyes were on the floor, and when he finally did look up, they were red-rimmed and glassy.

"No. No, no, no, no, no!" Mackenzie sat on the bed in a whoosh. It couldn't be. She couldn't be gone.

"I am so sorry," he said and moved toward her. He knelt on the floor in front of Mackenzie and held out his hand. In it was Analise's necklace. She never took it off, and Mackenzie never knew what it meant to her. But it didn't matter because now it was hers, and it meant never to take life for granted. She quickly clasped it around her neck and stood.

"I guess it's time to go outside." Mackenzie swallowed thickly and left the room, burying her tears yet again. She would let them fall when she wasn't expected to be leader to who knew how many wolves. When she didn't have to be strong. When she could just be Mackenzie.

As Mackenzie walked through the house, she heard the laughter of children playing and the familiar sound of crashing cars coming from a television in another room. There were wolves everywhere, in every room, while most were outside cleaning up the carnage from the night before.

"I don't want them just burned. I want a graveyard. I want everyone who lost their lives to be remembered," she said as they stepped onto the porch and watched hundreds picking up bodies and working together.

"I figured you would want something better than a mass grave. I'll have Teresa organize."

"Teresa?"

"Yeah, apparently she was Analise's contact. She fought on our side. She is really good at organizing and has been the go-to person since I carried you inside. She assigned someone to care for the kids, and then she assigned others to each side of the house to clean up from the battle. She even sent a few to the nearest grocery store to fill the van that was here with food to feed everyone for a few days. I think that might take more than one trip though."

Mackenzie smiled for the first time since she woke up. She could see Teresa taking charge, and she completely appreciated it. "Can you tell everyone to spread the word that I want to talk to them? Get them all out here where I can address everyone at once."

Liam nodded and kissed her head and went into the house. Teresa came out and hugged Mackenzie from behind, causing her to jump. "Sorry!" she said quickly.

"No, it's okay. Guess I'm still a little out of it. Thank you so much. For everything."

Mackenzie turned around and hugged Teresa properly. "I missed you."

"I missed you, too. What are you going to do?" she asked.

"Honestly, I want everyone to go back to their original packs. I don't want control. I mean that's why we stopped Margret. She wanted to control it all. It's not good for anyone."

"But that's why you would be a good leader. Because you see the danger in the power behind it."

"Thanks. Think you can round everyone up?"

"You got it." Teresa walked to the side of the porch and picked up a large megaphone and looked over her shoulder to Mackenzie with a smile, "This was in the basement. Still works." Then with a wink, she flicked it on, and her voice boomed out across the area to meet in front of the porch.

It only took a few moments for everyone to gather, much to Mackenzie's disappointment. She had hoped to have a bit longer to collect her thoughts and steady her nerves, but it was time.

"First, I want to take a moment to think of those we lost last night. No matter which side you were on, you lost someone you knew, you cared about, you loved." Mackenzie choked on the words coming out of her mouth.

"Now, I know that you are all here because I— because of what I did last night. I am here to tell you that I don't want to be Margret's replacement. I want every pack she took over to remake themselves. I want them to appoint a new leader, either by vote or by whoever was next in line before Margret. As for the Montana and California houses, the same goes for you, with the exception of anyone that might be related to Margret. If Geoff ever returns, he has no claim to anything. It is up to you if you want to welcome him into your pack. On your way back to the houses, spread the word that Margret is dead, and everyone is free to make their own choice for leader. I do ask that if you have the room and the heart that you consider bringing along one of the children who lost their parents in this horrible battle. I hope that it would be someone that at least knew their parents enough to tell them about them as they grow."

"What if we don't want to return to the house we came from?" someone asked.

"Then you can choose to be on your own, start a new pack with others who feel out of place in their old home, or follow me back to my father's land where we, too, will be deciding on a new pack leader. But the choice is yours. You may stay here for another night, but after that, you should move on with your lives. Thank you to everyone who fought by my side, and to those who didn't, I hope you understand now why Margret had to be stopped."

Mackenzie didn't wait for any comments back. she needed a moment to herself. Quickly, she ducked inside and closed the door. With every wolf outside, she slid down the wall and tucked her head into her knees, tired of being strong. She didn't sob loudly. She didn't wail or scream, but she did allow the tears to fall as she thought about all who had been lost over the past few months. She cried for the children who would grow up without their parents. And she cried for her sister, Lyla. She wouldn't leave her without a family. She couldn't.

It had taken nearly three days to get everyone to leave the Alaska house. Mackenzie had to settle more than one argument over who would be pack leader, which most of the time boiled down to a vote. She just hoped that it would work.

Darren's pack stood in two straight lines from the opening in the trees that lead to their camp all the way to the fire pit where he used to hold important meetings. It was where Mackenzie had attacked him the first time she saw her father. It was where he had asked the pack about her future amongst them. It was where he announced their immediate departure to fight the final battle as it had been named. As Mackenzie and Liam walked forward, the rest of the pack that traveled with her, joined into the line. With every person that she and Liam passed, they knelt down and raised a hand up.

When they reached the fire pit, every wolf stood and stood silently, waiting for her to speak. Mackenzie looked to each person until her eyes dropped down to the gap in the line and saw Lyla standing there, tears in her eyes and feet bouncing back and forth.

Mackenzie gestured her forward with a hand, and she bound forward and into Mackenzie's open arms in a flash. The sisters had held each other for a long moment before Mackenzie spoke to the crowd.

"I am so sorry to say that Darren died in battle. I do not know who had been in place to be his replacement for the pack, but I want you to know that I loved him and Nadia. I love my sister. I won't leave her behind. If you want me to leave, Liam and I will take her with us."

It was then that the whole pack again, dropped to their knees with their hand raised. "Liam," she whispered, "what is this? Why won't anyone talk?"

"I don't know," he said back just as quietly, his eyes traveling across the group of people before them.

"This is what happens when a new pack leader is elected. Daddy wanted you to lead if anything happened to him. He had told everyone before you left that if you returned and he did not, to respect you as the leader because that meant you had defeated the one person that he couldn't."

"Oh."

Mackenzie looked to Liam, and he leaned in, kissing her softly and whispered in her ear, "You can do this. You were born for this."

Mackenzie nodded and looked out at the people who had never turned her away. Who had never doubted her, who would be able to help her know her father more than she ever had before, and those who Lyla already saw as family.

"Thank you all so much. Please know that I will do my best to live up to the respect and expectations of you all and my father. I don't know exactly what I am doing, but I hope to learn from each and every one of you."

Everyone stood and moved forward, kneeling before her, pricking their finger with a needle and allowing a single drop of blood to hit the ground. They then stood and hugged her and moved so the next member could do the same.

In the end, Mackenzie decided to add her own blood to the ceremony.

"You have all sworn loyalty to me and given a drop of blood in symbolism. Now it is my turn. I swear my loyalty to you. To this pack. To my father's memory. To our future." She pricked her finger and allowed the drop of blood to hit the ground where the rest of the pack's blood puddled.

Everyone cheered, and Mackenzie wrapped one arm around Liam and the other around Lyla, and finally felt at ease. It was over. It was time finally to live the life she was meant to live.

EPILOGUE

Mackenzie watched as Lyla stood outside with her hands raised to the sky, enjoying the feel of the rain soaking through her clothing to her skin. She could see the perfect peace that rested on her face that being so close to nature brought to any Were's face when the full moon was upon them.

A text came through on her phone pulling her attention away from the window.

Good luck with Lyla tonight! I am sure it's going to happen!

Mackenzie laughed at Natalie's text. She had found her friend shortly after the final battle and moved her promptly into her pack. Natalie was going to be the go to person for the pack while she, Liam, and Lyla were gone.

I think so too. If you need anything, let me know. I will have signal for a few more hours.

Mackenzie put her phone back in her pocket and looked around their small house. Pictures lined the walls showing Lyla growing up and Mackenzie's journey as pack leader. It hadn't been an easy adjustment, but she had found her way. The pack was patient and understanding, and she learned to love every single member.

"Hey, the van is loaded with the roses. One for every fallen wolf." Liam had walked back into the house and wrapped his arms around her waist and pulled her flush against him. They had been married for seven years, and Mackenzie loved him more than she had the day they exchanged rings. The entire pack was in attendance as well as her mother and Liam's family. He had finally decided it was time to see them. Mostly because he felt his brother deserved to know what was inside of him. His father too, for that matter. His family welcomed him warmly, even if they didn't understand or even believe a word he said about being different now. He never said the word Werewolf, but he let them know he was too different for anyone besides them to know he was still alive.

They didn't care. All they cared about was having him back in their lives. And they loved Mackenzie as much as she loved them. Ben especially loved coming to visit each summer. Liam and Mackenzie were very careful not to have his visits coincide with a full moon.

"Look at her. I think it will be this month. She is nearly sixteen. I'm surprised it hasn't happened yet. But look at that. If that isn't the call of nature's magic to her, I don't know what is."

"You are probably right. We should get going if we want to make it to the Alaska house tonight. It will be the perfect place for her first turn if it is her time. There won't be a human for a hundred miles."

"You're right, let's go." Mackenzie and Liam locked up their house and headed out in the rain to gather Lyla and to go honor those who gave their lives to allow them their freedom eight years prior.

After hours and hours of driving, they finally pulled up to the old house that reminded Mackenzie of nothing, but the worst moments of her life. It never got easier, and she doubted it ever would. But she would never sell the house that she had legally claimed from Margret's estate after paying someone to forge documents giving her ownership. Not only of the house, but also of a quarter of the funds Margret had collected over the years. She divided the rest amongst all of the packs that had fought in the final battle.

She wasn't greedy with the money. She used it to pay for a headstone for every fallen wolf. The remaining had gone into a college fund for Lyla. She hoped by the time she was ready for college that her wolf would be under control.

"Come on, we only have a few hours before the moon rises. We need to place the roses," Mackenzie said, and the three of them placed a single rose on every stone with the exception of two. Darren and Nadia's stones got three.

Liam looked to the sky and said, "It's almost time."

"My skin is tingling like crazy!" Lyla cried out, peeling her clothing from her body then laying in the grass. Mackenzie knew what she was feeling. The draw to nature was something she had learned to control, just like her wolf. But the itch to feel it on every inch of her skin was still there.

Mackenzie shed her clothing and looked to the sky and said loudly to both Liam and her sister, "I love you!" The moon cast its glow across her body, and she freed her wolf.

She stood in time to see her sister's agonizing change from human to wolf for the first time. Her bones popped and cracked, and she cried out in pain. But when she was done, before her stood an absolutely stunning brindle wolf. Mackenzie smiled to herself knowing that her sister looked like her, and they both looked like the strongest and most loyal wolf she had ever known—their father.

Lyla didn't give Mackenzie a chance to reminisce. She ran off like a shot. Liam snorted, and Mackenzie did too, before chasing after her. Apparently, speed ran in the family, too. It was going to be a long night, but she was happy to know that Darren's spirit was there, watching his youngest daughter change for the first time.

THE END

ABOUT THE AUTHOR

Growing up, Adrianne couldn't get her hands on enough books to satisfy her need for the make believe. If she finished a novel and didn't have a new one ready and waiting for her, she began to create her own tales of magic and wonder. Now, as an adult, books still make up majority of her free time, and now her tales get written down to be shared with the world.

During the day, Adrianne uses her camera to capture life's stories for clients of all ages and at night, after her two children are tucked in bed; she devotes herself to her written work. Adrianne is living the life she always wanted, surrounded by art and beauty, the written word and a loving family.

As a young adult and new adult author, Adrianne James has plans to bring stories of growing characters, a little romance, and perhaps a little magic and mythology down the line for her readers to enjoy.

FIND ADRIANNE ON THE WEB

www.AdrianneJames.com

www.Facebook.com/AuthorAdrianneJames

www.Twitter.com/Adrianne_James